FROM THE DEEP

MICHAEL BRAY

For those of you who believe in monsters.

"Though it matches the audio profile of a living creature, there is no known animal that could have produced the sound. If it is an animal it would have to be huge — much larger than even a Blue whale, according to scientists who have studied the phenomenon."

- Unknown NOAA source.

"Of course it was a cover up. This thing was more than just an ice quake, if the public knew what we suspected it would have caused mass panic, so we released the 'ice quake' story and hoped it would stay down in the deep. We were wrong."

-Anonymous 2012

Ross Ice Shelf
Antarctica

At a staggering 487,000 square kilometres, the Ross Ice Shelf is the largest of its kind in the world. Rising an impressive 160 feet above sea level at its highest point, its mass continues deep below the water line. A low rumble splinters the silence of the frigid Antarctic air, as a huge section of the shelf shears away and tumbles into the ocean. A pod of orcas veer from the destruction as more than three hundred tons of ice impacts with the ocean.

The creature stirred.

Roused from its slumber by the sound, it opened its eyes and set forth to investigate, each movement of its flippers leaving a concussion wave behind as it moved into open water. Thousands of gallons of sea water filtered through the creature's body as it moved, allowing it to 'taste' the most miniscule vibrations of potential prey up to a hundred miles away. Swaying its head as it swam, the creature detected the fleeing pod of Orcas, able to pinpoint each of the seven whales to within an inch.

The Orcas sensed the giant closing on them and assumed a defensive formation, moving the calves into the middle of the pack. However, the creature was in search of a more substantial meal. It accelerated, angling towards the tail of the largest of the group – a twenty-foot male. The Orca was powerless to defend itself as the creature's backward facing serrated teeth slammed down, slicing through bone and blubber with ease. The incapacitated whale let out a pained moan as its frightened companions continued on, desperate to put distance between themselves and this terrifying new threat. The taste of blood sent the gargantuan beast into frenzy. It took a second bite, completely severing the wounded whale's fluke, spewing hot blood into the frigid waters. The dying orca's cries reverberated around the ocean as the leviathan creature began to gorge itself on its catch.

There was a new predator at the top of the food chain.

CHAPTER 1

Research vessel Neptune
Bering Sea.
62 miles off the coast of Alaska.

Relentless wind and rain battered the vessel as it struggled to stay on course. Andrews stared at the sonar, trying to ignore the nauseating movement of the boat as it ploughed ahead.

"We should have waited until after this storm," grumbled the boat's captain— a broad, barrel chested man with a thick black beard and steely grey eyes.

"Let me worry about the weather, Captain Smeet. You concentrate on keeping us on course."

"Easier said than done. We're getting slammed by the wind on the broadside and the hull is already thick with ice."

"Ice?" Andrews repeated, finally tearing his gaze away from the radar.

"It's seven below freezing," Smeet growled as he steered into a giant wave. "All this spray from the storm is turning into ice and sticking to the structure of the boat. The men are out there clearing it, but if we take on too much, we're dead in the water."

"But you have it under control?"

As much as he wanted to, Smeet didn't react to Andrews or his arrogance. The man had triple the going rate for him to pilot this floating asylum, and the money was more important than the satisfaction of putting him in his place, no matter how tempting an idea it was. Smeet stared at Andrews and tried to make sense of him. He was stick thin, and with his glaring blue eyes, expensive designer polo shirt and slick black hair, Smeet thought he would look more at home on a country club golf course than on the ocean.

"Captain Smeet," Andrews repeated, taking off his glasses as a shadow of a smile appeared on his lips. "The men *are* dealing with it aren't they?"

"Of course, but they aren't happy about it. You should have listened to my advice and gone out tomorrow. I don't know what's so important that it had to be today."

"It had to be today because I have waited for a repeat of this sonar hit for almost fifteen years, and I'm not about to be further delayed because of a little storm."

"I'd call twenty five foot swells and eighty miles an hour winds more than a 'little' storm."

"Aren't we paying you so much because you're the best? Or are you saying we should hire somebody more capable?"

"No," Smeet said, shaking his head, "no need for that. Just be aware of the danger."

"If this sonar hit is what I think it is, Mr Smeet, the seas will be the least of our troubles."

Andrews wanted to say it, if only to silence the arrogant captain's bleating, but it wouldn't help the situation. Instead, he smiled.

"Point taken. Now please, I have to get back to work. Keep us on course until I instruct otherwise."

Smeet scowled and did as instructed as Andrews turned his attention back to the radar. He checked his charts, double-checking their position. Happy they were still on track, he picked up the printout from the sonar spike from a few days earlier. To the casual observer it was no more than a monochrome squiggle. To him it spoke volumes. He had underlined the section of interest in red pen and scrawled next to it: *what are you?*

As the vessel vaulted over another wave, he only hoped they survived long enough to find out.

CHAPTER 2

Twenty-three miles away from the *Neptune*, the crabber *Red Gold* battled against the same storm. In the wheelhouse, Captain Sam Harris struggled to maintain control as the tiny boat was tossed around by the immense swells. A giant wave loomed out of the undulating horizon, blotting out the sky. The experienced captain steered into it, his stomach rolling as the hull smashed into the ocean as the wave passed under it.

Sam's brother, Joey, walked into the wheelhouse, his sea legs managing to make light of the rolling vessel.

"It's hell out there." He said as he perched on the bench behind the captain. "One of the new guys has already quit."

"God damn it, we can't catch a break with these greenhorns huh?" Sam muttered as he fought against the elements.

"It is what it is. Either way, we need to haul these pots and get back to Dutch before we get torn apart. How long until we reach the first pot?"

"Any time now. You better get ready."

Joey smiled, and lit a cigarette, billowing twin plumes of blue smoke out of his nostrils. "I'm always ready."

"I know you are. Just do me a favour. Be careful, okay?"

The tension in Sam's voice was palpable, and it made Joey's stomach knot a little.

"I'll get the crew prepped," he said, pushing aside his own growing fear. "Then we can haul this gear and get the hell out of here."

"Hey, Joey."

"Yeah?"

"Remember what I said. Be careful."

Joey slapped his brother on the back then headed downstairs to gather the crew.

CHAPTER 3

The four men stood by the hatch door waiting for the instruction to go outside. There was a brotherly camaraderie amongst Bering Sea fishermen, although tempers were often frayed due to the lack of sleep and threat of constant danger. With a one in four death rate amongst those brave or crazy enough to make a living on the ocean, the task for anyone new who joined the crew was a difficult one. Acceptance was only gained by sharing in with the backbreaking work and proving themselves strong enough both mentally and physically to captain and fellow crewman alike.

"Hey, Rainwater, how do you like your first taste of the Bering Sea?" Mackay chuckled as he shrugged into his yellow rain slicker.

"I've fished before you know, just not out here."

"Fishing or no fishing, nothin' can prepare you for this kind of hell. Just ask Grimshaw. He's already quit and we haven't even started."

"I'm not a quitter."

"That's what they all say. I reckon Grimshaw would have a different story to tell now – if he could pull his head out of the shitter long enough to tell it."

Rainwater forced his nerves aside and gave the middle finger to Mackay, and was even able to manage a wide grin.

"If your old ass can hack it, so can I."

"You ain't seen nothing yet, boy. Wait till the ice comes, or we hit some of the big waves. Maybe you and Grimshaw can bunk up together."

"Big waves?" Rainwater repeated, wondering how much bigger than the ones currently barraging the vessel could get.

"Oh yeah," Morales added, nudging Mackay as he put on his gloves.

"I seen waves top forty, fifty feet out here."

"Bullshit," Rainwater said, then saw with dismay that Morales wasn't joking.

"A few years back when I was fishing on the Kiska, we got capsized by a forty footer. We never knew anything about it until we were in the water. It hit us broadside and went through us like we weren't there. We were lucky to survive."

"And the dumb asshole decided to come back on the water," Mackay cut in.

"What can I say, I love it out here. Maybe we are all crazy eh? What about you, rookie, you think you can handle life on the Bering Sea?"

"As if he had a choice," Mackay interjected. "With daddy owning the boat, it was always gonna come to this, wasn't it, kid?"

Rainwater wondered why the comment had bothered him so much. He knew they were trying to get a reaction from him, and that giving the new guy – or greenhorn as they were called a hard time, was all part of the initiation to life as a crab fisherman. Whatever the reason, he didn't like to think he was getting an easy ride.

"I don't expect any special treatment out here."

"Is that why you changed your last name to Rainwater? You didn't want to be judged as a Harris kid?" Mackay said, watching for a reaction.

"I have my reasons. I want to be judged on my own ability, not because of the family name."

"Oh don't worry about that," Mackay said. "You will be on that bait station and knee deep in shit and fish guts before you know it."

"I can't wait," Rainwater mumbled, which seemed to amuse Morales and Mackay.

"Don't worry, kid," Morales said, "just think of the money you will make for this trip. They don't call it the hardest job in the world for nothing. Better hope daddy keeps us afloat eh?"

Joey joined them and walked to the outer door.

"Showtime ladies, let's go haul some crab." He said as he opened it and strode out on deck, allowing the fierce wind and rain to blast into the boat.

"Come on, rookie, let's get haulin'" Morales said as he lowered his head and walked against the wind.

Rainwater pulled the hood of his jacket over his head and followed the others outside.

As nauseous as he had felt when he was inside, it was nothing compared to the terrifying conditions on deck. The rain drove down hard enough to sting, and the wind roared almost as loudly as the broiling seas that tossed the crabber with abandon.

The process of crabbing on the *Red Gold* was usually a five-man affair, however, with Grimshaw already quit and seeing out the rest of the trip below decks, it was left to the rest of them to haul their gear and see if they had caught any crab. Failure to do so would mean nobody would be paid, and the entire venture could go under.

The reverse was that if the pots were full, they stood to make upwards of $30,000 each for their efforts. As always, Joey as deck boss operated the crane and pulley system, which would be used to drag the 90 lb crab pots out of the ocean. Mackay was on the hook, which he would toss to the floating buoy markers for each pot and reel them in. When the (hopefully full) pots were pulled out of the ocean, Morales and Mackay would guide the suspended steel and mesh container over to the sorting table. From there, it would be emptied, and the crew could sort through their catch, tossing back any juvenile or female crabs to ensure the grounds were sustainable in future and sending the precious cargo into the holding tanks in the ship's belly.

The task itself would be hard enough, but with the boat rolling and swinging under assault of the storm, and it made the potential for serious injury or death a very real possibility. As was customary with rookies, Rainwater was in charge of the bait table. His job was to cut and bag the pre-frozen fish, which would be used to bait the crab pots. He had already cut and prepared a huge amount of the frozen cod and could no longer feel his hands. It was something of a rite of passage, and he carried on without complaint. Everyone started their fishing careers exactly where he was now - prepping bait before eventually moving up the ladder.

"First pot coming up," Joey yelled, squinting against the wind and sleet.

Mackay set his feet by the four-foot high rail, ignoring the swirling certain death of the ocean below him, as the vessel swayed and drove through the waves. He threw the hook.

It arced through the air with expert precision, and even despite the violent seas and wind, landed exactly where the experienced fisherman wanted it to go, snagging against the buoy ropes that were attached to the crab pot that was sitting on the bottom of the ocean.

Mackay reeled in the line as Morales stood behind him, looping the rope to ensure it didn't tangle around Mackay's legs.

As the buoy was pulled against the side of the deck, Morales took it and hooked it over the winch spool, and Joey immediately started to haul the pot to the surface. Rainwater couldn't help be impressed at how the three of them worked. They moved as one, a well-practiced machine going about their business with frightening efficiency, despite being a man down and exposed to some of the most frightening and violent weather that the twenty- three year old had ever seen.

For the next two hours, the crew hauled their pots, stacking them on the deck of the boat as they were emptied of the valuable king crab. Their yield had been good, if not spectacular. Even though his hands had been numb for well over an hour, Rainwater continued to prep bait, stopping only when the sorting table was full of crab, so he could help in removing the ones that couldn't be sold and tossing them back into the ocean.

The storm had increased in ferocity, and now the boat was being broadsided by huge waves that were washing over the deck.

"How many to haul?" Mackay shouted above the bluster

"Three more." Joey said from behind the winch.

Mackay looked to Rainwater.

"What do you say, rookie, wanna throw the hook for this next one?"

Rainwater looked to his uncle, his father's twin.

"It's up to you," Joey shouted above the bluster. "Just don't screw it up and make us have to circle around."

Rainwater walked to the rail, flexing his hands to try to restore some warmth and feeling to them. He noted that the rail was only a little above knee height, and the briefest loss of balance or lurch of the boat could send him plunging into the ocean and certain death. As if reading his thoughts, Mackay grinned and handed over the hook, the last few hours' work having done nothing to remove his exuberance.

"You don't wanna fall in there, rookie. By the time we spin this sack of shit around to come back, you'd already be dead."

Rainwater tested the weight of the hook in his hand. It looked as light as a feather when Mackay was throwing it, yet, to Rainwater, it felt incredibly heavy and uncomfortable.

"A couple of things," Mackay said. "First, keep your feet on the ground. You don't wanna tangle this line around your feet and get pulled overboard. Second, don't throw the hook at the buoy. High seas, strong currents, throw it a little way ahead instead. The hook will snag itself when you haul it in."

Rainwater nodded, and Mackay stepped aside.

"One last thing," Mackay said with a grin.

"What?"

"Its bad luck for a rookie to miss his first throw, so make sure you snag it in one."

Rainwater squinted out into the darkness, trying to spot the yellow buoys against the undulating ocean.

"There it is, lad, throw the hook," Mackay shouted.

Rainwater threw, the hook arcing through the air. He was sure it was going to be a short throw, however the wind carried it behind the buoy. He began to pull it in, smiling to himself as the hook snagged the rope.

"Good throw," Mackay said, clapping him on the back as he helped to reel in the rope. Morales hooked the line onto the winch, which Joey activated, and pulled the steel pot that they all hoped would be stuffed with crab towards the surface.

"You might make a fisherman yet, Rainwater," Morales said as they waited for the pot to surface.

Rainwater grinned, thinking he might just find acceptance. The pot came up, and the three men cheered, as it was stuffed to the brim with king crab.

"Red money right there boys!" Morales said as they prepared to swing the haul on deck to the sorting table.

Rainwater grinned, and glanced out over the water, a landscape of rolling, undulating crests that barraged the boat. He saw the seventy-foot rogue wave immediately, heading towards them broadside against the wind. It looked more like a wake, but its sheer scale said it was impossible. His stomach tightened, as he knew it was going to hit them.

"Look out!" he screamed.

Morales looked up, and though the grizzled fisherman had seen it all, the terror in his eyes said this was something that even he was unprepared for.

"Holy fuck, down, get down!" Mackay yelled, and dropped to his knees behind the rail.

Rainwater was frozen, watching open mouthed as the wake came closer. Wake was the right word, because as impossible as it seemed, he knew it wasn't a wave. Both Rainwater and Morales saw it break cover, an arched blue-grey back that rose above the surface of the water. Rainwater had only an instant to try to comprehend how immense the creature must be. With nothing to compare it to, he could only stare.

" Morales..." was all he managed before the creature's back slammed into the underside of the fishing vessel, launching it fully out of the water as it passed.

The crab pot, still suspended from the winch, slammed into Morales, smashing his body with the same force of impact of being hit by a freight train. His body twisted through the air like a rag doll before it was swallowed by the rolling, black, Bering Sea.

Rainwater was thrown into the sorting table, his head hitting it hard enough to make white flashes explode in front of his eyes.

The boat slammed back into the water, the creature barely registering its presence as it went on its way. As soon as it touched down, it began to list, its portside dipping towards the water.

"We're going down!" Joey yelled, scrambling to his feet.

"Where's Morales?" Mackay said, shouting to be heard above the wind.

Rainwater couldn't speak, too afraid to do anything but try to process what he had seen.

Mackay shook him by the shoulder. "I said, where's Morales?"

"Overboard..." was all Rainwater could manage.

The portside rail was almost in the water, the boat listing at a sickening thirty-degree angle as it struggled to stay afloat.

"Come on, we need to get suited up," Mackay said, struggling to his feet and helping Rainwater back towards the interior hatch where Joey was readying the survival suits.

"Put these on," he shouted. "I need to get to the wheelhouse. You two get the raft ready, this thing will be at the bottom of the ocean within ten minutes."

With that, Rainwater's uncle was gone, heading back inside the crippled ship. Mackay and Rainwater started to climb into their bright red survival suits as the boat creaked and twisted closer towards its watery grave.

***

The wheelhouse was in disarray. Its windows shattered by the impact, the wind howled through the small room. Sam was in his seat, his bearded face set in a determined grimace as he tried to keep control of the vessel.

"Sam, come on, we have to get off before she sinks."

"I can keep us afloat."

"You can't, we're taking on water. The ship is gone. Come on, let's go."

"Maybe we can-"

"It's over. We need to get off the boat, right now."

"What happened?"

"Something hit us. Something big."

"Boat?"

"No, I don't think so. Call it in and let's get the hell out of here."

"Goddamn it," Sam spat as he sent the distress signal and followed his brother below deck.

Mackay and Rainwater were already suited up and had the self-inflating lifeboat ready to go. Joey and Sam hurried towards them, having to lean against the angle of the boat in order to stay on their feet.

"Come on, let's go," Joey said, as Sam looked around.

"Where's Grimshaw?"

The men looked at each other, expressions blank and frightened.

"Get that raft in the water," Sam said as he turned back towards the hatch.

"You can't go down there, it's probably full of water by now. It's too dangerous." Joey yelled above the wind.

"I'm not leaving anyone behind," he said, as he ran for the door and headed below deck.

The three men stood and looked at each other, and then to Joey, who as deck boss was now in charge.

"Do as he says," Joey said as he stepped out of his survival suit and headed after his brother.

Rainwater went to follow, when Mackay put a hand on his shoulder.

"Not you too. Come on, we need to get this thing into the water. I can't do it on my own."

Rainwater helped Mackay haul the self-inflating life raft across the deck.

"How long do we wait?" Rainwater shouted, trying to ignore how close the water was to spilling over onto the deck of the boat.

"Give them a few minutes then we—"

A huge explosion rocked the vessel from below, launching the rear of the boat out of the water as deck boards exploded into the air.

"We need to get into the water now!" Mackay yelled as the boat began to sink, the water finally clawing its way over the rail.

Smoke billowed out of the stairwell leading below deck, and from between the boards, flames licked at their feet as they were fed by the wind.

"My dad…" Rainwater said quietly, as Mackay pulled the ring to inflate the circular ten-foot rubber boat.

"He's gone," Mackay yelled as he dropped the lifeboat into the water. The vessel was now dipping, its stern dropping below the water line as the bow started to lift.

"I can save him, I—"

Mackay grabbed Rainwater by the shoulders of his survival suit and shook him.

"They are all gone, now get in the fucking raft!"

Rainwater hesitated, staring into the billowing black smoke.

"Come on dammit! When it goes, it'll go quick."

Rainwater hopped into the raft. Mackay followed, and the pair clung on as they were tossed about the ocean. They watched in silence as the *Red Gold* slipped beneath the waves, taking three of its crew with it.

Aboard the *Neptune*, Andrews hurried through the narrow corridors towards the bridge. Smeet was listening to the radio as he tried to pilot the huge ship through the storm.

"Why have we changed course?"

Smeet glanced at Andrews and was barely able to hide his disgust.

"We picked up a distress signal from a crabber a few miles from here. They need our assistance."

"This is a private charter. Let someone else attend to it."

"There are potentially people in the water, and we're the nearest ship for fifty miles."

"If some fool was stupid enough to get his ship sunk, I don't see why *my* time and money should pay for them to be plucked out of the sea."

"They could die from hypothermia if they have fallen into the water. I don't want that on my conscience."

"I don't care what you want. What *I* want is for you to stick to the course I instructed."

Smeet glared at Andrews, who took a compensatory step back.

"Well, in that case, let me tell you how it will go. We're going to pick up these people who need our help, and then I'm going to turn this boat around and take you back to port, where I want you off my ship."

"You were paid, in full, and in advance I might add," Andrews sneered.

"Oh, you will get your money back. Every damn penny. As of now, consider yourself an unwelcome guest on board my ship."

"Do you know who I am?" Andrews said, glaring at the captain as the colour flushed his cheeks. "This mission is too important to deviate from."

"Maybe to you," Smeet said with a disgusted smile, "but not to me."

"You can't do this, I'll talk to my superiors, they will—"

"Look, asshole, you might be some big shot government stooge, but frankly, I don't give a shit. This is *my* ship. *I'm* the captain, and *I* say we are going to help these people. If you don't like it, you can either start swimming or spend the rest of the trip confined to your quarters. It's up to you."

Andrews glared at the captain, his cheek twitching as he processed the information.

"Okay, captain, I suppose you seafaring folk are compelled to stick together. I won't cause any trouble."

"Glad to hear it."

"I do wonder if we would be wise to venture into seas that have already capsized one vessel."

Smeet shook his head. "You didn't seem too concerned about dangerous conditions earlier. Besides, it sounds like it might have been contact with another ship."

"Why do you say that?"

"The radio message said something hit them."

Andrews gave Smeet his full attention.

"Where did this happen?"

"A few miles due east of here. Coast Guard is grounded due to the weather so it looks like we're their best chance."

Andrews nodded, his mind already racing with possibilities.

"The message was clear, and it couldn't have been one of these rogue waves you mentioned earlier?"

Smeet shook his head "No, they were clear. They said something big hit them broadside. My guess is another boat got too close, although I would have expected them to throw a distress signal out too."

"What do you think it might be?"

"If you shut up and let me get to the survivors, you can ask them yourself."

Two slow hours passed in the rubber lifeboat. Rainwater looked at Mackay, who was sitting with his chin on his chest. He hadn't spoken for some time, and the bloody wound on his face had dried into a matted crust. Rainwater wanted to close his eyes, if only for a moment to take away some of the agony that had invaded his body. He was numb, his lips trembling as the boat was pushed wherever the tides chose to send it. He had activated the survival suit's transponder, which would give their location to any ships that came close enough. Now, all he wanted was to sleep, to close his eyes for a moment and rest.

He forced himself to focus, to pick a spot and stare at it. He chose his right foot, trying not to look beyond it at the dizzying, vertigo inducing motion of the lifeboat. His thoughts tried as best they could to wade through the thick soup that had invaded his brain. In his mind's eye, he could see the immense wake and the grey-green back of whatever had ploughed into them. He had seen something that defied belief, and knew now that the seas were no place for man. He lapsed into unconsciousness moments before the searchlights of the *Neptune* illuminated the life raft.

CHAPTER 4

Unnamed government facility
Washington D.C.

Andrews walked through the corridors of the vast grey building that officially didn't exist. It had no address, no registered owner, and no official title. A modest two stories high at street level, it also extended deep below the surface, acting as one of several secret locations designed to hold the president and his cabinet in case of emergency. He approached the unmarked elevator, giving a cursory glance to the multitude of security cameras that watched his every move. Shuffling his mountain of folders into one arm, he swiped his ID card through the reader at its side and placed his hand on the discreet panel beneath. Reading his palm print, the system opened the elevator doors and allowed him access. He waited as the doors closed and carried him to his destination eight floors below.

This meeting was a make or break. He was sure he had enough supporting evidence to convince his superiors. Despite the public opinion about alien conspiracies and knowledge of the existence of E.T., the actual and infinitely less interesting fact was that the government didn't believe in such things and were a stuffy, hard to convince bunch who cared only about politics, wars, and money.

The doors hissed open and Andrews was stopped at a security station where he was frisked for anything that could be construed as a dangerous weapon. Passing the checks, he was handed back his folders and allowed to proceed. Taking a moment to gather his thoughts, he took a deep breath and entered the meeting room, striding purposefully to the front. He set his double arm full of paperwork on the desk, and then paused, looking at the four men who were watching him with cold indifference.

"Gentlemen, my name is Doctor Martin Andrews, and I'm here today to talk to you about the situation to which by now, you all have been briefed, at least in a preliminary fashion."

The men looked back impassively.

Tough crowd, he thought to himself as he went on.

"Back in 1997, the National Oceanic and Atmospheric Administration detected an underwater signal, which was unlike anything ever recorded before. The signal was picked up by an array of deep water hydrophones designed primarily to monitor seismic activity. We dubbed it, The Bloop."

"What's so unusual about it?" asked a white haired, grey-eyed general, who was both cold and unreadable.

"Our analysis, which was concurrent with NOAA's own research, showed that the sound was thought to be organic in nature."

"Surely that's nothing unusual. The ocean is full of life," said the secretary of the defence, his tone implying that his time was being wasted.

"That's true, sir," Andrews said, "however, nothing about this signal was normal."

Andrews paused for effect, but if his audience was captivated, they were doing a great job of hiding it. He continued.

"This… 'Bloop', was thoroughly analysed and concluded to be not only organic, but made by a creature far larger than any species we currently know of."

"How big exactly?" the white haired major asked, his eyes showing a flicker of interest.

"Well, sir, if you imagine the blue whale is the largest known creature to inhabit the oceans at somewhere between eighty five and ninety feet, based on the signal we recorded, this creature would have to be at least three times that length."

"Are you saying this is some kind of god-damn dinosaur?" a thin, wiry man said from behind oversized glasses.

"No, not a dinosaur. An unknown species."

"Dr Andrews," the secretary of defence said, "if this is as big as you say it is, why has nobody ever seen it? Why has its presence not been felt? What I'm asking is how can this one encounter back in 97', lead you to such a speculative conclusion?"

"Well, sir, until a few weeks ago, we were prepared to dismiss the Bloop as an anomaly. Maybe an ice quake of some kind, or an expulsion of gas escaping from a rupture on the seabed. However, recent events came to light that changed things, which is why I come to you now."

"Go on," the major said, now giving his full attention to Andrews.

"Back in September, a huge portion of the Ross ice shelf in Antarctica fell into the sea. We believe the force of impact as the ice hit the water and the subsequent vibrations stirred the creature from some kind of long term hibernation"

"Forgive me, Doctor," the secretary of defence said with a smug grin, "I fail to see how this is anything other than speculation and fantasy. If you want to convince us, we need facts."

"I was getting to that, sir."

Andrews took a breath and continued.

"As I was saying, we think this creature was roused by the falling ice shelf from some kind of hibernation. Following the quake, we recorded another sound in the area that was at the same frequency of the Bloop. Later, partial remains of a killer whale were discovered close to where the signal emanated from."

"The ocean is a big place, surely you can't speculate that this creature killed the whale. It could have been a shark, or even another whale." The thin man in glasses said as he shot an agitated look towards the secretary of defence.

"Forgive my bluntness, sir," Andrews said, "but we do know. We recovered the carcass. Its entire lower half was missing. No shark would be able to do that. We also measured the bite radius of some of the wounds on the Orca, and although there was some decomposition and the feeding of other smaller scavengers to consider, the findings were astonishing."

"And what were they?" the general said, folding his hands on the desk.

"Well, sir, we estimate this creature would have a bite radius of around eighteen to twenty five feet.

"Impossible," the general said, rolling his wedding ring around his finger, "that's very hard to believe, Dr Andrews."

"I agree, but please, allow me to finish. Immediately following the ice quake, countless species of whales and fish altered their normal migratory and feeding patterns. When we analysed the changes, it was evident that all species from the smallest fish to the largest whales were trying to avoid something. A few weeks ago, I was on board the research vessel Neptune in the Bering Sea, attempting to track the source of the disturbance when a distress signal came in from a stricken fishing boat reporting something had hit them. We of course abandoned the search and responded. By the time we arrived, the boat had sunk, we did manage to find a life raft floating nearby which contained two survivors. Both men were hypothermic and close to death, however, one of them was mumbling about a monster that hit the boat."

"Did they survive?" The major asked.

"Yes. Both men were taken to a hospital in Anchorage for treatment and have since been released. The rest of the crew went down with the ship."

"Dr Andrews," the secretary of defence said, glaring at the scientist, "this still proves nothing. Talk of maybes and wild speculation isn't something that we are able to work with. What exactly are you expecting us to do?"

"I need finance to pull together a team and a ship to go to find this creature. To study it."

"Do you see this endeavour as a valuable use of government money?"

"Well, actually, I do sir. More so than the wars you continue to fund."

He regretted saying it immediately, and knew he had screwed up his chance. The secretary's face flushed, and he glared at Andrews as he spoke through gritted teeth.

"Well, fortunately for you, Mr Andrews, how that money is spent is a decision made way above your pay grade. For the record, I think you have seen one too many monster movies."

"If you don't do this, it will be a huge mistake. There is so much to learn here," Andrews said.

"I appreciate your warning, but you are wrong."

"No he isn't."

All eyes went to the only man at the table who had so far remained silent. He was slim, with black hair and a thin face. His eyes were dark, and he watched those around the table with palpable self-confidence.

"Who the hell are you?" the secretary of defence asked, as the man stood and walked to the front of the room, clasping his hands behind his back.

"My name is Russo, and I'm here to tell you that Dr Andrews is correct in everything he has said."

"Might I ask how you know this?" the secretary snapped, clearly not liking having his feathers ruffled.

"I'm afraid I don't answer to you."

"This is ridiculous, I have top level clearance."

Russo shrugged, and held the older man's gaze.

"I understand that, Mr Secretary. Please try to understand that *everybody* answers to somebody. For now, I would appreciate it if you would be quiet and let me explain."

Russo returned to his seat and picked up a stack of folders sealed with the presidential crest, handing everyone around the table a copy and giving the final one to Andrews.

"Now, gentlemen, if you would be so kind as to open those documents, I will explain all about Project Blue and how it ties in to the funding Dr Andrews is requesting."

CHAPTER 5

Rainbow Bay Beach
Australian gold Coast

The scorching sun burned down on the juvenile sperm whale that had beached itself some five hours earlier. Twenty six year old marine biologist, Clara Thompson and her team of volunteers had been working on freeing the trapped animal for some time, and were close to returning it to the ocean.

"Dexter," she yelled to her assistant as she replaced the wet towels which covered the whales back. "Hose her down again, we need to keep her skin moist."

Dexter looked at his boss and nodded, not having the heart to tell her that the animal's chances of survival were slim. Clara had seen beaching's before, but the last couple of weeks had seen a worrying increase in the phenomena. Often there were plausible explanations. Confusion on the animal's part or due to following smaller, more nimble dolphins into the shallows had accounted for similar incidents in the past. Even sonar pings from submarines had been known to cause confusion in certain species and cause them to beach themselves in error, and yet, something about this most recent bout of them concerned her. It was too much, too many different species at the same time. It wasn't enough to make mainstream news, not when there were pointless celebrity feuds to report on, or wars in faraway countries to glorify. However, in the close community of marine biology, the stranding's had certainly raised a few eyebrows, and now one had happened on her doorstep.

Clara had a slim, athletic body, and bronzed, freckle dashed skin from a career spent mostly outdoors. Her eyes were green and her hair a stunning shade of red, which even tied and hidden under her baseball cap still stood out in the blazing Australian sun.

"How long until that bloody crane gets here?" she snapped.

"It's inbound. Within the hour I expect." Dexter replied, glancing at the tide that was lapping around the whale's underbelly.

He picked up the hose as Clara worked on digging a channel around the animal to help return it to the ocean. A crowd of onlookers had gathered and were watching intently.

"We can't wait much longer," she said, glancing at the weakened animal. "We need to try to do this by hand."

"I thought you said that was a last resort?"

"This is the last resort. Get some of those rubberneckers to help us."

Thirty minutes later, the group managed to drag the whale back into the ocean. They whooped and cheered as they watched the animal swim away. Clara stood, hands on hips, breathing heavily from the exertion.

"Think she'll be okay?" Dexter asked as he stood beside her.

"I hope so. She seems lively enough."

The pair started to walk back up the beach, when they heard the commotion behind them.

The whale they had rescued had re-beached itself, only this time it wasn't alone. Clara and Dexter watched as dozens of whales, dolphins, and even sharks launched themselves on the beach, thrashing as they tried to distance themselves as far as they could from the water.

"Jesus…" Dexter said as he watched wave after wave of fish lurch out of the water.

Clara didn't reply. Instead, she stared out beyond the beach full of stranded marine life, to the calm blue ocean beyond.

"What the hell is spooking you all?" she muttered to herself under her breath.

CHAPTER 6

Kodiak town,
Kodiak Island,
Alaska.

Lying off the southern coast of Alaska, Kodiak Island is the second largest of its kind in the entire United States. Mountainous and heavily forested in the northern and eastern regions, yet treeless in the south, the island is pocked with numerous natural bays, which are used by the local fishermen to shelter their vessels when the nearby Bering Sea unleashed one of its frequent violent storms. The island also boasted a rich wildlife reserve, and was populated by a community who almost exclusively work in or around the thriving fishing industry.

Because of its location within the sub polar oceanic climate zone, Kodiak's 6,000 residents are subjected to long, cold winters that test even the hardiest of the fishermen who make up a vast bulk of the local populous.

Valerie Harris looked out of the window of her house across the bay, and clutched the photograph of her late husband a little tighter. Although death itself wasn't a surprise out on the water, the fact that the Harris family were so well known, and had been for generations, made the local interest aspect worthy of the newspapers paying particular attention to the story. Valerie looked at her children as they ate breakfast, Tyler who was three, and Tess who had just turned five, would never know their father. Never get to find out what a wonderfully warm, kind man he was, and for that, she was angry. She closed her eyes, and rested her head on the cool glass of the window, feeling guilty about the dark thoughts that had drifted back into her mind.

She had bought a bottle of vodka, and set aside a stockpile of pills. Twice now, she had gone as far as opening the bottles, but hadn't found the strength to go through with it, mostly because of the love she had for her children. The voice in her head that had given her the idea to end it all in the first place, was making ever more convincing arguments that they would be better off without her of late. As she stood there, it started once again to ask those questions she was never able to answer.

What would happen when the money ran out?

What would happen when the house got repossessed because she couldn't afford to keep up the mortgage payments?

What would happen when the children grew older, and their unconditional love for her morphed into resentment and hate?

She closed her eyes, and clenched her fists, determined not to put them through such an ordeal. She did, however, wonder how long it would be before the voice in her head became the one she turned to for help, and that idea frightened her. All she could do was to take things one day at a time and hope she made it through.

And if the day came where she couldn't?

She looked at her children, and choked back more tears. She would have too. It was the only way.

CHAPTER 7

Sunset Cliffs,
California

"Go on, Tommy, stop being such a pussy," Alex goaded as he treaded water and squinted to the cliff top.

Tommy ignored his brother and looked at the ocean some fifty feet below. It had started as a game of dares, each of them daring the other to do things more and more extreme in the hope of causing their sibling to back out. First, they had dared each other to steal a magazine from the local store, then to run across the street without stopping or changing direction to see if they could make the traffic swerve to avoid them. So far, they had each done everything the other had suggested, however, now as fourteen year old Tommy looked at his brother from the edge of the cliff, he didn't think he could go through with it.

"Tooooommmmyyyy," Alex goaded as he kicked onto his back and spat water in the air.

Tommy stared out at the beautiful, pale blue of the Pacific Ocean, and shifted his weight, his feet starting to burn on the hot surface. He knew the jump was safe. The water here was deep, and he was in no danger of hitting rocks or anything else that could end his life or leave him in a wheelchair. Still, he wasn't great with heights, and as he looked down on his brother, his stomach knotted.

Alex was making chicken noises as he kicked and splashed in the water below.

"Okay, cut it out." Tommy yelled, the irritation in his voice just about masking his fear.

He took a deep breath, and psyched himself up to make the jump. There was no question of him wimping out. He would never live it down, especially as he was older than Alex was by almost a year. He took a couple of steps back, exhaled, and calculated his run up.

Three running steps, then jump.
Easy.

He felt a powerful surge of adrenaline as he took his run up, half considering trying to perform a mid-air somersault in order to try to shut Alex up and prove he wasn't afraid.

He saw the shape out of the corner of his eye as he was about to leap, and although he tried, couldn't stop in time. It was huge. A deep, dark shadow under the water that was angling towards Alex. Tommy half jumped, half fell towards the water, his brother's mocking now secondary to the thing that was heading towards them. He told himself it was a whale, yet knew it was way too big. Impossibly big. His thought process was cut short as he hit the water, tumbling and spinning as he submerged.

He kicked to the surface, gasping for air as his grinning sibling swam over to him.

"What the hell was that? You screwed up whatever you were trying to—"

"Swim!" Tommy blurted, kicking towards the beach.

"What the hell?"

Tommy put his head down and kicked hard, vaguely aware that his brother was following. He could see the beach, near, and yet seeming so very far away. He spared a glance over his shoulder, and a fresh surge of adrenaline raced through his body.

The wake was closing in on them. It was impossibly large, impossibly wide. Tommy thought he could see the ghostly shape of a mottled grey body below the surface as whatever it was closed on them.

He turned towards the beach and lowered his head, kicking with everything he had. Alex was alongside him now as the two boys swam in unison.

Tommy felt the blessed touch of the sandy ocean floor as they reached the shallows. Coughing and spluttering, Tommy charged up the beach, his brother in tow. He turned to look out at the water, and saw the immense shape that had followed them peel away and head back to the deep. The displaced water rolled towards them, sending a freak wave up the beach, soaking sunbathers and children who complained as they scrambled to higher ground. Alex had his hands on his knees, panting as he tried to regain his breath.

"What the hell was all that about?" he asked between ragged gasps.

Tommy didn't answer. He could only stare out into the ocean and try to make some sense of what he had seen. "Hey," Alex repeated, "what is it?"

Tommy shook his head, and vomited noisily into the surf.

CHAPTER 8

Freeport town,
Kodiak Island,
Alaska.

At 120 feet in length, the *Victorious* was far bigger than most of the other commercial fishing boats on the dock. The ship was a heavily modified whaler that had been transformed, ready for Andrews and Russo to proceed with their operation. Below its unassuming grey hull, a state of the art command centre had been installed, as had living facilities for up to a crew of twenty. On this particular trip, there would be just twelve. Andrews waited until the boat was securely in its berth, smoothed his jacket, and walked down the ramp onto the dock. He took in the town, casting his sunglass-covered eyes over the homes that were scattered up the hillside. The wind was cold and smelled of salt, and the incessant scatter of seagulls was already starting to give him a headache.

There was a weather beaten and grizzled fisherman checking crab pots at the end of the dock. Andrews angled towards him, unleashing his best smile as he approached.

"Excuse me, sir," he said smoothly, "I wonder if you could help me? I'm looking for someone."

"Aye, you wouldn't be here otherwise." The old man said, not looking up from his task.

"Do you know where I might find Henry Rainwater?"

The old man paused, cupping his hand against the sun as he stared at Andrews.

"You mean the Harris kid?"

Andrews nodded. "I was lead to believe he goes by the name of Rainwater now."

"So he says, but he'll always be a Harris round here. You here about the business that killed his pop and uncle?"

"I'm afraid I can't say, all I can tell you is that it's imperative I speak to him."

The fisherman stood and wiped his grimy hands on his shirt.

"Well, all I can tell you is that he ain't said much of anything to anyone since he got back from the hospital. Hell, he ain't even left the house. Nobody has seen him anyhow."

"And where is the house, exactly?" Andrews asked, pulling a notepad out of his pocket.

"I ain't sayin' nothin'. Not till I know what you want."

"It's imperative I speak with him."

"That may be, but I still ain't about to tell you where he lives. As I said, the kid won't talk anyway."

"How do you suggest I find him?"

"Ain't my problem. You could try Belgrave point."

Andrews wrote it in his diary. "Thank you, sir, and where is that exactly, is it far?"

The fisherman shook his head and laughed as he lit a cigarette.

"It ain't a place. It's a bar up the hill there. Ask for a guy called Mackay. He was on the boat, and if he's drunk enough, his tongue might loosen enough to talk."

Andrews slipped the notebook back in his pocket.

"What if he's not there?"

The old man smiled. "He will be."

"How can you be sure?"

"Because, that's pretty much the only place he's been since the accident. Spends all damn day by himself, drinking till' someone has to carry him home. He ain't been the same since he got back from that damn trip."

"You think he'll talk to me?"

The fisherman looked Andrews up and down, and shrugged.

"Who knows? Might cost you a few drinks to loosen his tongue. I'll tell you this though, whatever happened out there has done something to him."

"What do you mean?"

"Well, he was always happy go lucky, you know full of piss and vinegar. Had a mouth on him that would usually get him into trouble. Since he came back... I don't know. Man's changed."

"In what way?"

"He's quiet. Doesn't say much to anyone anymore. Just sits staring into space. You know what's even more odd?"

"Go on."

"Just before the trip, he bought himself a boat. Took him the best part of six years to get the money together. All he would ever talk about was running his own boat. The second he came back, he goes and sells it for less than half he bought it for."

"Any idea why?"

"Who knows, "shrugged the fisherman. "Scared maybe. Who can blame him after almost dying? The ocean isn't something to be screwed around with."

Andrews nodded and looked past the fisherman.

"Where did you say this bar was?"

"Up the hill there. You can't miss it. Big white building."

"Thanks."

"Welcome, although I wouldn't expect him to say much."

"Maybe, maybe not," Andrews said with a slimy grin. "I guess we will have to see won't we?"

The fisherman nodded as Andrews set off up the hill.

The Belgrave point bar was set back into the hillside, and as the fisherman had said, it was hard to miss. Andrews walked into the dimly lit building, taking a few seconds to let his eyes adjust to the gloom. There were a dozen or so fishermen spread around the tables, all indulged in their own private conversations. Andrews took an instant dislike to the place as he approached the bar, which wasn't helped by the icy stare of the barkeep which Andrews suspected was reserved for strangers like him.

"What can I get you?" he asked bluntly.

"I'm looking for someone. A man called Mackay. I need to speak to him."

"That's him over there."

Andrews looked to where the barkeep had motioned at the man hunched over at the corner table.

"What's he drinking?" Andrews asked.

"Whisky. That's about all he drinks these days."

"Pour him another, I'll take one too."

***

Mackay didn't look up from his empty glass as Andrews approached, or say anything when he sat opposite and set the fresh drink in front of him.

"Mr Mackay?"

"Who's asking?"

"My name is Andrews, and I would like—"

"You a reporter?"

"No. I'm with the government, and I want to talk to you about the accident that claimed the lives of—"

"Forget it. I don't wanna talk about it."

"Mr Mackay, the accident needs to be investigated, and we need to find out the truth."

"The truth..." Mackay repeated as he took a sip of the drink Andrews had bought him. "The truth is the boat sank, and my friends are dead."

"Is that why you won't go back on the water?"

Mackay finally looked at Andrews, and for a second, it seemed he was going to lunge across the table. Instead, he shook his head and took another sip of the whisky.

"You don't know shit. I have my reasons for staying on dry land."

Andrews leaned close, and lowered his voice to a whisper.

"You saw something, didn't you?"

Mackay watched, offering no reply. Andrews pressed on.

"You saw something out in the ocean, and whatever it is scared you, didn't it?"

"Yes," Mackay said with a sneer. "I saw my friends die. Nothin' more, nothin' less."

"You can tell me the truth, I believe you."

"Look, mister, I don't know who you are, and I care even less. All I can tell you is if you don't shut up and leave me alone, I'm gonna finish this drink, drag you outside and beat the shit out of you. Understood?"

"Okay," Andrews said, "I hear you loud and clear. Just remember, I'm only looking to find out the truth."

Mackay drained his glass and looked at Andrews with a glassy, half-coherent stare. "I don't care about whatever it is you're looking for. Just leave me alone."

Andrews stood and pushed his chair under the table. He reached into his pocket and pulled out a business card, which he placed on the table.

"If you wish to speak with me, don't hesitate to call."

"I already told you, pal, I got nothing to say to you."

"I know. Keep the card just in case."

"Whatever you say, buddy," Mackay said as he picked up the card, looked at it, then tossed it back on the table.

"Just one more thing," Andrews said as he fastened his jacket. "The other survivor, Henry Rainwater... any idea where I might find him?"

"You *might* find him anywhere, but where he is I don't know. Just get the hell out of here and leave us be."

Andrews nodded, ignoring the icy stares of the other patrons as he made his way to the exit. Even though it was a small town, finding one man would be difficult, especially if it was a man who didn't want to be found. He wondered if Russo would have any ideas, and was about to head back towards the *Victorious*, when he saw the newspaper stuffed into the top of the waste bin. He pulled it out, and looked at the headline.

FUNERAL FOR BROTHERS LOST AT SEA.

Andrews looked at the photograph of the grieving woman, crying at the graveside, then at the caption underneath

Widow, Valerie Harris, mourns her husband Joey, who along with his brother Sam and deck hands Hector Morales & Alex Grimshaw were killed at sea in last week's tragic fishing accident. See page 7.

Andrews skimmed to the relevant page. Three quarters of it was filled with a long lens photograph of the funeral, and the mourners standing around the four coffins. Andrews skimmed the article, hoping against hope that the usual insensitivity of newspapers would pay dividends. The final paragraph of the article gave him exactly what he was looking for.

...Mrs Harris, of 344 Chestnut Drive, was not available for comment at the time of writing...

Andrews grinned and tossed the newspaper back into the bin.

CHAPTER 9

344 Chestnut Drive
Freeport,
Kodiak, Alaska

Valerie Harris walked around her home like a ghoul. Without the children to provide her the distractions she needed to get through the day, the bottle of vodka and the two full bottles of prescription painkillers on the kitchen counter looked particularly inviting.

Her way out.

Her exit strategy.

One that if not for the children, she would have taken already.

There was a knock at the door. She ignored it, unable to cope with another visit from one of her neighbours or a well-meaning do-gooder wishing to pass on their sympathy, and at the same time get a fresh batch of gossip about the Harris widow to spread around their circle of friends. The knock came again, louder and with more urgency. To continue to ignore it would mean more people would come and interfere, perhaps accurately guessing that she was considering ending her pathetic existence. She strode to the door and opened it. For a split second, she thought it was Joey, so similar were they in appearance now that he had started a beard.

"Hi, Valerie. Can I come in?"

She nodded and stood back to allow him in. Rainwater walked into the sitting room, clasping his hands behind his back as he looked at the photographs on the wall of his father and uncle.

"I didn't see you at the funeral." Valerie said.

"I couldn't be there… It didn't feel right."

"They would have wanted you there. You're all we have now."

"I shouldn't have left them. I should have gone back."

"We can all talk about should and shouldn't. It doesn't change anything. They're still dead, Henry."

He nodded and turned back to the pictures on the wall.

"Can I get you a drink?" She asked.

"I'll take a coffee, if you have some."

"I have it. Go ahead and take a seat."

Henry nodded, but didn't sit. He picked up a photograph of his father, uncle, and himself as a five year old on the deck of the *Lisa Marie,* named after his late mother. Rainwater's father had retired the boat following her death, and it had been in dry dock ever since. Setting the photograph back on the mantle, he walked to the kitchen.

Valerie was leaning on the counter, dabbing the corners of her eyes with a tissue.

"It's hard isn't it?" he said quietly, as his eyes slid to the vodka and pills on the work surface. Valerie saw them and scooped them up, shoving them into one of the overhead cupboards.

"I'm not about to do anything stupid, if that's what you think," she snapped.

"I didn't say anything. Please, I didn't come here to fight."

"I miss him, Henry. I mean, I'm used to him being away at sea for weeks at a time but this is different, I keep waiting even though I know he's never going to open the door and come back home."

"I'm sorry, Val. I truly am. I miss them too."

"Not enough to keep the family name though." He knew the bitterness in her voice was fuelled by grief, the words still cut deep.

"Look, I have my reasons. Dad and I didn't always get on. You have to understand how hard it is to live up to his name, to follow in his footsteps. I didn't want that pressure."

"Why did they die, Henry? Why didn't you make him get in the damn lifeboat?"

"I'm sorry."

"Sorry doesn't pay the bills, it doesn't answer the kids when they are asking when daddy is coming home. Sorry doesn't cut it."

"I don't know what you want from me, Val. This wasn't my fault."

"I don't blame you for the accident, I blame you for not being there for us after. Turning up at my door now doesn't make up for you missing the funeral and abandoning us when we needed you the most."

"I just needed some time…"

"It's not all about you. What about me? What about my kids?"

Rainwater stared at the floor.

"I'm sorry," he repeated, hating himself for not being able to think of anything more constructive to say.

"Look, I don't mean to take it out on you," she said as she wiped her eyes. "I'm sick of well-wishers and people asking me if I'm okay. I'm struggling here, Henry. I don't know what to do."

Rainwater nodded, wondering how to best approach the subject that had been the reason for his visit.

"I spoke to Mackay. He came to the funeral." Henry ignored the bitter edge in her voice, deciding he didn't want to upset the grieving woman.

"He told me all about you and the crazy stuff you were babbling in the hospital."

"I was delirious with hypothermia. What did he say?"

"He said you were babbling about something in the water, something big that smashed into the boat and caused the accident. He says you're crazy."

"Mackay had no right to say that to you. If he has a problem he can ask me about it himself."

"How?" she shrugged. "Nobody could find you. Nobody knew where you were."

"I needed to clear my head, I needed to think."

"And leave us all to deal with the funeral arrangements in the process?"

"I'm sorry, I really don't know what else to say."

"So I see." She snapped, setting the cup of coffee on the counter in front of him.

"So," she said, as she looked him in the eye, "was it?"

"Was what?"

"An accident."

"You know what happened."

"Why do I get the feeling you know more than you're letting on?"

"I don't think this is the right time…"

"What did you see out there, Henry? I know you saw something, I can see it in your eyes. You Harris's are bad liars."

"Look, I didn't come here to argue or to heap any more stress on you. I came here to clear the air and to ask a favour."

"Ahh, here we go. The real reason for the visit."

"Look, Val," he said sharply, his anger taking over, "you're grieving, I get it. I am too. Even if taking it out on me makes you feel better it's not right. I lost them too. I appreciate how hard it is for you, I really, really do, but it's no picnic for me either. I keep replaying it in my head, and wishing I had died instead of them. I screwed up by not forcing them onto the boat, but you know what they were like. They would never leave with someone still on board. They were trying to do the right thing."

"And now I'm alone."

"We both are." He said quietly.

Another silence followed, as the two stood and sipped their drinks.

"So, what was it?" Valerie asked.

"What was what?"

"The favour you wanted to ask me. The reason for coming out of wherever you have been hiding."

He sighed and lowered his head, wondering if he had picked the wrong time to visit.

"I'm sorry," she said, running her hands through her hair. "I didn't mean to snap. I haven't been sleeping well."

He saw it happen, the slump of her shoulders as all the fight went out of her.

"Look, I think this is probably a bad time," he said, setting his cup down. "Why don't I come back later?"

"No, no it's okay. Just ask me whatever it was you came here to ask."

Henry hesitated, and looked Valerie in the eye.

"It's about the Lisa Marie. I want to use it."

"Why?"

"It's just something I have to do. Please, don't ask me anymore. Just let me take the boat."

She smiled and tried to make eye contact, but he lowered his gaze.

"It's true isn't it? You think you saw something out there?"

"No. That's not what this is about."

"What did you see? What's out there that has you so scared?"

"I'm not scared, and there is nothing to tell."

"You're lying. I can see it in your face."

"Valerie, please, don't ask me anymore. Let me take the boat, no more questions, okay?"

"No, not until you tell me what you need it for."

"I can't. Not yet."

"Fine. Then no boat."

"Valerie—"

"No, Henry. If you want to take the Lisa Marie, you are going to tell me why, and what actually happened."

"You don't understand, I'm doing this for you. You don't need the stress."

"Who the hell are you to tell me what I do and don't need? I want the truth, is that too much to ask?"

"Look, calm down, I'll come back later, I—"

She slapped him hard across the face and recoiled instantly, drawing breath and lifting her hand to her mouth as the room fell silent.

"Henry, I'm sorry."

"I guess I deserved that." He said as he rubbed his cheek.

Valerie sat heavily at the kitchen table and put her head in her hands.

"I don't hate you, Henry, and I don't blame you. I just want to know what happened to my husband so I can start to get over his death."

Rainwater hesitated, torn between getting it off his chest and how ridiculous what he saw would sound. "The night the *Red Gold* sank wasn't an accident." He said, choosing his words carefully.

"What do you mean?"

"Something hit us. Something big."

He watched for her reaction as she processed the information.

"Tell me what you know."

Despite his every intention of telling her what had happened when he had arrived, he had been caught off guard and unprepared for how badly she was coping. He didn't want to put her through any more pain.

"No, this isn't fair. I'll hire a different boat. Forget I asked."

"What gives you the right to keep it from me? Tell me what you're hiding."

"Look, all I know is the people we love are dead. I know you probably think I'm the biggest prick in the world right now, believe me, I'm only doing this to protect you."

"It's not your job. It's not your right. I can tell something is bothering you. Spit it out. Be a man for once."

"I'm sorry I couldn't save them." He whispered, and then before Valerie could say anything else, he set his cup on the counter and left without looking back.

CHAPTER 10

South Pacific Ocean
5 miles off the coast of New Guinea

The majestic 92-foot blue whale glided through the ocean, moving with ease through the black depths. It had acknowledged the presence of the creature that had been stalking it some five hours ago, and was now tiring as it further increased its speed to try to put some distance between them. With no natural predators, the blue whale wasn't accustomed to fleeing from anything, it had however, sensed the immense size of this new threat, and had abandoned its previous course to try to avoid a confrontation.

The whale made for the surface, its need to breathe every twenty minutes forcing its decision. Its pursuer had no such need for oxygen, and increased its speed, closing the distance between itself and the blue to half a mile.

The whale breached, ejecting a great plume of spray before diving again, changing course towards the coastal shallows in the hope of shaking its mammoth pursuer. The creature accelerated, the attack ferocious and violent, its bite shearing away a portion of the blue whales fluke fin. The Blue increased its speed, heading for the shallows with more urgency.

The creature angled away, readjusted its position and attacked, the second bite more infinitely more devastating than the first, shearing away the whale's entire ten-foot flipper with a single bite. The wounded whale emitted a pained moan, and tried to propel its crippled body through the ocean.

The creature devoured the fin, its body quivering as it consumed the mass of bone and blubber, sending it into frenzy. It could sense the water was becoming shallow, yet the creature's instinct to feed was stronger than its self-preservation, and it pursued the crippled whale relentlessly.

It attacked again, this time its bite shearing away a section of underbelly, and in turn, releasing a bounty of blood and entrails into the ocean. The creature fed, gorging itself on its meal as the dead whale drifted out of range into the shallows and onto the beach, where blood red waves licked against its mutilated remains.

CHAPTER 11

Greendale Cemetery
Freeport,
Kodiak, Alaska

It was the first time Rainwater had seen the grave of his father and uncle, and was surprised to find he wasn't as upset as he expected he would be.

"I wondered when you might show up here."

Rainwater spun his head around and nodded to Mackay, who was standing behind him, hands thrust in his pockets.

"I'm just here to pay my respects."

"Aye, and not before time."

They were silent, and Mackay walked closer, standing beside Rainwater.

"It's still hard to believe isn't it?"

"Yeah, it is." Rainwater said softly.

"Missed you at the funeral."

"I had my reasons."

Mackay didn't push the point, and the two stood in silence.

"In the hospital, I heard some of that crazy shit you were saying."

Rainwater glanced at Mackay then exhaled, his breath pluming in the chilly morning air.

"I saw something. In the water."

"You didn't see anything." Mackay said, glancing at Rainwater.

"Something hit us, something big."

"Cut it out. We were hit by a damn wave, nothing more."

"It wasn't a wave, it was a wake. Morales saw it too."

"Morales is dead. Don't drag him into this when he can't defend himself."

"I'm not dragging anyone into anything. We both saw it just before it hit the boat."

"Bullshit." Mackay said, walking away. Rainwater followed.

"Why don't you believe me? You were there."

"It was a wave. A damn freak accident. Why can't you accept it instead of spouting off this sea monster bullshit?"

"I'm not lying."

"You didn't see shit. Your mind was playing tricks on you. All you saw was a wave, a big one and something in your head has concocted this sea monster story."

"You saw it too, didn't you?"

Mackay broke eye contact, and started to walk away.

"I didn't see anything."

"You did," Rainwater pressed, grabbing Mackay by the shoulder and spinning him around.

"You saw it. The thing that hit us."

"Don't dare try to pull me in with the same crazy bullshit you were spouting. I heard you in the hospital, spouting off about giant wakes and fucking Godzilla coming out of the ocean and sinking our boat."

"I'm not lying, why the hell would I?"

"Guilt? Who the hell knows?"

"Guilt at what?"

"For leaving them, for getting in that damn life raft."

"You got in it too," Rainwater screamed, shoving Mackay in the chest. "You got in because you saw what I saw, and you didn't want to be on that boat any more than I did."

"Don't you stand here and talk to me like some kind of veteran fisherman. You're a rookie. I spent years on that damn boat. They were like my family. It's enough they are dead, without you making these dumb fuckin' claims about sea monsters."

"I know what I saw!"

"Let's say you did," Mackay said, his face twisted into a scowl. "Let's say you saw what you say you did, and it was responsible for sinking the boat, what good will it do to shout from the rooftops about it? Why not let things heal normally without damaging the legacy of your family?"

"I can't do that!" Rainwater screamed.

"Why not?"

"Because I have to find out what caused it. I have to know if I was right."

"You go back out there, and you're going to get yourself killed."

"Maybe so. At least my conscience would be clear. Anything has to be better than living in denial like you."

"You son of a bitch," Mackay bellowed, and tackled Rainwater to the ground. The two rolled around the floor, each trying to land blows on the other.

"Cut it out!"

Valerie hurried from her car to where the two were fighting, glaring at them as they got to their feet and brushed themselves down.

"I think we all need to talk." She said.

"What about?" Rainwater asked.

"About the man from the government who just came to see me and was asking all sorts of questions about you."

"What did he want to know?"

"Not here. Back at the house. You better come too," she said to Mackay, "your name came up more than once."

The three of them sat around the dinner table in Valerie's kitchen. Rainwater and Mackay did all they could to ignore each other, the tension between them heavy and uncomfortable.

"The man who came to see me today was asking questions about the accident. More specifically, asking about both of you and what you might know."

"What did you tell him?" Mackay asked.

"I didn't tell him anything, but he was pushy. Said he was some kind of government contractor or something. He asked a lot of questions about you, Henry. He wanted to know where you were, how he could reach you. He said it was a matter of national security. What the hell are you mixed up in?"

"Let me guess," Mackay sneered, "he was here about your bloody sea monster."

"What are you talking about?" Valerie asked.

"Oh, I thought he'd have told you by now. He seems to think the accident was caused by some kind of monster slamming into the side of the boat."

"Is this what you were here to tell me earlier?" she asked. "That's why you wanted the Lisa Marie, isn't it? To go back out there and find it."

"This guy is a fucking idiot." Mackay bellowed.

Rainwater felt a surge of rage, and before he knew what was happening, he was on his feet, pointing at Mackay.

"You might be best to keep your mouth shut before I shut it for you."

Mackay grinned, and stood, inviting Rainwater to him.

"Come on you little shit. Try it. Come on and see what happens."

"Both of you stop it!"

Valerie's words went unheard as both men sized each other up.

"Take it outside if you wanna fight. You don't do it in my house."

"You heard the lady," Mackay said with a wide grin. "Let's take this outside."

"Come on, let's do it." Rainwater said, striding towards the door.

Whilst Rainwater's back was turned, Mackay picked up one of the dining chairs and slammed it into him, and in one smooth motion opened the door, grabbed Rainwater by the jacket and threw him outside, following and kicking him hard in the stomach. Valerie was screaming at them to stop, but Mackay was like a man possessed. He beat on Rainwater, the younger man vastly out skilled by Mackay. The fight was both short and incredibly one sided as Mackay delivered a vicious beating. Breathless and with Valerie screaming in his ear, he stood and was suddenly overcome with shame.

"I'm sorry, I didn't mean it," he panted.

"Get out of here, just go."

"I'm sorry."

"Get the hell out of here. Joey and Sam would be ashamed of you."

"It's him," he said, pleading his case. "He's crazy. All this talk of fucking sea monsters. Why can't he leave it alone?"

"Maybe it's all he has." She shot back, glaring at him as she started to cry.

Mackay looked from Valerie to Rainwater, then back to Valerie.

"I'm sorry," he said, his bottom lip trembling as he spoke. "I loved them too. They were like family."

"Henry *is* family. The only one I have left."

"I know, but he ain't perfect. You call him family when he won't even use the name. You wanna ask him when he comes round if he's a Harris or Rainwater. Kid needs to make up his mind and cut it out with these damn stories."

Mackay strode away, leaving Valerie to help Rainwater to his feet and back to the house.

CHAPTER 12

The island of New Guinea
Pacific Ocean

Freeman paced the beach barricade, pausing to wipe the sweat from his brow. The scorching temperatures had turned his pale skin an ugly shade of red, and the portly man checked his watch for the twentieth time in the last five minutes.

On the other side of the barrier, a large crowd of locals and tourists were rubbernecking and trying to get a look at the remains of the blue whale that was stinking up the beach. Freeman had been sent to make sure the Marine biologist they had called for got an undisturbed look at the remains. He pushed his glasses back up his sweaty face, and glanced at his watch again. The stench of the dead animal was awful. He had been told not to touch it, and to erect screens around the carcass to keep the curious eyes of the public off the body. That was a day ago. Freeman hoped their Marine biologist was there before Andrews himself was, otherwise, he suspected he might be in for a verbal dressing down which he was both too hot and too tired to take. His attention was caught by a skinny man with glasses and a nerdy, awkward gait who pushed to the front of the barricade. Freemen would have bet his bottom dollar that this was his biologist. His interest lasted only a second before he shifted his gaze to the smoking hot redhead who was following him.

"You must be Thompson, the Marine biologist we sent for." Freeman said, thrusting his hand towards the bespectacled man.

"Actually, that's me." Said the redhead, giving Freemans hand a professional double pump and releasing him. "I'm Clara Thompson. This is my assistant, Dexter."

"My apologies, this heat is baking me alive. I'm Gus Freeman, I'm the one who called you."

Clara nodded, half looking over Freeman's shoulder to the screens erected further down the beach.

"So, what do we have here? What was so urgent to have the government fly me in all the way from Oz?"

"Whale carcass," Freeman said, pulling a gap in the barrier to allow Clara and Dexter through. The trio began to walk towards the screens as Freeman continued to speak.

"It washed up here a couple of days ago. Some guy found it whilst he was walking his dog, we closed the beach after that. As far as I know, nobody has seen the remains yet."

"So why did you ask for me? Does New Guinea not have marine biologists?"

Freeman came to a halt, and as Clara looked at the awkward, sweating official, she half felt sorry for him.

"Look, I was told to get the best, and your name came up pretty much everywhere I searched."

"This all seems a little extreme for a whale carcass. Why all the secrecy?"

Freeman fidgeted, and wiped his arm against his brow.

"Well, frankly, I would rather not say."

"I can't help you if you don't tell me what we are dealing with." Clara said, trying to sneak a look between the screens.

"Oh, sorry, I think you misunderstand. We know what it *looks* like happened, I would rather you see for yourself without me clouding your judgement."

Clara flicked her eyes to Dexter, and she could see her curiosity mirrored in his face.

"Why do I get the feeling I'm about to see something unusual?"

Freeman grinned without humour.

"Lady, you don't know the half of it. Come take a look."

Freeman led them around the screen, and even though she had visited every corner of the earth and thought she had seen pretty much all there was to see, she still drew a sharp breath when she saw what lay beyond the screens.

"What the hell did this?" she asked, unable to take her eyes from the carcass.

"Well, frankly, we were hoping you could tell us." Freeman said as he stood beside them.

The remains of the blue whale dwarfed them where it lay half in, half out of the water. Dozens of seagulls were feeding on its body, as others still circled overhead. Although it was unusual, Clara had seen evidence of blues being attacked. Sometimes, particularly aggressive pods of Orcas had been known to attack if they were desperate enough. Although not in this case. Even at a glance, she knew it was no Orca attack.

The entire lower half of the whale's stomach was missing, its fleshy blubber fanned out over the sand, sloshing and rolling in the gentle tides. What looked to be a huge bite had been taken out of the animals flank, and one of its flippers was missing.

Clara tried to take it all in, but her eyes kept drifting towards the bite.

"When did this wash up?"

"Couple of days ago." Freeman said as he squinted at Clara. "What do you think?"

"I don't know yet. Has anyone interfered with it since it was found?"

"No, that's how it washed up. Damn seagulls might well have helped themselves to a bite or two, other than that, it's been sealed off and under guard."

Freeman nodded to the rotting remains. "What could do that, in your opinion?"

Nothing I know of.

She almost said it, and then clamped her jaw closed.

"It depends. I need to make a few initial examinations."

"Go right ahead, if you can stand the smell." Freeman said, grimacing and shooting the dead whale a venomous look.

Clara turned to Dexter. "Start taking some pictures, all angles."

"On it," Dexter said, slipping off his backpack and looking for the camera.

"Hand me the tape measure will you?" she said as Dexter rummaged in his pack. He found it and handed it to her, and she approached the carcass, fanning the mass of droning flies away from her face as she took a closer look. Her instincts screamed at her to go directly to the bite, but she wasn't sure where she stood with Freeman, and so she walked instead to the stumpy remaining flesh of the flipper and crouched in the sand, leaning closer to examine the wound. She knew what her eyes were telling her, the facts didn't tally with what she knew as possible. With a frown, she stood and looked at the remains.

"Looks like a fully grown male. Size can only be estimated due to decomposition and extensive tissue loss, but I would say eighty five to ninety five feet in length."

Dexter started to snap photographs as she walked towards the deep wound on the whale's side.

"Death appears to be due to massive blood loss from injuries consistent with attack by a large predator."

She glanced at Freeman who stood sweating with his hands on his hips.

"Is it a bite?" he asked.

"Hard to say. My first instinct would be to say that it's far too big, and there is nothing out there that could inflict such a wound."

"Looks like a bite to me, if you don't mind me saying." Freeman said as he wrinkled his nose at the smell.

"Appearances can be deceptive. Remember, Mr Freeman, this creature could have been dead for days before it washed up here. Any number of predators could have fed on this animal."

"Why there though? Wouldn't they have bitten it elsewhere?"

She had asked herself that same question, and because she hadn't yet formulated an answer, declined to give Freeman one. Instead, she turned to Dexter.

"Hang five with the photos for a minute, and help me measure this..."

Bite

"...Wound," she said, stopping herself from saying the wrong word. Dexter set his camera in the sand, and jogged to Clara, grabbing the tape measure. Even as they went through the motions of taking the gaping wounds measurements, she was now certain it was a bite. She had learned to read such things as an average person might read a book, but this particular book looked to be written in a brand new language, because it made no sense. Dexter knew it too, she could see it in his eyes as they took their measurements. When it was done, she took a step back and simply stood, staring at the whale and trying to make sense of what she was looking at. Freeman approached, his presence foretold by his musky, sweaty odour as he stood beside her.

"So, what do you think?" he asked, glancing at Clara, who was still staring at the whale.

"I'm not entirely sure."

"It's a bite, isn't it?"

She turned to Freeman and took a sip of her bottled water.

"It looks like one, and if it is, that opens up a whole host of problems."

"Such as?"

"Well, for starters, the wound is twenty eight feet across and nine feet deep. If it's a bite, we need to rewrite the history books."

"What do you mean?"

She hesitated, wondering if she should say what was on her mind.

"I mean, if that is a singular bite from one animal, which at this stage it appears to be, you're looking at something of unbelievable size."

Freeman glanced at the wound, and back to Clara. "Please, explain what you mean."

"If this is a bite, Mr Freeman, then based on the radius and depth of the wound, we are talking about an animal which is over three hundred and fifty feet in length, and weighing three to five hundred tons."

"That's impossible," Freeman said, his eyes wide. "I mean, there isn't anything in the ocean big enough is there?"

"As far as science knows, no," Clara said quietly "For as much as I would love to suggest otherwise, this does appear to be a bite inflicted by a huge, and as yet, unknown animal."

"I think," he said as he looked at her, "you better have a word with my boss. He might be able to give you some more information about this...situation."

Freeman took out his phone and dialled a number as Clara and Dexter looked on. She tried to gauge the conversation, but Freeman walked away, taking his sweaty stench with him and leaving them for the time being, alone.

"What do you think?" Dexter said quietly.

"I think we're in over our heads here."

"You're telling me. That's one hell of a bite. Something ate the crap out of this animal."

"What are your first thoughts?" she asked, keeping a close eye on Freeman.

"Looks like something big. From the early examination of the wound, I'd say whatever did this has teeth between twenty and thirty inches long."

He shook his head and flashed a nervous smile. "Hell, even as I say it, the whole thing sounds implausible."

"Well," Clara said, glancing at the carcass, "if it helps, I drew the same conclusion. There's something out there, and it's big and aggressive. I think whatever it is, it's responsible for all the beaching's we have seen of late."

"You think it's so dominant that it might be scaring the marine life into beaching itself?"

"It would make sense. It certainly fits with everything else."

"So what's our next move?"

"For now, we keep our suspicions to ourselves. Last thing we need is to be frozen out of this. Let's see what this guy's boss has to say."

Dexter nodded, and spoke under his breath. "Heads up, he's coming back."

The pair waited as Freeman walked back towards them. He was squinting at the sun as he stopped and exhaled, the phone still held in his hand.

"My boss asks if you would be willing to meet him."

"What does he want?" Clara asked.

"He wants you to join his team."

"What team?"

"The team that is going to find whatever attacked this whale."

"Tell your boss we would be happy to meet with him and discuss it in person." Clara said.

Freeman nodded, and held the phone to his ear.

"They said yes." He said simply, and then listened as he was given instructions. Clara turned away from Freeman and looked at the giant carcass on the beach. She tried to imagine the scale of the kind of creature that could incapacitate such a goliath of the seas, but try as she might, she couldn't see it. It was too big, too improbable. Hell, it was impossible, even if the facts were right in front of her.

"Dr Thompson," Freeman said, snapping her back to reality as she turned towards him.

"What is it?"

"He wants to know if you are able to meet him today."

"When?"

"Right now. He can send a helicopter to pick you up in thirty minutes. From there you will be transported by plane to his location."

"And where is that exactly?"

"Alaska."

CHAPTER 13

East dock
Freeport,
Kodiak, Alaska

Rainwater cast his eyes to the sky. The clouds were a threatening shade of deep grey, and as he looked beyond the relative calm of the harbour, he could see vicious whitecaps rolling in increasing velocity as the ocean threw wave after wave towards land.

"You getting on or not?"

Rainwater turned to see Mackay walking down the dock. His stomach involuntarily knotted with fear, yet he didn't get the impression Mackay was there to dish out another beating. Instead, he waited as the former soldier stood beside him and looked at the *Lisa Marie.*

"How's the eye?" Mackay said, flicking his gaze towards Rainwater's swollen cheek.

"It's fine. Looks worse than it is."

"Some good memories on this boat," Mackay said, smiling reflectively "This is where I cut my teeth as a greenhorn. Nobody would give me a job, said I was too old at thirty to start life as a fisherman. Sam gave me a shot anyway. I spent the best years of my life sleeping, puking, and working so damn hard I wished I was dead on this boat, and I wouldn't have traded it for the world."

Rainwater said nothing, and waited as Mackay lit a cigarette, then looked out over the bay.

"I was deck boss for a while you know," he continued. "A few years back your uncle had a falling out with your father. Said he was done with fishing. We thought it would blow over, but he was a stubborn one, and he left the boat. For three seasons, I ran things alongside your father. Course, we all knew Joey would be back, we didn't know when. Some of the best memories I have were on this old girl."

"I don't remember much of this boat. I was only a kid the last time I was on it."

Mackay nodded "I remember. You were a whiny little bastard."

Rainwater looked at Mackay and was about to protest, when he saw the older man was smiling.

"Hell, even back then you hated being out on the water. You couldn't get back on dry land soon enough. I think your dad understood that fishing wasn't in your blood the same way it was his and his fathers before him."

"I get it, I'm a failure. You don't need to remind me."

"You ain't no failure." Mackay said, glancing to Rainwater then back to the *Lisa Marie*. "That wasn't what I was saying. What I mean is, you just ain't a fisherman. Nothing wrong with it. Hell, some might say it makes you the most sensible of us all."

"Well, it doesn't matter now anyway. I don't think I can do this. Hell, I don't know what to do. You were right, Mackay. I should shut up about this and get on with my life."

"If you had said that yesterday, I would have agreed. Truth is, I'm starting to think maybe you have a point."

"What do you mean?" Rainwater said, turning to face Mackay.

"Well, it seems to me this fella who went to see Valerie was asking a lot of questions about the accident. Normally, I wouldn't think twice about it. Some folk are just nosy, can't keep out of other people's business. This guy seemed different."

"Different how?"

"You gotta remember, I was in the forces for twelve years before I got out and started working for your dad. I know military when I see it, and this guy stank like high end government."

"What would the government want with you and Valerie?"

"It wasn't really us he was interested in, it was you. That got me thinking about the stuff you were saying about this thing you claim hit us. Maybe this Andrews guy knows more about it than he's letting on."

"That's a bit of a stretch."

"Well, there's more. I called an old buddy of mine from the forces. Served with me in Iraq. Anyhow, he's pretty high ranking, so I asked him to snoop around for me and look into this guy."

"How did you know who to look for?"

"The guy gave me his business card. Anyways, this buddy of mine took the info and made some enquiries. It turns out this Andrews guy is working with a slimy piece of shit called Russo."

"You know him?"

"In a way. He was responsible for funding cuts to my unit when I was serving in Iraq. Long and short of it is that we didn't have enough body armour to go around. My squad got ambushed during patrol and the three of my guys who didn't have vests were killed. My CO told me to leave it alone, said it was just a case of casualties of war. I knew Russo was responsible and I ain't never been good at holding my temper. I knew I shouldn't have done it, but I went to his office and before he could try to worm his way out of it, I punched the motherfucker square in the mouth."

"Holy shit, what happened?"

"He got a bloody nose, I got kicked. Dishonourable discharge. Thanks for the years of putting your life on the line, Mackay, but this prick in a suit wants you out."

Mackay grinned, and shrugged his shoulders.

"I was about done with the army by then anyway. Seen too much shit, spent too long fighting other peoples wars. I will tell you this, if this Russo guy is involved, you can bet your ass there's an angle in it for him."

"What else did your contact dig up?"

"Well, he couldn't find much. A lot of it was locked tight, and he didn't have the clearance. All he knows is that Russo and Andrews have commandeered a ship and the government have thrown a ton of money at them to do whatever it is they intend on doing. He couldn't say for sure, it seems they are looking for something, which was enough to make me interested as it is, but there's more."

"Go on."

"Well, you know when we were adrift in the lifeboat after the accident, and we assumed we were picked up by the Coast Guard?"

"Yeah."

"Well, it wasn't. It was Andrews who picked us up. He was looking for something in the exact area where you say something hit out boat. By the time he'd come back to the hospital to question us, we'd checked ourselves out. The only reason he couldn't find you when he came looking is because you aren't registered as living here anymore. Now I'm a realist, but I also don't believe in coincidence, and things are stacking up here that makes me think maybe you might not be as crazy as I thought."

"So you believe me?"

"Do I think you saw a sea monster? No. That's something I can't buy until I see it for myself. I do believe that whatever you saw is the thing Russo and Andrews are looking for, and that's enough for me to be interested. Maybe some new piece of military kit that has gone rogue. A sub maybe, I don't know. Whatever it is must be important to have the government sniffing around like this."

"I don't get it, if it was Andrews who found us, why keep it quiet? Why ask us later on about the accident if he was there?"

"Exactly. Nothing about this situation sits right. I get the feelin' we have only scratched the surface."

"I still don't understand why top line government would be involved in this. Maybe we should get in touch with them, see if we can work together."

"I don't think you understand. If Russo and Andrews want to find this thing, I want to get there first."

"Why?"

"Because I still owe that asshole one. You might think I wouldn't be so bitter after all these years, but you'd be wrong."

"I thought you didn't believe me?"

"I said I'd have to see it for myself, and I ain't ever gonna do it from here on dry land."

"It's no good," Rainwater said, shaking his head. "If they have the resources you say they have, and the expertise, we don't stand a chance."

"They're soldiers and pencil pushers. Not fishermen. We know the seas, and that gives us the advantage."

"Maybe I should go with them. I'm no fisherman either, you said so yourself."

"Maybe it's time you learned. What I'm saying is, if you really want to find out what this thing is, I'll come out and help. Maybe you'll prove me wrong and I'll see this monster with my own eyes, although I suspect it won't be anything quite so dramatic when we get to the bottom of it."

"I don't know if I can do it. The thought of setting foot on that boat scares me, Mackay. I keep thinking about the accident, how close we came to dying…"

Mackay nodded.

"It's normal to be scared. Fear keeps you on your toes. If you don't conquer this, it'll eat at you until there is nothing left."

"I don't think I can do it."

"You will."

"Why so confident?"

"Because despite whatever you choose to call yourself, you still have Harris blood running through your veins. You belong on the water, even if you don't know it yet."

A mixture of pride, nerves and fear surged through him as he looked at the boat rocking against the dock.

"It won't be enough with just us, we need more help."

"I might know a guy. He's ex-army too, but he knows about hunting things. He a tough son of a bitch, spent some time in Japan working on a whaler and also did some safari stuff in Africa in between tours in the forces."

"We aren't hunting lions here, Mackay."

"I know that, my point is that he knows the way to hunt things. He's our only option anyway, so it was a case of take it or leave it."

"So where is he?"

"Flying in today as it happens. We recently got in touch again and had been planning to meet up anyway. I asked him to come and see if he can help us."

"You don't want to leave right away?"

Mackay shook his head.

"Not without prepping first. We should head out in a day or two. It gives us a chance to make some kind of plan instead of going out into the unknown."

"I'm not sure this is anything we can plan for. Not really."

"Doesn't hurt to be prepared though, kid."

"I suppose."

"Let me make a few calls, see what I can arrange. In the meantime, you need to get your shit together and be ready for when we leave. If there's one thing I know about Russo, it's that he doesn't fuck around when he has a job to do."

CHAPTER 14

The Victorious
Dutch Harbour,
Alaska

Andrews paced in the meeting room, waiting for his guests to arrive. Russo was pushing to get things underway as soon as possible, and, anxious not to upset the man who had ensured that the trip was funded, Andrews didn't want to be the one to let him down.

Freeman knocked on the door and entered the room, followed by Clara and Dexter.

"Miss Thompson," Andrews said, striding to meet them and extending his hand.

"I'm Doctor Martin Andrews, thank you for coming to meet me. I trust the journey was comfortable?"

"It was fine, thank you. I certainly didn't expect the private jet. Seems you were in a hurry to get us here."

"Indeed I was. We have much to discuss. Please, take a seat." Andrews gestured to the large meeting table.

As Clara and Dexter took their seats, Andrews pulled Freeman aside. Clara watched as the two shared in hushed conversation, following which, Freeman left quickly, closing the door behind him. Andrews took his seat and folded his hands on the table.

"My colleague emailed me the findings of your investigation on the remains of the Blue whale. I thank you for your observations."

"I wanted to discuss them with you in person when I got here. Mr Freeman was pretty forceful about sending them ahead of me." Clara said, making no attempt to hide her annoyance.

"I'm sorry about that, as I'm sure you understand, we are on a strict timetable here."

"Maybe *you* are. As a rule, I don't appreciate being bullied for answers, especially before I have had sufficient time to analyse the results."

Andrews smiled. Clara remained neutral.

"My apologies. I don't wish for us to get off on the wrong foot here. We asked you to come because you are said to be the best in your field. You were the one and only name on our list. I can only ask you to forgive my urgency. As you by now know, this situation is unique to say the least."

"Well, until you tell me exactly what I'm dealing with, we aren't going to get anywhere. Why did you bring us here?"

"Your findings about a potential predatory attack to the whale carcass are in line with our own observations."

"I'm sure you could have confirmed that by telephone."

"This is a confidential situation. An unsecured telephone conversation wasn't an option I'm afraid."

"You do intend to tell people about this? To warn them?"

Andrews squirmed and offered a strained smile.

"You know as well as I do that the public would panic if they suspected something in our oceans was capable of such a violent attack, not to mention the impact to the fishing and shipping industry. They would demand action, and until we have an answer to give them, it's important to remain discreet."

"I don't think the public would react as badly as you seem to think. In fact, maybe it would be better if people were told that the oceans might not be a safe place to be right now."

"You don't understand as much as you think," Andrews said as he looked at them in turn.

"Then let's not waste any more time." Clara shot back "Tell me what you know and I'll see if I can help you."

"You have to understand this is, as I said, a very sensitive subject. Due to the nature of this operation, I need to ask you to work with us with the limited information I am authorised to provide."

"I'm not sure I *do* understand. Do I get access to the research or not?"

"Well," Andrews said, choosing his words carefully, "the subject matter of this investigation is highly, highly confidential. We have our own team of scientists and experts involved already who will deal with the more... sensitive aspects of the investigation. We would only require you for certain clarifications and confirmations of our findings."

"You either want me in or you don't. I won't play second fiddle."

"I'm afraid there are limits to the information I can give you."

"Then we have nothing to discuss. I can't be expected to consult with you without access to all the information."

"Don't make any hasty decisions," Andrews said, offering a wry smile. "There are other marine biologists who would crawl over broken glass for an opportunity like this."

"That may be so," Clara shot back with a smile of her own. "As you said, I'm the best, and I don't think you would be prepared to settle for anything else."

"You have, if you don't mind my saying so, a very high opinion of yourself." Andrews said, his face a mixture of admiration and frustration.

"No, I just have respect for my work, and think you should too. You valued it enough to fly me out here to talk to you. To then deny me access to the research is an insult."

"We don't need you, Miss Thompson. Let me make that perfectly clear right now. We can easily manage with someone else."

"I'm more than happy to walk away from this if I need to. Believe me, I'm interested in helping, just not as some out of the loop lackey."

"I don't believe you would have come all the way out here if that was the case. You're as desperate as the rest of us to find this creature."

"I don't think you would have flown me all the way out here if you weren't desperate for my help."

"You're wrong."

"I don't think I am."

"By all means, feel free to leave. If you can't work with us, then we will have to make other arrangements I'm afraid."

"Okay. No problem." Clara said, standing. "Come on, Dexter, it's time we were going."

Dexter looked from Clara to Andrews then stood and followed her to the door.

"Wait," Andrews said, the desperation in his voice impossible to hide.

Clara turned to face him, folding her arms as she waited for him to speak.

"What is it you would need exactly? To stay, I mean."

"Full disclosure. I'll need real time access to every part of your research."

"I can't do that," Andrews said, shrugging. "My hands are tied."

"Then good luck with the mission." Clara shot back and turned back towards the door.

"Hang on, just give me a second." Andrews stammered, standing and crossing the room to meet her.

"Okay, let's say I can get you full mission access. You will both need to sign a non-disclosure agreement about anything you see, read, or hear.

"No problem. I'm a professional, and NDA or no NDA, I would have kept the findings private. Before we go any further let me make something clear right now. The first inkling that something is being withheld from me, I'm gone. No second chances. You're right when you suggest this is a fantastic opportunity. Even so, I won't put my professional reputation on the line for anything, even a secret as big as this one. Got it?"

"Yes, I understand," Andrews sighed, showing a rare moment of weakness. "I need to make a few calls and get those NDA's readied. I'll have Freeman show you to your rooms."

"When do we leave?" Dexter asked.

"Within the hour."

"Just one thing," Clara said, trying to keep her expression neutral despite the butterflies in her stomach. "I'm right aren't I? About this being some kind of new species of predator."

Andrews simply looked at her blankly.

"First things first. Let's sign those NDA's then we can talk."

CHAPTER 15

The Ocean Mist
18 miles off the coast of Hawaii

The 48-foot long humpback launched itself out of the ocean, its 70,000 lb. body crashing down in an eruption of spray. The passengers on board the Ocean Mist gasped, cheered, and took photographs as one.

"Did you get it, Herb?"

Herbert Keller looked at his wife of forty years, and scowled.

"Of course I did. You don't have to ask me every damn time."

His wife, Maude, nodded. Although it could be easily mistaken as an argument, this was the way they normally spoke to each other, their interactions mostly a series of irritable swipes. Both in their seventies, they had decided post retirement to see a little of the world. Herb had suggested Hawaii, hoping the warm temperatures might make the arthritis in his elbows and knees a little easier to bear. He had spent many years in the Navy, and so whales were something he had seen before, but he was a younger, stronger man back then, and the black hair and sharp eyes he had last time he was out at sea, had long since become grey and dull respectively. It wasn't the kind of trip he had imagined, but knew the whales were a spectacular sight for Maude, who apart from the occasional visits to see family in Texas, had never really seen the world. His joints were starting to ache, and the overcrowded boat was doing nothing to help his mood. He was looking forward to getting back on to dry land and sitting by the pool, soaking up some sun and sipping a nice cold beer.

"Make sure you get some good ones," Maude pressed, looking over the top of her glasses. "I want some shots for the photo album to show Alice and the grandchildren."

Another whoop erupted from the fellow passengers, and both Maude and Herb looked out to see the white wake on top of the water.

"See, Herb? You missed it!"

"God damn it, woman, will ya get off my case? I got the damn picture first time around. It's not as if you are gonna see anything different."

"Did you get a video of it?"

"No," Herb sighed, "not yet."

"Switch to the video camera and get one before we miss it."

Herb let the camera hang loose around his neck as Maude handed him the Sony camcorder.

"Make sure you zoom in. Oh and-"

"Maude, please. Give it a rest. I know how to work the damn thing."

"Well make sure you pay attention, it will be up again in a minute."

Herb shook his head, knowing well enough that to argue was fruitless. He caught the gaze of one of the other passengers, a man who like him was complete with nagging wife. They shared a silent moment of kinship, a look which said 'buddy, I feel your pain.' Feeling the dagger like glare from Maude, Herb hit the record button on the camera and turned back to the ocean, awaiting the arrival of the next breaching whale. He didn't have to wait long, and as they watched, the humpback once again soared majestically out of the water, turning in mid-air as it began to crash towards the ocean.

Herb recorded, sure the footage might be enough to give his hearing aid a rest from the constant abuse, when he saw the second breach. The crowd gasped as the creature emerged, directly below the humpback. It came out of the water, a flat, wide mass of barnacle encrusted grey flesh. The beast's snout hit the humpback in mid-air, sending the animal spinning off course as it smashed into the water. The crowd gasped as the creature continued to rise from the water. Its body was lined with tentacles much like a squid, but these were the size of tree trunks. It turned in mid air and reached its array of tentacles towards the dazed humpback, which had just impacted the water. The tree-trunk tentacles enveloped the stricken whale, as the creature came down on top of it, sending a huge thirty foot wake racing away from its impact point. The wave reached the Ocean mist in seconds, sending the vessel into a sickening, lurching roll.

Now, the people who had been gasping and cheering were screaming and clinging on as the boat came perilously close to capsizing. Herb grabbed Maude's hand, and hooked his free arm around the guardrail that ran around the edge of the boat. He was sure they would go over, and for a moment, all he could see was the crisp, blue Hawaiian sky as he clung on to both the rail and his wife.

He heard people falling, sliding, and screaming. Just when it seemed they wouldn't be unable to stay upright, the wave passed underneath them, and the boat righted itself, rocking and lurching as it slammed back into the ocean.

Gasping, Herb sat on the bench, his arm in agony from the effort of clinging to the railing. Maude sat beside him, staring out into the ocean at the white wake where the creature had slammed back into the water. Of the whale and its attacker, there was no sign.

"Herb, what was that?" Maude asked, unable to keep the tremor out of her voice. "Herb, answer me. What was it?"

"I don't know," he croaked, then looked at the camcorder, still gripped in his hand. "Whatever it is, we have it on video."

CHAPTER 16

344 Chestnut Drive
Freeport,
Kodiak, Alaska

Rainwater stood out back on the decking, enjoying the quiet as he smoked a cigarette. He looked over the lush trees that sloped uphill behind the house, and closed his eyes as he tried to calm his nerves. The last few days had been a whirlwind of activity, and in less than an hour, they were scheduled to head out to sea. The only problem was now the day had arrived, Rainwater still wasn't sure he could go through with it. He wondered as he listened to the seagulls in the distance and felt the bite of the wind at his face, if he had done the right thing. When it was just going to be him, he could accept the risk. Now things had escalated, and the one-man trip that had been in his head initially, had become a four-person voyage. Mackay had been good on his word.

His hunter friend had been flown in, and to say he wasn't what Rainwater expected was an understatement. He had been sure the man would have been a square jawed, tobacco chewing silent type, but he couldn't have been more wrong. Instead, Richie Morrison was a tall, gangly man, who was bald apart from a ring of black hair around the back of his head. Rainwater thought he looked more like an accountant or banker than an ex-army hunter. The only thing that gave any indication of his true nature was his eyes, which were dark brown to the point of appearing black, and seemed to stare through you rather than at you from behind thick glasses. Morrison was a man of few words who had a methodical approach to working. During the last two days, he had barely said a word to anyone. Mackay and Rainwater had given him a full account of what had happened on the boat, each telling it from their individual point of view. He didn't speak or interrupt to clarify anything. He simply made notes in his journal, occasionally casting his thousand-yard stare on Rainwater when he spoke. When all was told, Morrison stood, tucked the journal under his arm and told them he would work out the best place to start looking. Earlier that morning, he had arrived at the house with a rolled ocean chart and told them to be ready to sail to the location he had marked.

Rainwater glanced at his watch.

It was time.

He finished his smoke and went back inside the house.

Valerie was waiting in the sitting room, wringing her hands as she watched him check his bag of clothes and supplies.

"It's not too late to change your mind," she said as he pulled on his orange rain slicker.

"Let's not go over this again, please."

"Look, I don't want to fight with you. I think on some level that I understand why you're doing this. There's no shame in staying."

He didn't answer. Instead, he pulled on his beanie hat, and picked up his rucksack, slinging it onto his shoulder.

"Just be careful, okay?"

Rainwater paused, and turned to her.

"I'm scared, I won't deny it."

"Then don't go."

"I'll regret it if I don't."

"You might regret it if you do. You're your own man, Henry. You aren't your father, or your uncle. Don't do this because you feel you have to."

"This isn't some ego trip, it's something I have to do. I have to see it with my own eyes."

"For what? What good can it do?"

"I don't know, and that's the truth. I just have to know once and for all."

"Even if you die?"

He lowered his head, and then turned towards the door.

"I have to go. Mackay will be at the dock by now."

"Call it off. There's been enough death in this family already."

"We both know I can't do that."

"What am I supposed to do whilst you're gone?" she said, fighting to keep her composure.

"Stay strong. We'll be fine."

"You sound like your father."

He adjusted his bag on his shoulder, and jogged down the porch steps.

"Look after yourself, Val. Remember what I said. Stay strong."

As he made his way away from the sanctuary of the house, he felt his stomach roll at the first sight of the ocean and the boat that would carry them to whatever fate awaited them.

***

"Ah, here he is," Mackay said as Rainwater approached the boat. At the stern, Morrison was making the final adjustments to the harpoon gun that had been installed, the cannon like device bolted to the deck on a steel framed tripod. "Top of the range harpoon gun, acquired by our hunter friend." Mackay said. "If this fuckin' fish of yours is out there, we will drag the son of a bitch right into the bay."

Rainwater knew he should have stopped Mackay, told him that both the harpoon and the boat were vastly unequipped for the task ahead. Instead, he forced a smile and nodded.

"I want you to meet our engineer," Mackay said, then shouted into the boat.

"Hey, Ox, get up here."

The man who came out of the cabin better fit the picture of how Rainwater imagined Morrison to look before he met him. He was short and broad, with muscular arms. His skin was so dark it had a purple sheen. His head was completely bald, which was complimented by a thick beard. The man paused to wipe his oily hands on a rag, and then climbed onto the dock.

"Ox, this is Henry." Mackay said.

Ox and Rainwater shook hands, and the short man flashed a wide white grin.

"Mac here tells me we are going fishing for something big."

"Yeah, you could say that," Rainwater replied, noting with dismay that nobody on board seemed to appreciate the magnitude of the task ahead.

"Well, wherever we need to go, this boat of yours is fit to get us there. She was in pretty bad shape if you don't mind me saying so. I managed to fix her right up. She's ready for anything."

"Then I guess we are too." Mackay said. "Hey, Morrison, you ready to go?" Mackay shouted.

Morrison looked at the three of them on the dock with his dead man's stare and gave the briefest of nods, then returned to examining the harpoon gun.

"Man, that guy don't say much does he?" Ox said quietly.

"It's just his way. He's actually a really funny guy when he ain't working." Mackay said.

Rainwater couldn't imagine the word 'funny' could ever apply to someone so perpetually miserable and uptight as Morrison.

"We might be wise to get moving before this weather turns." Ox said as he eyed the clouds that were rolling towards them.

Mackay nodded. "Aye, best if we make a move." He said, and then followed Ox on board. Rainwater stayed where he was. His feet felt like lead weights, and he wasn't sure he would be able to move. The engines spluttered to life, as Mackay shoved his head out of the wheelhouse window.

"Come on, Cast us off and let's get the hell out of here."

Rainwater unhooked the bow and stern lines, and with a tremendous force of will, hopped over onto the boat and stood by the rail. Mackay began to maneuverer out of the harbour. As Rainwater watched the town of Freeport begin to shrink away from him, he wondered if he would ever see it again.

CHAPTER 17

Russo walked down the corridor of another one of the governments many un-named, non-existent buildings, and regarded the file in his hands about the people he was about to interview. He looked at their photographs, and read the hand written notes alongside them.

Herbert and Maude Keller. Both early seventies & retired. The notes said the pair had been reluctant to give over much information, not knowing the little they had given, names and dates of birth had been enough. Russo had in front of him their entire lives on paper, pulled in seconds from the thousands of databases the world over to which he had access. He had everything about them from social security numbers, employment records, bank account information, even the details of the couple's children and grandchildren. A lot of it he hoped he wouldn't need, especially as long as the conversation remained pleasant. Russo always found if the questioning had to take a more interrogatory feel, throwing in a barely veiled threat using specific details of a close family member to those being questioned was invariably successful. Russo noted as he approached the holding room that the Man, Herbert, had a military record. He had served in Nam, and hopefully, would recognise the importance of maintaining national security. Russo closed the file and paused outside the holding room, fishing a roll of mints from his jacket pocket. His stomach quivered, and he opened the package quickly and popped a mint into his mouth. Taking a few seconds to compose himself, he entered the room.

The Keller's were seated on one side of a stainless steel table. The room was windowless, and apart from the overhead strip light and air conditioning unit, was empty. They watched Russo as he closed the door, smiled, and sat opposite them.

"It's about god-damn time," Herb said, scowling at Russo. "We have been here for hours, and my damn joints are playing up and I—"

"I apologise, Mr Keller. I was unfortunately delayed. I'm special agent James Russo. I'm in charge here."

He shook hands with Herb, while Maude only offered him an icy stare.

"I don't know why you're keeping us here." She said, narrowing her eyes at Russo.

"Mrs Keller, I really do apologise for the way you have been treated. The men responsible have been reprimanded, however, as you may appreciate, this a highly sensitive situation."

"See, Herb, I told you. Its aliens!"

"Shut up Maude, it's not god-damn aliens." Herb hissed, and then turned back to Russo.

"I'm ex-military, Mr Russo, so I certainly know the drill."

Buddy, you don't know shit.

Russo smiled. "Well, sir, I'm happy to converse with someone who provided such a great service to our country."

Herb swelled with pride, straightened in his chair, and pushed his chest out.

"Now, Mr Keller—"

"Herb. You can call me Herb."

"Well, Herb, as I'm sure you're aware, this is a matter of national security. We have suspected the existence of this creature for some time, although we are yet to see it in the flesh."

"We have video footage if you'd like to see it?"   "You have video?" Russo said, feigning surprise.

"Sure," Herb said with a wide, proud grin. "Maude, give me the camera."

"No Herb, you don't know who this man is." "God damn it woman will you give me the camera. This isn't just some guy, he's from the government."

"Well, I don't care if he's Abraham Lincoln, he ain't getting the camera."

"Maude just give me the camera!"

Russo watched the exchange, the friendly smile still etched onto his lips as he thought about how to proceed if the old bag didn't hand over the footage. He was debating between either dropping in one of those veiled threats to a close family member, or because time was of the essence, taking his government issued sidearm from the holster under his jacket and putting a bullet in-between the old crow's eyes. He was spared from making either call when Maude handed the camera over to Herb, folded her arms, and scowled at both of them. Herb powered on the camera and handed it to Russo.

"There you go, just press the playback button on the side."

Russo took the camera, and played the footage. The clip lasted less than half a minute. As Russo watched, he couldn't help but feel a surge of adrenaline and excitement. He watched the footage again a second and third time.

"This is remarkable."

"Ain't it just?" Herb said with a grin. "It's big huh?"

"I wonder if you would mind if my colleague made a copy of this footage? As I said, it's a matter of national security."

"I understand, sir," Herb said, reverting to full military protocol.

"What do we get out of it?" Maude spat.

"Shut up, Maude." Herb hissed, shaking his head and flashing an apologetic look at Russo

"No, Herb, we discovered the damn thing. Surely, we should get a reward, or get to name it or something?"

"Maude," Herb said with a sigh, and looked about to resume their argument when Russo stepped in.

"Mrs Keller, I do appreciate your concern, however, this goes far beyond anything I'm able to tell you. I would appreciate your cooperation in this matter. As I said, it's a matter of national security."

"Don't mind her, sir," Herb said with a shrug "She's been in a bad mood all day. You go ahead and make a copy if that's what you need to do."

"Thank you, sir, you have made a valuable discovery and assisted in a matter which concerns the safety and security of this country. You should be proud."

"I might be retired, but I'll always be a soldier, sir."

"I can see that, "Russo said with a smile. " I'm sure you were a real asset to the service. If you two would excuse me for a moment, I'll have my colleague make a copy of this footage, then have one of my men drive you wherever you wish to go."

"Thank you," Herb said, giving Maude the look that said she should show some gratitude too. "We would really appreciate it. We are staying over at the Four Seasons in Kona."

"Oh, really? I hear it's a beautiful resort." Russo said with a smile, keeping up the game. He, of course, already knew where they were staying. A team of his men were already clearing out their room and proceeding to check the couple out. Erasing the tracks. Removing the evidence. He marvelled at just how good at his job he was. Herb was talking, telling them all about their holiday, and the resort. Russo nodded in the right places and smiled accordingly, he could only think of the footage on the Keller's camcorder. To know of the creature's existence was one thing. Actually to see it with his own eyes made things seem more real. He waited for a gap in Herb's monologue, and then interjected.

"Well, Mr and Mrs Keller, I feel we have already taken too much of your time. If you will excuse me, I'll have this footage copied, and we can get you back to the rest of your holiday."

Russo stood and shook Herb's hand.

"Thank you again, sir. Your cooperation will not go unrewarded."

Herb bristled with pride as Russo left the room. He closed the door and approached the agent who was waiting a little way down the corridor, handing over the camera.

"Copy the footage. Send a copy to Andrews and bring the other one to me."

"Yes sir."

"Have the other passengers being questioned?"

"They have. Their stories all match. They all saw it."

"Nobody else had footage of the creature?"

"No sir. We checked."

"Good. Gather them together and dispose of them."

"Dispose of them, sir?" The agent said, eying Russo carefully. "These people have families who will be looking for them."

"I know that. Sometimes, we have to do things for the benefit of the greater good. Take the whaler out to sea and sink it. Make sure the bodies are on board the boat when it goes down, and then inform the news agencies of the accident. Remember Agent Sloane, this is what we are trained to do. Someone has to do the dirty work. The sacrifice of a few will greatly benefit the many. Remember that."

"Yes sir."

"Did you commandeer everyone's phones and cameras?"

"All of them, sir."

"Good. Start building the backstory. Send messages to family and friends to say they were going whale watching. Remember the drills, make it plausible, and make it believable."

"Understood." Sloane said as he started to branch off down a separate corridor.

"Oh, and Agent Sloane."

"Yes sir?"

"No bullets. I don't want anything traceable about their deaths. They are expected to be drowning victims. Make sure that's how it happens."

"Don't forget the Keller's. I want them dealt with first."

"Yes sir. I'll take care of it."

Russo nodded, and checked his watch. He would just have time to grab a bite to eat before he flew out to Alaska to meet Andrews. He walked down the corridor, whistling to himself as he tried to decide what to have for lunch.

CHAPTER 18

Lisa Marie,
Freeport,
Kodiak, Alaska

"God damn son of a bitch!" Ox said as the *Lisa Marie* spluttered to a halt just outside the harbour. He was covered in oil and hydraulic fluid and was working unsuccessfully at repairing the leak. Mackay headed to the engine room.

"I thought you said this thing was sea worthy?" "Screw you, Mackay, it's not my fault. Damn hydraulic line is busted."

"Better here than out there I suppose. Can you fix it?"

Ox nodded "I'll only be able to patch it up. We need to turn around and head back to the dock so I can repair it properly. We don't want this thing to break in the middle of a storm and have the ocean start tossing us."

"I was hoping we wouldn't have to turn back." Mackay said, walking over to Ox, picking up a spanner and starting to loosen the bracket holding the hydraulic line to the hull of the ship.

"Why not?"

"Rainwater."

Ox nodded as he tried to stem the flow of hydraulic fluid.

"I noticed. The kid looked scared. I didn't think he was gonna get on the boat."

"That makes two of us," Mackay sighed. "How long to fix it?" he said, nodding to the cable gripped in Ox's massive hands.

"Repair job here should only take a few minutes. Once we get back to the dock, it depends. If I can get all the stuff I need, just a couple of hours."

"Okay," Mackay said, setting the spanner on the floor and clapping Ox on the shoulder. "I'll leave it with you and tell the others what the situation is. Let me know when we are good to go."

Mackay walked towards steps that led to the upper deck, when Ox called to him.

"Hey, Mackay, you know this is all bullshit, don't you? This trip I mean. I wonder why we are even bothering with it."

"It's his way, and it's something the kid feels he has to do. Without his dad or his brother here, I feel like it's down to me to help him."

"Way I see it, Mac, you don't owe that kid anything."

"I was *there,* Ox. I was there when it happened, it's hard to explain, I just have to do this, not just for him, but also for Sam, Joey, and Morales. Hell even for me."

"You do know its all bullshit though, this sea monster talk?"

Mackay hesitated, then grinned, even though inside his stomach knotted. "Yeah, or at least I hope it is. Otherwise, we are getting in way out of our depth here."

"Jesus, Mackay, some things never change do they?" Ox said with a wide grin.

"Not for us. Come on, let's get this thing back to dock, and I'll buy you a beer."

"You can buy me two, asshole," Ox replied, then turned back to his work.

The repair work took longer than expected. The *Lisa Marie* had been back in dock for six hours, and its crew had ventured off the boat to kill a little time, leaving Ox working on replacing the hydraulic lines.

Mackay and Rainwater had gone to grab a drink and a bite to eat at Belgrave point. They had invited Morrison, but he had declined and had stayed on the ship to pour over his charts. They were about to order another round of drinks when Ox walked into the bar, his clothes and hands streaked with oil.

"Repairs are done, but we're blocked in."

"What? By who?"

"Some dick in a big ass boat. He won't move it until he's loaded up with supplies. Looks like we're waitin.'"

"Like hell we're waiting." Mackay said. "Let's go see who this guy thinks he is."

The three walked to the dock, Mackay's rage bubbling over as he saw the *Victorious* completely blocking their exit.

Without breaking stride, he began to walk up the loading ramp.

"Who the hell do you people think you are? Get this fuckin' thing moved or—"

Men clad in army fatigues swarmed around the top of the ramp, pointing their weapons at Mackay and blocking his progress.

"Can I help you?" A voice said from behind the soldiers. They parted as Andrews approached the loading ramp.

"Yeah, you can help me by moving this oversized –" Mackay stopped and looked at Andrews, who was unreadable behind his sunglasses.

"Mackay, isn't it?" Andrews said.

"Aye, that's me."

"You seem a little more coherent than last time we met."

"Aye, well I was drunk and you weren't blocking me in, neither of which I can say now."

Andrews was about to answer when he looked beyond Mackay and saw Rainwater and Ox standing on the dock.

"Well, Mr Mackay, it seems you found the man that I could not."

"Lucky me."

Andrews waved away the solders around him, and then called down to the dock.

"Mr Rainwater, it seems you are a hard man to find. I wonder if I could have a word with you?"

Rainwater walked up the loading ramp, standing beside Mackay.

"What is this about?" He asked, as Andrews gave him a quick once over.

"It's about the thing I suspect brought us both here."

"Only thing that brought us here is the fishin,' pal."

"Indeed," Andrews said with a humourless grin, "and what kind of fish, I wonder, are you looking for?"

"That depends on how long it takes for you to move this bloody boat and let us out of here." Mackay shot back, glaring at Andrews, who for his part appeared unconcerned. He was now giving Rainwater his full attention.

"It seems we both have something in common, Mr Rainwater."

"I can't think what."

Andrews smiled and took off his sunglasses.

"Because we have both seen this thing and know what we're dealing with."

Rainwater felt a chill run down his spine.

"Seen what?" he asked anyway, wishing Andrews would turn his penetrating gaze somewhere else.

"Our big, big, fish."

"Is that why you wanted to find me?"

"It was. I thought we might both benefit from sharing information and working together."

"We have our own boat, and our own business to attend to." Mackay said, trying to interject.

Andrews looked at the *Lisa Marie* and chuckled.

"I appreciate your bravery, if nothing else."

"What did you want to talk about?" Rainwater said.

Andrews looked at Mackay, then back at Rainwater with raised eyebrows.

"He knows all about it. Whatever you need to tell me, you can tell him."

"As much as I wish that were the case, I'm afraid in the United States government, we don't have the luxury of being so free with our information."

"It looks like we have nothing to talk about." Rainwater said, and turned to walk away.

"We know where to find it." Andrews called after him, prompting Rainwater to stop mid stride and turn back.

"Go on," Rainwater said cautiously.

"Not here, it's not secure. Come aboard and we can talk in private. Your friends are welcome too, of course."

Mackay and Rainwater exchanged glances.

"No thanks, we'll take our chances." Rainwater said before turning and heading back down the ramp.

"Crustecmosi Gigantis we've dubbed it. Three to four hundred feet in length, eight to ten tentacles, two flippers, and fluke similar to a whale. Twin rows of serrated backwards facing teeth, which measure anything from twenty-five to thirty inches. We know where it feeds, and we also know how to trace it."

"You don't need us then do ya?" Mackay said, wondering if the world had gone mad overnight.

"No, we don't," Andrews agreed, flashing his predatory smile. "Wouldn't you prefer to know what you are dealing with rather than splash around and get in our way?"

"Just because you work for the government doesn't mean you own the ocean. We can go where we please." Mackay said, glaring at Andrews.

"That's true, however, I do have command of this boat. I'm also dealing with a matter of national security, and have the authority to do whatever is necessary to ensure the task is done without interference."

"You fucking government stooges are all the same," Mackay said shaking his head. "Why don't you cut the 'national security' shit, and spit out whatever it is you are trying to say."

"Well, Mr Mackay, in the interests of clarity. If I deem you to be compromising this mission, I will have no hesitation in putting your boat on the bottom of the ocean. Clear enough?"

"Crystal," Mackay grumbled.

"So, under the circumstances, perhaps a chat would be the best solution all around?"

Rainwater nodded. "It seems so."

CHAPTER 19

California,
10 miles off the coast of Venice beach

Zimmer's muscles flexed as he raced the fifteen-foot sailboat through the water. He had been taking part in the annual Venice Beach international boat race for the third successive year, but until today, had never led. Now, the twenty six year old German turned the boat slightly, feeling the rush of acceleration as it cut through the water. His nearest challenger was three-time world champion, British born, Ben Green, who had suffered technical trouble earlier in the race, and for the last mile or so, Zimmer had been steadily increasing his advantage at the front. There were over sixty entries for this year's event, and popular opinion was that it was going to be a two horse race between Green and his bitter rival, Jonas Haim, who as expected, was right with Green as they tried desperately to close the gap.

Nobody however, had expected Zimmer, a fifty-to-one outside bet, to become such a fly in the ointment. As he carefully repositioned his one man sailboat, Zimmer half wished he had placed a bet on himself for the win, and then reminded himself there was still a long way to go and his arms and back already burned with the efforts of his exertion.

Zimmer could see the next buoy marking the route ahead, and angled towards it. After he had made the turn, he would be heading against the wind, which would make things infinitely more difficult for the remainder of the race, however, he was confident he could pace himself against Green, who still seemed to be struggling with his boat. The main threat would likely come from Haim, who looked to be shadowing Zimmer at a distance and waiting for his chance to strike. Gulping a shallow breath of air, Zimmer passed the buoy and pulled the sailboat into a graceful turn, as he set out towards his next waypoint. He hoped his stamina would last the distance. With the sun in his face, Zimmer lowered his head and increased his efforts.

The near four hundred feet behemoth lay on the ocean floor, allowing the currents to flow through its body as it rested. It hadn't fed for twelve hours, and although it could sense the other sea life on the outer edges of its territory, it was reluctant to expend the needed energy by pursuing them. With the ability to slow its metabolism by regulating the tempo of its pickup truck sized heart, it was able to sustain itself on the energy stored in the fatty sacs below its forward flippers.

It's near slumber was disturbed by the series of vibrations which were making their way directly towards the creature and into its territory. Its simple brain compelled the creature to defend the waters it had claimed as its own. It pushed up from the seabed on its array of tentacles, and with one powerful flick of its fluke, was racing to intercept.

Until they had made the turn, Ben Green had been pretty sure he was losing his edge. He was world number one, ranked as the best in his profession, and as a result, losing was unacceptable. Although not as glamorous as football or motorsport, he still lived his life under an ever-growing mountain of pressure and expectation. He had sponsors to keep happy, as without them, there was no money, and without money, there was no racing. There was also the personal pride that came with testing himself against the best in the business. He'd been leading the race until a twisted line had caused his main sail to malfunction, dropping him back into seventh place. He'd recovered to second, and had now dropped back to third. Ahead of him by around twelve feet was his main rival, Jonas Haim. The press had made more of their rivalry than actually existed. In reality, they were actually friends, although it was a distant relationship built on respect. They knew well enough that controversy brought viewers, and with it money, so they both took every opportunity to play up their non-existent rivalry in order to make the show more exciting. What Green didn't expect however, was the performance of Zimmer, and he was starting to think he had underestimated the young German who was a good forty to fifty feet out in front on him.

He wondered if now at thirty-six, age was starting to go against him. Certainly, his body was less able to cope with the stresses of racing like it used to, and although he was still a regular winner, his performance edge was undeniably reducing. He asked himself if this was how it happened, and when the first signs of age knocking on the door start to tell you maybe it's time to start slowing down. Time to think about passing the torch to the younger generation like Zimmer and the other up and coming stars of the future, or if he should go all out to try and bag one last title, one last chance to squirrel away enough money to make his life comfortable. He was aware that the working life of a sportsman is short, and he also knew he didn't have enough eggs in his nest to take his foot off the gas yet. He saw that Zimmer was starting to struggle with the headwind, perhaps a sign of his inexperience. Green increased his speed, pulling alongside Haim, leaving a good distance between himself and his rival. They were both closing on Zimmer quickly, and he positioned his boat to go alongside him, Haim taking the opposite flank. Perhaps he had fixed his issue, or the sight of the two closing in had spurred him on. Zimmer now also increased his pace, and the boats were three abreast as they cut through the water. Green smiled.

He lived for these moments.

He was starting to edge ahead when he saw something explode out of the water ahead of them.

It looked like a wall at first, a greenish brown barrier that had thrown itself out of the ocean. He had only a split second to comprehend the impossibility of what it actually was, but by then, it was too late. Its near thirty-foot jaws opened, and Ben Green was looking down a deep red maw of serrated teeth.

Zimmer had seen it too, and because he was already in the zone, was able to react fastest, veering the boat to the left in the hope of avoiding the immense mass as it launched toward the trio. Zimmer's boat collided with Haim's, and the pair was ejected into the water. Green was not so lucky, and barely had time to register that his life was about to end when the creature bit down, devouring both Pilot and boat in one powerful bite. Blood, bone, and sinew quivered down the creature's gullet, and its dim brain told it that it had mortally wounded the creature that had dared enter its territory. Mistaking the thirty-one other boats competing in the race as the death throes of a single creature, the animal went into frenzy.

The water bit into Zimmer as he struggled to regain his senses. He drew breath as he saw the full size of the creature as it passed. It was beyond comprehension. His head broke the surface and he let out a gasping cough as his lungs took in much needed air. Haim had also surfaced, and was in the process of pulling himself back into his boat.

Zimmer thought Haim had the look of a man who had peeked into hell and was trying to come to terms with what he saw, and he supposed, as he kicked towards his own boat, he probably looked pretty much the same. He pulled himself out of the water and glanced over to Haim.

"Jonas," he said breathlessly as he looked across the water to his rival, "did you see it?"

Haim nodded and even from ten feet away, Zimmer could see that his rival was in shock.

He was about to speak again, when they both heard the splintering crack from behind them. They looked just in time to see the marbled, arched back of the creature duck beneath the waves, taking one of the following boats with it.

"We have to get out of here," Zimmer said.

Haim didn't respond, he simply sat and watched the creature as it systematically destroyed the other boats that were now crashing into each other and changing course wildly, as they tried to avoid the beast. The air was filled with the sounds of screaming and splintering wood & fibreglass as the creature continued to rampage.

"Come on, this is our chance to get out away," Zimmer pleaded. Haim was unmoving. All he could do was sit in his boat shivering and staring at the carnage.

"I'm going," he said with finality. Haim didn't respond, and left with no choice, Zimmer set sail alone, aiming at a diagonal for the coast. He lowered his head, and found a current of air that drove him forwards, his speed quickly building as he raced towards the beach.

It had attacked the pod of creatures that had invaded its territory, and now it detected only one. Even though it was fleeing, the enraged creature spun around to pursue it, pushing through the splintery and bloody debris of the sailboats that it had destroyed.

Jonas Haim watched as the immense wake surged past his boat, pushing it a further fifty feet out to sea as it chased Zimmer. He looked on open mouthed and shivering, and was still unable to comprehend what had happened.

Ahead, Zimmer had noticed it too, glancing over his shoulder as the great wave of water closed the distance to him. Despite the fear, he smiled, because the adrenaline junkie in him found a sick excitement in the situation. The race he had been competing to win was now meaningless. This race was for his life. The wind was strong behind him, and the boat was flawless in its precision as it cut across the ocean, the ride smooth and as close to perfect as Zimmer could have ever hoped.

Don't look back, don't look back, don't look back.

He repeated it in his head, but couldn't help a quick glance over his shoulder. The wake had halved the distance to him, and he thought it would be a pretty close call as to whether he would be able to get to the beach before the creature got to him.

Forget it, focus on the beach, and focus on maintaining the speed. Get to the finish.

The voice in his head was right, and he did as it instructed, making minute adjustments to the angle of his sail, and ignoring the burning in his back and shoulders from his efforts. He knew he was approaching the shallows, and with it, as the water became less stable, he knew the breaking waves would slow his progress. He didn't look, and didn't have to. He could sense the creature behind him, and knew time was up. Unsure if it was by instinct or awareness, he veered the boat sharply to the right, almost coming to a stop as he changed course. A split second later, the giant exploded out of the water, its jaws slamming on the space that he had occupied seconds earlier. He laughed, or maybe it was a scream. He couldn't tell the difference anymore. He spun the sailboat back towards the beach, which was tantalisingly close. He could see people watching, pointing, and taking photographs. He aimed towards them, wondering when the water would be too shallow for the creature to follow.

The creature turned its massive body around and closed within striking distance. Infuriated by missing its first attack, its confusion lasted only seconds, as it instantly relocated its target. With a flick of its tail, the creature was upon the boat, attacking side on and launching out of the ocean in an explosion of spray, crushing the fibreglass hull like kindling. It thrashed its head from side to side as it swallowed its catch before circling away from the shallows and back to deeper waters.

On the beach, Michael Zimmer fell to his knees, exhausted, as a crowd of onlookers surrounded him. He had pushed beyond what he deemed to be his limits, and by steering the boat away from the beach, and then jumping out to swim to safety, he had bought himself enough time to ensure his survival. Now he was safe, the weight of what had happened crashed down upon him, and he began to shake. He heard distant voices from those around him calling for help, some comparing video footage. None of that mattered to Zimmer. All that mattered was the feel of the sun on his back and the sand under his knees. Everything else seemed incidental.

"We need to call the police," he gasped between ragged breaths.

"It's done, dude, police are on their way. I think we're gonna need the damn army for this though."

Zimmer squinted to the bronzed man standing in front of him. "You saw it?"

"Damn straight we did. We all did. What the hell was that, man?"

Zimmer shook his head, and got gingerly to his feet. "I don't know, but someone needs to close the beaches."

CHAPTER 20

"What is it exactly that you want from me?" Rainwater asked Andrews as he looked at him across the table.

"I want to know what you saw. Any detail, however small could greatly help us."

"I doubt anything I could tell you will be anything you don't know already."

"Perhaps, perhaps not. Until you tell me, we won't know."

"Is that why you brought me in here on my own?"

"It is," Andrews said with a slight flicker of a smile. "Your friend seems quite aggressive."

Rainwater didn't answer, so Andrews went on.

"You know none of them believe you, don't you?"

"Of course I do, I'm not stupid. I just think it might be better that way. If they knew, they wouldn't have come."

"And yet, here we are, both willing to risk everything to find this magnificent creature."

"Have you seen it?" Rainwater asked.

"Not in the flesh as such, but on video, yes."

"I thought as much."

"Why do you say that?"

"Because, if you had you wouldn't be doing this."

"I've been searching for this creature for years. Long before you managed to get in its way. Anyway, what about you? Why are you risking your life again to look for it?"

"I have my reasons."

"I would like to hear them."

"If you must know, I want to find it to prove to myself that I'm not crazy."

"I can assure you, the creature is real. I can show you video footage of it. At least that way you can stay at home and not risk your life and that of your crew."

"I think if you had seen this thing in the flesh, you wouldn't be so arrogant."

Andrews's cheek twitched and darkness flashed in his eyes as he looked at Rainwater.

"And I think you give this creature too much credit. What happened to you wasn't a deliberate act. You were in the wrong place at the wrong time and suffered an unfortunate loss. Let it go. Put it down to the power of nature."

"I figured you'd say something like that."

"Oh, and you are now an expert on these animals?"

"No, not by any means, I have seen it and I respect what it can do. I have to go out there. I need to find it. I need to conquer it."

"You sound afraid."

"I am afraid."

"Then take my advice. Let it go. Let the professionals deal with it. You don't need to be out here."

"Would you let it go if you were in my position?"

Andrews showed a brief glimmer of a smile and leaned back in his seat. "You don't speak like a fisherman, if you don't mind me saying so."

"I have no idea what you mean."

"I mean, with you there is intelligence and level headedness, which might be better suited in another profession."

Rainwater straightened in his seat as he watched Andrews pace the room.

"What are you suggesting?"

"I'm suggesting you could do far better than head out to sea with a less than competent crew, and pitiful equipment with which to attempt to find this creature and put more lives at risk."

"I already told you. I'm not going to stay home and let this thing eat away at me inside."

Andrews grinned, as he approached the table, sitting opposite Rainwater.

"No, what I'm suggesting is you join us here. Help us. We have the best equipment, the best staff. Trust me, if anyone will find this creature, it's us. If you are really intent on locating this creature, let me help you do it."

"At the same time, you can keep an eye on me and keep control of whatever knowledge goes in or out, right?"

"That's a little dramatic, but in essence, yes."

"No thanks."

"Are you absolutely certain? I would advise you give this some serious thought, especially considering what you are up against, and what you could stand to lose. The ocean is a lonely place. Who knows what could happen out there?"

"Are you threatening me?"

"Call it friendly advice. You are in over your head here. Despite what you might think of me, I like you, Mr. Rainwater. You don't beat around the bush. I don't want you to get mixed up in something you are certain to lose."

"Lose? I didn't realise we were playing a game."

"In my experience everything in life is a game."

"I'll take my chances."

"Why?" Andrews said, leaning on the table and staring at Rainwater. "For some family honour code or bragging rights to let those close to you know you weren't hallucinating? Why is it so important to you?"

"It's simple really. I want to find it, and I want to kill it. I need to know its dead. I need to see first hand that it can never do to anyone else what it did to me."

Andrews's expression changed. His eyes narrowed and he flashed a wide, uncomfortable smile. Rainwater thought this was his first glimpse at the *real* Andrews, the one hidden behind the friendly, helpful exterior. When he spoke, his voice was low and laced with threat.

"I should warn you, any notion of harming this creature will not be tolerated. We have absolute power to do whatever is necessary to capture this creature unharmed."

"Capture? I thought you were just trying to find it?"

Andrews grimaced. He knew he had said more than he intended to.

"I've heard enough. We're leaving." Rainwater said as he stood and strode to the door. In the next room, Mackay was sitting at a table along with Clara and Dexter.

"You need to be smart, think about your options." Andrews said as he followed Rainwater out of the room.

"Options? If you had seen this thing up close like I have, you would know there is only one option, and that's to kill this damn thing."

"What's happening?" Mackay said, standing and glaring at Andrews.

"This asshole plans to capture this thing, not kill it."

Clara and Dexter joined Mackay and Rainwater in staring at Andrews.

"Look, we all need to calm down and take a moment to relax, it was a slip of the tongue, and that's all."

"Bullshit it was," Rainwater said.

"Is this true?" Clara said, watching Andrews carefully for a reaction.

"You know as well as I do that our objective is to find and observe this wonderful creature."

"You're lying, pal." Mackay said, taking a step towards Andrews. "I can smell it on you. You fuckin' government pricks are always hiding behind bullshit excuses."

"Look, let's all calm down, okay?" Dexter said, trying to diffuse the tension. "Maybe we should all just take a breath and relax."

"I don't need to relax," Rainwater said. "I need to go find this thing."

"Then what?" Clara said, watching him just as intensely as she looked at Andrews.

"I'm going to kill it."

"That's barbaric," she shot back. "This is a unique species which needs to be studied. I was assured that was the reason for my being here."

"And it is. Mr Rainwater here is mistaken." Andrews said, his smile faltering.

"If you believe that, you'll believe anything. Come on, Mackay, let's get the hell out of here."

Mackay opened the door leading to the deck.

"Remember what I said. Don't get in my way." Andrews said as he followed them.

"You do what you have to do, and I'll do the same." Rainwater said over his shoulder as he headed down the loading ramp.

"What makes you think you can compete with us out there?"

Rainwater stopped and turned towards Andrews.

"Because you might have the technology, and the brilliant scientists, we have one thing you don't."

"Oh, and what might that be?"

"We know the water. We know what it will throw at us."

"Water doesn't scare me."

"I know," Rainwater replied, "which is why we have an advantage."

CHAPTER 21

Venice Beach
California

Milton Cooper had worked for TSBS for seven years, and this was by far the most ridiculous story he had ever been asked to cover. He was looking to secure the anchor job, something where he would work from the studio and become a familiar face in people's lives at six o clock every weekday. For now though, he was stuck with the always on the move roaming reporter role. He was the one who was forced to cover what the company referred to as 'human interest' stories, which more often than not were the stories that nobody really took too seriously. He picked up the handheld mirror and squinted at his reflection where he crouched in the back of the news van. Milton was tall and gangly, and despite being the wrong side of thirty-five, he still held up pretty well. He had sandy hair that was still full and free from grey, and smooth skin, which was – as yet- line and worry free. He adjusted his tie, put on his game face and clambered out of the van.

Melina, his camera operator was waiting outside. She was in full business mode now, but the dark haired, English born, twenty three year old Asian, had a softer side, which most of her colleagues rarely saw. She grinned as he approached, and he felt his chest quiver a little.

"This is bullshit," he said, giving an exasperated shrug.

"It's work," Melina replied.

"We shouldn't be out here doing shit like this, Melina, we've paid our dues. We should be working out of the studio."

"Hey, at least this way we get to travel. I know you, Milton. Within six months, you'd be sick of the sight of the studio and be clamouring to get out to jobs like this." She touched his arm gently as she said it, and he had to fight off a flurry of those pesky emotions that he felt towards her. He blinked and looked at his expertly shined shoes.

"Sorry… it's just… I get frustrated that's all. I would make a great anchor for the six o clock news. The execs have been dangling the carrot at me for years now, and yet, here I am, about to report on a god-damn sea monster sighting."

He shook his head as he looked at the expanse of sand in front of him, which was jammed with people, police, and rival TV crews.

"Well," She said, following his gaze, "it looks like we aren't the only ones with a crew out here. I saw a CNN truck parked up the beach."

Milton grunted, only half listening. He was more concerned with the damage the sand would do to his shoes, and wished he had brought his pumps.

"Hey, I'm talking to you," she said softly, clicking her fingers in front of his eyes. He looked at her and as always, those old feelings tried to rekindle until he quashed them and broke eye contact.

"Sorry," he said, forcing a smile of his own, "I guess I'm being a moody asshole today, that's all."

"Milton, I get it, I really do. Like it or not, this is the job we have been asked to do, and we have to do it."

"I know, but I wish someone in the office would take notice. I work hard, I'm a model employee."

"If you really want something in this world, you don't wait for someone to give it to you." She held his gaze, her dark eyes mesmerizing to him. "You have to go out there and take it."

"What do you mean?" he asked, wondering if she was referring to the job, or how he had dealt with their brief fling.

"I mean you need to get out of your comfort zone. Think outside the box. Force them to acknowledge your talents."

"How do I do that?"

She shrugged "Who the hell knows. You have to do *something*. Give it some thought, okay?"

He nodded, and turned his attention to the beach.

"Okay, let's get this piece recorded and get the hell out of here. It's too damn hot."

Melina grabbed her camera. "Let's do it." She said, and followed as Milton walked onto the beach.

They set up with the crowd of onlookers behind Milton, who made a few minor adjustments to his tie, and then looked into the camera.

"Okay, we're rolling, start whenever you're ready."

He took a deep breath, broadened his grin, and began.

"Godzilla. Jaws. Cthulhu. Moby Dick. All leviathans of the deep, which fortunately for us, are creatures drawn from the wild imagination of authors and screenwriters. That was at least, until, today. This is Milton Cooper for TSBS, coming to you live From

Venice beach California. Here amid the bronzed surfer bodies and beautiful people, a creature is claimed to lurk in the ocean…"

He was on autopilot, going through the motions in order to present the report, whilst looking beyond the camera towards Melina. His heart pinched a little because he had let her through his grasp, and at his age, he didn't think he would ever get another chance with someone like her again. He dismissed it, and the thought of Melina was replaced by the idea of getting a drink. Something cold and alcoholic that he would regret the following day, an idea that quickly escalated from one drink to a determined plan to get absolutely shit faced, and why not? It's not like anyone at the station would miss him. He broadened his grin and continued his lighthearted report about the alleged monster sighting.

He had found a quiet bar off the beach, and having changed out of his suit and sand filled shoes, was now incognito in knee length shorts, sandals, and white t-shirt. He was on his second beer chased with Jack Daniels, and still felt no better about his life. He was grateful that the bar was at least quiet and cool, and from his seat in the corner, he was happily drowning his sorrows. He drained the bottle, finished the Jack, then walked to the bar, disappointed to find his legs were still steady and the euphoric numbness of being drunk was still nowhere close to arriving. He waited, staring at the bartender, who was absorbed with watching the flat screen on the opposite wall. Milton was about to bang his glass on the bar to get his attention, when he too looked at the TV, and changed his mind.

The amateur footage was shot from the beach, and though it was shaking and unstable, showed the entire miraculous escape perpetrated by Zimmer, as the huge wake followed. The footage showed a huge…*something* charging just below the surface of the water, taking Zimmer's boat as the young German vaulted overboard and swam for the beach. The footage was replayed, zoomed, and in slow motion. Milton watched open mouthed, and cursed himself for neither researching the origin of the story or bothering to consider it might be a serious chance for him to actually do something worthwhile. Certainly, the CNN reporter who was now on screen seemed to be taking it seriously, his tone sombre and serious as he speculated on what might be lurking in the depths of the ocean. The entire feel of the report was a million miles away from his own, cheesy, campy, hammed up effort from earlier. He felt angry, ashamed and frustrated, and all thoughts of drinking himself unconscious were gone. The footage on screen was now an overhead shot of the ocean, where several overturned and splintered sailboats bobbed in the surf. The news bar across the bottom told the devastating news:

FORTY KILLED IN BOAT RACE. ATTACK PERPETRATED BY CREATURE OF UNKNOWN ORIGIN. GOVERNMENT UNAVAILABLE FOR COMMENT.

Milton licked his lips, and snatched up his phone, taking his eyes away from the screen only long enough to punch in Melina's number. He stared at the television whist he waited for the line to connect.

"Melina? It's me." He said as she answered. "You know what you were saying earlier about thinking outside the box? Well, I think I just had an idea."

CHAPTER 22

Andrews poured another drink as he watched the television footage of what had now been dubbed 'The Venice beach monster attack.' He shook his head and whistled through his teeth, as he toyed with what to tell Russo when he arrived. There was a knock at the door, immediately followed by Clara entering the room. She sat in one of the plush leather chairs set up in Andrews's quarters, and for a moment, said nothing.

"So," she said, "when were you going to tell me this was more than an observation mission?"

"I told you everything I'm able to. All I need you to do is help me locate it. After that, you won't need to get involved anymore."

"That's not what we agreed," she snapped, a flush of hot anger blooming in her cheeks. "Full disclosure. That was the deal."

"I told you everything I'm able to. You have to appreciate that this situation goes way above my pay grade."

"I don't care about how high up the chain this goes, I want some clarification about your intentions."

"The expectations haven't changed. We are to locate this creature as soon as possible in order to ensure public safety."

"Public safety? Funny how it only became an issue since the incident on Venice beach this afternoon."

"It's no secret we wish this had been kept out of the public eye. Now more than ever, we need to act quickly."

"Or we could leave it alone."

Andrews leaned forward in his seat, paused to consider his words, and continued.

"Clara, you are brilliant and highly respected, so I won't insult your intelligence by lying to you. However, you must understand that I can't divulge certain things. I'm simply not authorised. Once my colleague arrives, by all means, ask him anything you wish to know. Until that time, I can't give you any more information."

"When does he arrive?"

"He's here."

Russo walked into the room, clad in a sharp looking suit. He nodded to Andrews, and looked at Carla, devouring her with his eyes.

"You must be our curious scientist," he said, striding confidently across the room and extending a hand.

"Marine biologist," she countered, shaking his hand.

She trusted her initial instincts when it came to people, yet found her opinion of Russo to be mostly neutral. He smelled of expensive aftershave and soap, and when he removed his jacket, she saw he was much more muscular than he had at first appeared. He crossed the room and poured himself a large brandy, then sat opposite Clara, watching her with a half-smile. There was intensity to his gaze that would come across as attractive, if not for the fact that it instilled fear in her instead.

"I was just asking what your intentions were towards this creature," she said, forcing herself to keep eye contact. "I'm not comfortable heading out until I know definitively. He wouldn't tell me."

"And rightly so," Russo said with a grin, "as he wasn't authorised. I, however, am."

"Okay, so you tell me. Are you looking to capture this thing or observe it?"

Russo took a sip of his brandy, set it on the table and looked at Clara. "Miss Thompson, let me personally assure you of our intentions. The question of capture did arise for a time, however, under the circumstances, we thought it was both an unnecessary risk and in truth, a dangerous option considering the sheer size of the creature."

"He seemed to think capture was still on the cards." She replied, nodding at Andrews.

"I can assure you, Miss Thompson, he was wrong."

"So you're just going out to observe it? You guarantee it?"

"I give you my personal assurance that our mission is one of observation. I have no intention or desire to put the lives of anyone on board this vessel in danger. We simply want to assess the threat this creature may pose so we can consider future action."

"You ought to tell that to those other guys, the ones that intend to kill it."

"Other people?" Russo said, his eyebrows raised as he looked towards Andrews.

"Nothing I couldn't handle," Andrews said, squirming under Russo's gaze. "A group of fishermen. We had words."

"When?" Russo asked, now training his icy stare on Andrews instead of Clara.

"About three hours ago." Andrews said. "I'll give you a full report shortly," he added.

The two remained locked in eye contact, then Russo nodded. "Of course, thank you."

He turned back to Clara, and grinned. "Well, if there is nothing else, Miss Thompson, Mr Andrews and I have much to discuss."

"No, that's all I needed to know," she said, standing and taking a second to look at both men.

"Thanks for the reassurance."

As she crossed the room, she imagined she could still feel Russo's eyes crawling all over her, and felt a strange compulsion to run. She fought it off, and remained calm as she left, closing the door behind her and cutting off Russo's line of sight.

The instant she was gone, Russo turned to Andrews.

"Tell me about this fishing boat."

Andrews filled Russo in about Rainwater and Mackay. When he had finished, Russo stood and paced the room, allowing the information to sink in.

"We can't compromise Project Blue. That has to be our first priority." Russo said, sitting and taking another sip of his drink.

"I thought you said it was off, and that we were just observing?"

"Come on, don't be so naïve. Do you really think the government would sink millions of dollars into funding this project if we were to break to the will of a scientist? No. I'm afraid not. I simply did what you should have. I told her what she wanted to hear."

"All I wanted to do when I first pitched this idea was to observe it. Hell, I just want to find it. Things only changed when you came on board."

"And for that you should be grateful. Until I stepped in, the chances of this project being funded was less than none. You should keep that in mind."

"Even so, we need to be careful. With the way the media are treating this, every half-assed adventurer with a boat will be out looking for this thing. It could be a problem."

"They don't concern me. Most of them will sail around getting into each other's way. However, this Rainwater situation is a worry. He has encountered it, and you can bet he will start looking in the same kind of places as us. "

"I imagine a lot of the people out looking for it have aspirations of killing it. What makes him so different?"

"Because those others who are out there haven't seen it yet. If they had, they wouldn't be out on the water. This guy though, he's seen it up close. It almost killed him when it took the lives of his father and uncle, and yet, he's back out on the water trying to find it. Like it or not, that kind of determination should be respected, and be of more than a little reason for concern."

"What do you suggest we do?"

"For now, nothing. They aren't a priority. If they start becoming a problem, then that might change. Project Blue is to go ahead as planned."

"Let me ask you something off the record," Andrews said.

"Go ahead."

"Do you think it's possible?"

"Project Blue?"

"Yeah."

"Not only do I think it's possible, I'm willing to risk all of our lives to prove it."

Andrews had no answer. Satisfied, Russo grinned.

"Anyway, enough of the melodrama. Let's get underway before our temperamental biologist changes her mind."

Andrews called the captain and gave the order to cast off, and then poured himself and Russo a fresh drink. Outside the door, Clara stood, and chewed over the conversation she had overheard. At first, she was angry at being deceived, then that was quickly replaced by curiosity, which was transforming into obsession. As she walked towards her room, she asked herself the same question.

What the hell is Project Blue?

CHAPTER 23

Famous for its often inhospitable weather, it was a rare calm day on the Bering Sea. The sky was blue and cloudless, and the boat cut smoothly through the water as they continued the search. Rainwater was by the radar looking over Morrison's shoulder at the green hued display.

"Do you have to stand there?" he grunted.

"I'm just looking."

"Look, I'll tell you if we get a signal, until then, can you go somewhere else? I can't work with you hovering over me."

"Sorry, man, no harm intended," Rainwater grumbled, then headed to the wheelhouse.

Mackay was piloting the boat, one foot propped on the control unit as he smoked his way through another pack of cigarettes.

"Another long day today, lad, eh?" he said as Rainwater sat beside him in the co-pilots chair.

"It's a big ocean."

"It's a big fish we're looking for too." Mackay shot back with a wink. "I just hope we're looking in the right place."

"I thought your guy knew what he was doing?"

"He does, or so he tells me at least."

"You don't believe any of this do you?" Rainwater asked as he looked out at the vast expanse of water.

"Well, the way I look at things, I have spent a long time on the water all over the world. I have seen whales. Sharks. Dolphins. Even sea snakes more than twenty feet long. I can't imagine something as big as you say could be swimming around out there without someone coming across it."

"I saw it, Mackay. I saw the wake."

"I know what you say you saw, but it was dark. Raining. You were tired. The mind can play tricks with you out here after a while. I don't doubt what you *think* you saw, I just don't think it will be as spectacular as you are expecting."

"So what *do* you think I saw? Andrews is after *something* out here."

"I think maybe it might be a big whale out there. Maybe a giant squid, nothing as big as you are claiming. Nothing the size you say this thing is could live for so long without us knowing about it."

"Morrison says it could have easily existed without us knowing. Hell, it *did* exist without us knowing."

"Aye, well, it seems that asshole on the other boat is as caught up in all this as you, so maybe I'm the dumb one after all. He seems the type to do anything to get what he wants."

"You think he'd really try to sink us if it came to it?"

Mackay shrugged and tossed his cigarette butt out of the open port window. "Depends if you believe in conspiracy theories, I suppose. A guy I knew back in the forces, swore all of our technology came from an alien spaceship the government deconstructed back in Roswell. Says without that craft, we wouldn't have microwaves, mobile phones, silicon, or half of the other things we take for granted."

"I didn't take you for a conspiracy theorist."

"I didn't say *I* believed all that shit, my point is there are plenty of people who do. The internet is full of people who claim all sorts of stuff. That the government was responsible for John F Kennedy's assassination, or killing Marilyn Monroe, or even of engineering 9/11. My point is, we don't know what this guy is willing to do."

"So what do we do about it?"

Mackay shrugged as he lit another cigarette.

"Way I see it, there isn't much we can do. We're out here in the middle of nowhere on a small boat, which has long since seen its best years. If this prick decides to blow us out of the water, there ain't' a whole lot we can do to stop him."

"What do you suppose he wants with it?" Rainwater asked.

"If this thing actually exists, my best guess is that our wonderful government is looking to find it because they see something to gain. In my experience, everything related to people like Andrews comes down to either war, money, or both. Whatever it is, you can bet your ass they won't stop until they get what they want. If we get in the way, don't be surprised if they blow us out of the water and call us collateral damage."

"You think we're in danger, don't you?"

"Maybe, maybe not," Mackay said with a shrug of his shoulders. "There ain't much we can do about it now, other than see it through to the end."

"Why did you agree to this if you knew we could be at risk?" Rainwater asked.

Mackay exhaled a plume of blue smoke from his cigarette, and then turned to face Rainwater.

"In all honesty, I've been asking myself the same question since we came out here. Is it a sense of duty to the son of a good friend? Maybe. On the other hand, maybe I'm curious to know if our boat was sunk by this fish of yours. Either way, I'm here by my choice. You don't have to feel guilty about it."

"I hope we find it soon. The waiting for something to happen is worse than if we actually hit."

"Well, you better get used to the calm. Looks like there's a bitch of a storm coming in tonight. It could be a rough few hours."

"How bad?"

"Tropical storm bad."

"Have you been in one before?"

"Yeah, and I'll be straight with you. If you think conditions were bad on the night the *Red Gold* went down, it was a picnic compared to this. I only hope you know what you are doing, kid, otherwise, we could all end up at the bottom of the ocean.

CHAPTER 24

The California coastline had exploded into a melting pot of frantic activity. Driven into frenzy by the media coverage, docks and jetties everywhere were overcrowded with people, all desperate to get out to sea in search of what was now being dubbed the 'sunshine state monster.' Boats of every conceivable size and shape were being loaded and prepared to head out to sea. Some were setting out with the intention of killing the creature and were readying dynamite and harpoons. Others were content simply to try to find the creature, and many opportunist skippers were charging curious civilians extortionate sums to join in their adventures.

Milton walked down the dock, struggling to cope with the explosive heat. He had hoped that by heading out early, he might avoid the crowds. Unfortunately, it seemed everyone in California had the same idea.

Melina was waiting for him by the boat he had hired. She looked stunning, dressed in a red vest top and jean shorts, and he couldn't help but let his eyes linger on her as she loaded the last of her camera equipment onto the boat. She took off her sunglasses and greeted him with a bemused smile as he arrived.

"I thought you said it would be quiet this morning?"

"I thought it would be. It's like a damn circus. Seems like everyone who has ever seen Jaws thinks they are Roy fucking Scheider."

"The world's gone monster crazy. What did you expect?" she said, giving him a smile that made him melt a little inside.

"I expected it to be a little less... frantic."

"Well, whatever the crowds are like, I have to say, I'm impressed."

"Oh yeah? With what?" he said, making sure to stand a little taller and push his chest out a touch.

"With you. With getting the network to agree to this. I'm surprised they went for it."

"You told me to think out of the box, so I did. What do you think of the boat?"

She stepped back and admired the fifty-three foot state of the art vessel, which was equipped with the latest in cutting edge sonar and fish finding software.

"I love it. Do you suppose we can keep it?" She said with a wink.

"Who knows, if we're the first to get footage of this thing, then maybe."

Melina smiled, and the two stood and looked at the vessel as it bobbed against the dock. "Well," Milton said, clapping his hands together, "we better get moving. I'm hoping to have this thing found in time to hit the six o clock news."

"That's optimistic," Melina replied, as she slipped her sunglasses back on and climbed onto the boat. "Where is the rest of the crew?"

"No crew, just us on this trip."

Melina frowned, and for the first time seemed a little uncertain. "Don't you need specialist operators for the underwater cameras?"

"Relax, I have it covered. We only need to film a static shot. Point and shoot. That wasn't worth the five grand or more these so called specialists were charging. Do you have any idea how in demand they are right now?"

"Still, we don't really have the experience to do this ourselves."

"Nobody is expecting us to film some kind of National Geographic documentary here. We just need to snag footage, the *first* footage, so we really need to be making a move. Trust me on this, okay?"

"Okay, what's the plan?"

"Way I figure it," he said as he hopped from the dock onto the boat, "is that we head away from the coast."

"Any reason?"

"Yeah, I did some research. Before the attack on the boat race, there were a series of beaching's and whale carcasses reported that washed up all across the Californian coast. I marked the positions on a map and I'll be damned if it doesn't look like a pattern."

"I'm impressed, really impressed." She said with a wide grin.

"It seems our creature feeds every few days, which means by now, he should be out looking for something to eat. We will find him, and film him from that," he said, pointing behind her.

"Please tell me that's not a shark cage."

"The best money can buy," Milton replied, striding over to the steel sections of cage and laying a hand on it. "This is our ticket to the next stage in our careers, Melina."

"I don't like this, Milton. This is how people end up getting in over their heads. You were the one who said these people are acting like Roy Scheider. Do you remember what happened to Robert Shaw?"

"Come on, that's just fiction. It's perfectly safe."

"Look, I know I said you needed to do something to get noticed. It doesn't have to be this extreme. As you said, a shot from the surface will be fine. I assumed you would be lowering those underwater cameras from the surface. I didn't think you would ever consider going down there."

"It does have to be extreme," Milton shot back, a little snappier than he intended.

"No, it doesn't. I'm all for going out and trying to get footage of this thing, just, let's do it from the boat. We don't need to get up close and personal."

Milton sighed, and looked out over the crystal blue California waters, then back at Melina.

"You know, maybe you're right. I'm sure we can get what we need from on board the boat."

"Exactly," she agreed, "let's just get our footage and get back here in one piece."

"Agreed," he said, happy that she had bought the lie.

"Glad to know we're on the same page."

"Aren't we always?" he said it with a deliberate flirtatious edge, testing the waters. Her small half smile wasn't at all discouraging, and he proceeded to untie the line holding them to the overcrowded dock.

"Well, let's get to it. Feel free to go ahead and grab a drink. The bar inside is fully stocked."

"Network really splashed out on this huh?"

"Hell yes, they want the exclusive on this. They pretty much gave us free reign to spend what we need to get the job done."

"Well, if it's on the network, who am I to turn down a free drink on such a beautiful day?"

She winked at him, and he wondered if it was suggestive or innocent. Either way, he thought it was going to be a hell of a trip.

CHAPTER 25

The *Victorious*, vaulted over fifteen foot waves as it ploughed through the East Siberian Sea. Andrews was sitting in the wheelhouse trying not to spill coffee all over himself. Russo simply stared out of the window, his face twisted into a grimace.

"I thought this expert of yours was certain we'd find it out here," he growled.

"The ocean is a big place. It was always going to take time."

"We don't have time. We have obligations towards certain parties who are relying on us locating this animal."

Andrews took a careful sip of his coffee, and followed Russo's gaze out of the window at the rolling seas.

"Surely they understand we can't make this thing appear out of nowhere. They have to give us time."

Russo whirled on Andrews, his face contorted into a grimace.

"You convinced everyone you knew where to look. That you had an expert who would help you pinpoint the creature within a matter of hours. That's what you said."

"I never said anything about a couple of hours. I said I would find this thing and I will. Hell, it took the entire might of the government ten years to find Osama Bin Laden, I'm sure your bosses can give the two of us a little more breathing space to do what we need to do."

"We need answers. I need something tangible that I can report back with."

"I get that, really I do. The truth is, this isn't an exact science. It will take as long as it takes."

"Oh, that's okay. Let's waste more valuable government resources whilst we wait for this thing to show," Russo growled.

"Take it easy, there's no point in getting yourself agitated."

"There is every reason. I have a job to do. If you and your people aren't up to the task, I'll have to get someone who is."

"That's not necessary. The marine biologist will locate the creature. You have my assurance. She's good. Just give her a little more time."

"Then where is she? Where is your superstar marine biologist whilst we're floating around out here in the middle of nowhere?"

"She's plotting our next move right now as it happens. Jesus, Russo, relax. I'll go talk to her and see if I can get an update."

"Do it. Make it clear to her I want results and want them now."

"Understood. I'll make sure she understands the urgency."

"Actually," Russo said as he turned towards Andrews, "I'll do it myself."

"I can handle this."

"The fact I have to press you on this says otherwise."

"Look, I get it. You need to see something happen. I'm not some slouch or freeloader. I'm as desperate as you are to find this thing."

Russo looked at Andrews and sneered. "You are nothing like me. Nobody is."

Andrews wasn't a man often lost for words, yet, this was one of those rare occasions. He stood and stared at Russo, unsure how to react. The tension was broken when Dexter walked into the wheelhouse.

"I, uh, just came to plot our next search location."

Neither man responded, as Dexter sat at the small table and unfurled his charts.

"I have work to do. We can continue this conversation later."

Andrews had heard enough anyway, and headed below deck, leaving Russo staring out of the window at the rolling landscape of broiling ocean.

CHAPTER 26

The 238 foot Russian made Kilo class submarine drifted through the murky depths off the Siberian coast. An older spec submarine, the Kilo class was still used for drills and training purposes, both of which were taking place today. The sub could house a crew of up to fifty-two, yet for this particular training exercise, there was less than half that on board. Commander Alexi Valentin shifted position, folding his massive arms as he looked at the trainee crew. The forty six year old was at one time, one of the brightest prospects in the Russian army. A leg wound sustained during a training exercise in the Siberian wilderness had put a stop to his active service career, and so he had spent the last twelve years putting new recruits through their paces. His fierce reputation was enough to ensure that the recruits toed the line, and if it didn't, his intimidating presence did. He was broad, and at well over six feet tall, he seemed to fill the submarines narrow corridors as he made his way through the labyrinth like maze. He kept his hair short, a blonde buzz cut, and he glared at his recruits through harsh eyes, which were a brilliant, if cold, shade of blue.

They were in seven hundred feet of water, and Valentin thought most of the trainees might yet make the cut.

"Okay," he said in his native tongue, his voice reverberating around the cramped operations room. "Descend to seven hundred and fifty feet and begin a sonar ping test."

The sub dived deeper into the freezing waters and not for the first time, Valentin hoped the old girl held together.

"Seven hundred and fifty feet, sir," one of the new recruits said as he looked at the commander.

"Very good. Begin ping test."

"Yes, Commander."

The creature had registered the presence of the submarine, but because of its size, it had kept a respectful and cautious distance.

Some two thousand feet away it was resting on the seabed, its mouth open as it fed on billions of tiny micro bacterial organisms, filtering them out using a sophisticated retractable plate at the back of the throat. As the seawater raced through the filter, the organisms were collected in their millions, and then when full, the creature would retract the net like appendage, devouring its meal.

The first sonar ping reached the goliath beast in seconds, sending it into a furious rage. It lurched from the sea floor and raced towards the sub, mistaking the sonar as a challenge from an aggressive rival.

"Commander, sonar has picked up an object moving towards us."

Valentin strode over to the radar station, leaning over the console and looking at the streak accelerating towards them.

"It looks like another sub." He growled and turned the navigator. "Radio in to base, find out if there are any other drills in the area. Do it now."

Valentin turned back to the sonar, and tried to figure out who it could be. He thought it might have been the Koreans. Ever since the EU restrictions were placed on them, they had blatantly flaunted their efforts to attain nuclear and military independence. Whatever it was, it was coming straight for them, and Valentin felt a rare surge of adrenaline. He watched as the signal closed in, and it was either through instinct or through experience, he understood this was no sub.

"Stop pinging." Valentin ordered, waiting as the junior officer obeyed.

"Should I attempt to establish contact, sir?" the officer asked.

Valentin shook his head. "That won't do us any good. Whatever that thing is, it's organic."

Even though they were fresh out of the academy, the recruits knew better than to question their commanding officer and instead, flicked concerned glances at each other as the object drew closer.

"Shut down everything, all operations bar life support."

The recruits were frightened enough to obey immediately, and within seconds, the submarine was silent, its control room bathed in a red glow from the emergency lighting.

Everyone, including Valentin, held their breath and waited.

Seven hundred feet away, the creature slowed, approaching the submarine cautiously. It moved alongside, mouth open as it tasted the water around the motionless vessel and tried to assess if it was a threat or not. It rubbed its snout against the cold steel hull, and retreated.

"Commander, what is it?" one of the junior officers asked, his eyes showing the fear that they all felt.

"I don't know. Some kind of whale maybe."

"Sir, that's not possible, it's bigger than the sub."

"I know," Valentin said, watching the radar.

He thought he knew what it was. He had seen the stories of the creature sighted off the coast of California, and had believed them to be nothing but fantasy. Now, as he stood sweating in the tight confines of the sub, he believed every word of it. He strode over to the radio, and was about to call in to base, when the operator yelled the words any submersible captain dreads to hear.

"Brace for impact!"

Valentin jogged to the radar display to see the creature, represented by a green smudge on the screen racing towards them.

"Full speed ahead! Hurry, it-"

Valentin was cut off by the explosive sound of metal buckling as the sub lurched violently, tossing Valentin off his feet and into the navigator's control console.

He struggled to stand, blinking away his confusion as alarms started to sound through the sub.

"Damage report," He barked. "Give me the damage report now!"

"We're breached in the rear compartments, Commander, taking on water." One of the trainees croaked.

"Get us out of here, now." Valentin snapped.

"We can't, sir, both screws are offline."

All eyes fell onto Valentin, and for once, he didn't know what to do. Aware that the creaking hull of the ancient submersible was the only thing separating them from certain death, He gave the only possible order.

"Take us to the surface," Valentin said.

"But, sir-"

"Do it now."

"Yes, Commander."

After attacking the sub's hull, the creature had decided it was neither edible, nor a threat, and had begun to retreat, leaving the stricken submarine where it was. It was time to feed, and the creature was about to start hunting when the subs ballast tanks whirred into life, making the vessel buoyant and taking it to the surface. Enraged by the persistence of its rival, the creature raced at full speed towards the boat, mistaking the crippled vehicles attempt to surface as an act of aggression. Valentin realised too late what was happening. Before he had time to react, the near four hundred foot missile smashed nose first into the already weakened outer structure. The entire rear end of the thirty-year-old submarine sheared away, flooding the interior chambers with thousands of gallons of seawater. Valentin and his crew of rookies never stood a chance, as the submarine imploded, its mangled remains spilling debris and bodies into the water and sank towards the bottom of the ocean. Satisfied its prey had been vanquished, the ravenous creature snapped at the floating debris spilling from the sub, then set off towards its usual warmer hunting grounds. It was time to feed.

CHAPTER 27

Clara lay on her bunk in the darkness, plagued by the gnawing feeling that something was desperately wrong. Beside her on the floor, partially illuminated by the moonlight, was a large map. From the research she had done, she had narrowed the creature's possible location to three places, none of which was where they currently were. She had deliberately guided them to the wrong region because she needed time to think. As sure as she was that she could keep Andrews chasing shadows for as long as she needed to, Russo was a different beast altogether. He was clever, crafty, manipulative, and driven, and it was him alone that had made her reluctant to lead them to where she actually thought this creature may be. She also wanted to know more about what Project Blue was. She had been in some conflict about what she was about to do, and now thought she had built up enough courage to go ahead. It had all been worked out. Dexter was in the wheelhouse under the pretence of pouring over some new underwater charts. His real purpose for being there was to keep an eye on Russo. She checked her watch in the gloom, the illuminated display telling her it was a little after nine.

It was time.

Before she could change her mind, she got up, exited her cabin, and walked down the corridor to Russo's room. Without hesitation, she slipped the door open and went inside. Even at a glance, it was obvious the room was inhabited by a man with a military background. Everything was pristine - what she would deem to be overly neat. She looked at the bed and knew if she had a coin and dropped it on the cover, it would bounce.

Russo's briefcase was by the bathroom door. She hesitated. Right now if she were caught, she still hadn't done anything wrong. That saying about what curiosity did to the cat popped up in her mind for a split second as she walked towards the case. She crouched and snapped open the clasp. Neat brown folders were lined up inside with the same obsessive tidiness that was on display through the room. She carefully removed them and began to skim through, hoping whatever she was looking for would jump out at her when she saw it. The first few were nothing special. News reports and profiles on the creature, requisition orders to hire the boat, and profiles on the crew, she and Dexter included. Curious and angry, she skimmed her own file, wondering what they were saying about her. There was nothing in there but the most basic of information pulled from public records. It offered a very one dimensional and flat profile of her as an individual. She half suspected this was how Russo viewed everyone. Either way, the sheer volume of information they had been able to gather without her permission was staggering. Conscious that time was of the essence, she moved on. There was a file on the *Victorious*, expenses forms for the duration of the mission, documents on the mass beaching's, and a report about an incident involving a whaler that had sunk off the coast of Hawaii, killing all on board. None of it was out of the ordinary, and there was no mention of Project Blue anywhere to be seen. She replaced the folders and was about to close the case when she noticed an extra pocket which was hidden against the seam of the lining. Without allowing her rational inner voice to interject, she reached in and pulled out the folder that was nestled inside. She knew immediately this was what she had been looking for. The pale brown folder was stamped in red ink with the words 'EYES ONLY', and she hesitated before opening it.

She asked herself if she really wanted to know, if she really want to get involved. If not, now was the time to go back to doing what she was hired for. Before she could talk herself out of it, Clara opened the folder and started to read.

PROJECT BLUE

P/N: 85485743234

CONFIDENTIAL

As her eyes devoured the words, her adrenaline morphed to horror at what Russo was planning to do. She had to tell someone about this and put a stop to it. She closed the folder and shoved it back in the briefcase, now more afraid of Russo than she was before. Standing to leave, she turned towards the door, a scream launching into her throat which she somehow managed to swallow.

Russo was watching her from the doorway, a cocky half smile on his lips.

"You probably shouldn't have done that."

"I want off this boat. Take me back to shore."

"I'm afraid I can't do that."

"You can't keep me here," Clara said, striding towards him.

"Yes, I can. Give me your phone please."

"Screw you, I don't answer to you." She was shaking, yet it was more from anger than fear.

His face changed. She wasn't sure what it was, but there was a subtle shift that made her even more afraid than she had been already.

"Don't force me into doing something we'll both regret. Phone. Please."

In no position to argue, she handed over the handset and watched as Russo removed the battery, and then pulled out the sim card.

"You can't keep me here as a prisoner. You still need my help." She said, her voice wavering as she spoke.

Russo grinned, his friendly mask firmly back in place.

"Prisoner? That's a little bit dramatic."

She looked at him, still afraid to move. He laughed, a short deep bark that sounded decidedly unnatural coming from him.

"You look terrified! What, did you think it would be like in the movies, where I would shoot you on the spot and throw you overboard? The real world isn't quite so exciting I'm afraid."

"Then let me go."

He held up his hands and turned to the side.

"Be my guest." He said, clearly enjoying every second of her discomfort.

She walked towards the door, and turned to squeeze past him. Their bodies touched as she brushed past, and just as it looked like she would be free, Russo slammed his arm against the doorframe, blocking her in. They were now inches apart, and Russo leaned close, whispering in her ear, his minty breath hot on her cheek.

"You are treading a very thin line, Miss Thompson. Rather than looking into things which don't concern you, perhaps you might be served better looking for the thing we're paying you to find."

He smiled and leaned back, lowering his arm so she could squeeze past and into the corridor. She walked away, trying not to let him see her shaking, or the tears which were threatening to escape as she hurried towards her room.

"Time to stop wasting our time, Miss Thompson. Either find us our beast, or I will be forced to get someone in who will."

CHAPTER 28

Gulf of Alaska
13.20pm

Ox gritted his teeth and strained his arms as he tried in vain to control the fishing rod.

"Easy," Rainwater said with a smile, "you might have something big here."

"Feels god damn huge," Ox grunted, straining against the tension of the wire.

"For someone who hasn't fished before, you are doing okay."

"That's all well and good, now what the hell do I do next?"

"Relax, give out a little slack."

"I thought I was supposed to be reeling the damn thing in?"

"You are, but you have to let the fish tire itself out first."

Rainwater grinned and watched as Ox did as he was told.

"You think this guy knows what he's doing, Rainwater?"

"Who, the fish?"

"No, man, not the fish. This Morrison character. First, he has us out in the Bering Sea, and now we're changing direction again. It don't seem like he's a man with a plan that's all."

"At least we're moving away from the storm. The reports are saying it's looking like a nasty one."

"Yeah," Ox said, squinting at the sun. "Truth is, storm or sun, I'm starting to get tired of this trip. Next time we stop for fuel, I might well stay on shore and let you guys get on with what you need to do."

"And miss the California sun?" Rainwater said with a grin.

"It's not that, man." Ox said as he worked the reel. "I don't know what we're trying to prove here. To be honest, I thought this was all bullshit, an excuse to get away from the wife for a few days, but now…"

"You didn't believe it, and now you do, right?"

Ox relaxed his grip on the fishing rod, allowing the reel to unfurl as the unseen catch made its escape. He turned towards Rainwater, his brow furrowed into a frown.

"Look, man, don't take it personally, it's just... well, who would? Sea monsters and shit ain't real. Or at least that's what I thought. Now it's all over the news and I'm not so sure we should be screwing with this thing. I'm an engineer, not an adventurer."

"Look, Ox, it's alright. You don't have to be here if you don't want to be. This isn't your fight, I understand what you're saying."

"Can I ask you something?" Ox asked, squinting against the sun.

"Shoot."

"Why don't you forget all this? You seem like a good guy. Maybe you shouldn't be out lookin' for somethin' that could kill you. Seems to me life's too short to flirt with death all the time."

Rainwater walked to the stern and leaned on the transom, looking at his grubby sneakers for a moment as the boat sliced through the ocean.

"I don't really know how to explain it," he said eventually. "It's something I have to do."

"You must have a reason though, right? Nobody does shit like this without a damn good reason."

"I just know I have to find this thing."

"What then, man? What happens when you find it? I'm sure as shit this little boat ain't gonna be enough to stop it. Not if it's as big as the news reports are saying."

Rainwater had no answer, and so looked out to sea, enjoying the feeling of the sun as it warmed his face.

"Not that it matters anyway," Ox added. "Because this dude who is meant to be guiding us after this thing, don't seem to have a damn clue what to do."

"Interesting." Morrison said as he walked out on deck. He took a pack of cigarettes out of his pocket and lit one, looking out to sea as he did so. Ox and Rainwater shared a quick glance, then waited and watched Morrison smoke.

"This creature," he said between exhales, "has been feeding in warm Californian waters, which is where we're heading now. However, most of the disturbances to marine life have taken place in colder climates. The Siberian and Bering seas, which is why we were checking that area first. I thought the Bering Sea was a perfectly logical place to begin. My best guess is our fish feeds every two to three days. Something of that size would have to take on an extraordinary amount of energy from feeding, and so my hope now is to catch him in the act, so to speak. That's why we're changing direction again. The recent series of attacks, beaching's, and whale kills, certainly suggests we are heading the right way."

"Hey, man, no offence, I was just wondering what the score was." Ox said, flicking his eyes towards Rainwater, who was watching the conversation unfold.

"It's just that… well, you don't say much that's all."

"I don't have much to say. My job is to track this fish. Not make small talk."

"Come on, man, we're all stuck on this boat together, no harm in getting to know each other."

Morrison said nothing. He stared at Ox and shrugged his shoulders.

"All you need to know is that it won't be long until I locate this fish. What happens when we find it is anybody's guess."

"You must have an idea of what to do, right?" Ox said, glancing at the ocean then back to Morrison.

Morrison grinned, enjoying Ox's nervousness. He walked towards the transom and sat beside Rainwater, and then with a sigh, pulled out his tobacco tin and started to hand roll a cigarette.

"Well that all depends. I have hunted pretty much every predator on the planet over the years, and one thing I have learned, is that you can never take them for granted. Man takes great pleasure in convincing himself it's the superior species, but you can never discount nature. Any animal that feels threatened is apt to strike first and strike to kill."

Rainwater couldn't help but get drawn in, and ventured to ask a question himself.

"What's the most dangerous thing you have ever hunted?"

Morrison didn't answer at first. He simply finished rolling his cigarette, shoved it into his mouth, and lit it, inhaling deeply as Rainwater and Ox waited.

"There are a lot of dangerous things out there that's for sure, without question, the most dangerous thing I ever hunted is man."

Rainwater and Ox exchanged glances, and Morrison saw them and flashed a subtle smile.

"Relax, I'm no murderer. It was in Afghanistan. Hunted me some Taliban. Some of the boys liked to snipe em' from a distance. I always liked to get in up close and personal. You better believe I was good at my job. A lot of the guys hated the heat, whereas, I couldn't get enough of it, burning under the sun with the snakes, waiting to bag a terrorist or two."

"How many did you…hunt?" Rainwater asked quietly, noting the definite shift in atmosphere.

"Who knows," he shrugged as he worked his cigarette, squinting against the sun as he looked at Rainwater. "Twenty? Thirty? Forty? All I know is there were a lot. After a while, the numbers don't really matter. You know what the best part was?"

He widened his grin to show his uneven teeth.

"Guess what my country gave me for my service? A medal? A commendation? No, they gave me a dishonourable discharge. Said I was too volatile to be kept in active service. Seems even in war, you aren't allowed to kill too many of the enemy."

Although Rainwater thought it was probably a good move from the army's standpoint, he wasn't about to say so. Instead, he pressed for more information.

"What happened then?"

"I threatened to appeal, and because the government were already taking a ton of flak for going to war in the first place, they paid me off and threw me into a shitty office job where they could keep an eye on me. Pushing a pen behind a desk was never for me though, even though some say I look the part. See, the thrill of the hunt never goes away. Some might say otherwise, but they'd be lying. It's always there."

He inhaled again and blew smoke out of his nostrils.

"I tried to reason with them, told them I wanted to get back out to making a difference. Of course, they didn't want any of that. They moved me around, put me into a few other roles they tried to make sound important, but they were really only wanting to keep me quiet and out of the way. By then, I'd had enough, so I told them I wanted out. I half expected them to try to bend over backwards to retain me, but the bastards seemed relieved and couldn't wait to agree. Just like that, I was a free man in a world I had fought for, but didn't understand or fit into."

"What did you do next, man?" Ox asked quietly.

"As I said, the thrill of the hunt is a hard one to replace. Especially when you throw in rejection from the country you risked your life for. I started drinking. First out of boredom, then out of necessity to try to forget that my life had gone to hell. Pretty soon, it wasn't enough, so I started with the drugs. Let me tell you, it didn't take long to spiral out of control. I got about as low as it's possible to get, and although my body was screwed up and my brain was fried, no matter how much I drank, no matter how much coke I snorted, no matter how close to the edge I tried to exist…"

He shrugged and lowered his eyes as he exhaled deeply. "Well, it never got anywhere close to that high of hunting."

Rainwater shifted uncomfortably as he looked at Morrison. He was still unable to get over the fact this man who looked more like some kind of well-spoken investment banker, was a seasoned hunter and war veteran. It was as if nothing but Morrison existed. Somehow, the rocking of the boat and the salty breath of the ocean had faded into the background. Both he and Ox were hooked on the slender hunters words.

"After that," he continued, "after spending so long at the edge flirting with throwing yourself off, it doesn't take long to realise it's a game you are never gonna win. I saw a doctor, hoping to get some help getting off the crap I was pumping into my body. He told me I shouldn't be alive, and the drink and drugs could finish me off if I didn't stop straight away. Believe me, that's the kind of thing that makes you sit up and take notice."

"What did you do then?" Ox asked.

"I left the office and got wasted. I had this belief I was untouchable and those things the doctors said didn't apply to me. It took something drastic to make me see that I wasn't invincible." He smiled and took another drag of his cigarette. "I had a stroke. Pretty bad one too. Lucky for me someone found me in time and dragged me to the hospital. I had pissed my pants and was so out of it that I didn't know what had happened until a few days later. Doctors put me on an enforced rehab plan for both the drugs and alcohol addiction, and also to try to get my fucked up left side back to some kind of normality. It was hell, let me tell you, but I'm tougher than I look, and although I'm not completely recovered from the stroke, I'm clean as far as the other shit goes. Have been for a while now. With all that behind me, I needed a change of scenery, so I travelled, drifting from place to place. I hunted Bears in Oregon, Lions in Africa. Did whatever I could to try to get that natural buzz back."

"Did you find it?" Rainwater said, finally starting to understand a little of what made Morrison tick.

"Find what?"

"That feeling. The thrill of the hunt."

Morrison snorted a laugh and looked at Rainwater, shaking his head.

"Not yet. Not so far anyway. It's like chasing shadows, but I'm trying. I suppose it's just me replacing one addiction for another. Mackay might have you think he found me, but believe me, if it wasn't on this boat, you can bet your ass I would still be out here now, doing this exact same thing and hunting this creature. I'll tell you this though, some of you might be in for a bit of a surprise."

"What do you mean?" Rainwater asked.

"Oh, not you," Morrison said with a thin smile. "I can see in your eyes you know what we're dealing with. The rest of you..." He looked at Ox as his smile spread further across his face. "Well, some of you are in for a rude awakening."

"Why?" Ox asked, unable to hide the panic in his voice.

"Because, even though I have hunted pretty much everything on this planet that could kill a man, this thing scares me. We're in its domain now, its territory. You can all forget about being the superior species. Out here, we're nothing. It's us or it, life or death. There's something poetic about that, don't you agree?"

"You sound like you want this thing to kill us." Ox said, glancing at Rainwater then turning his attention back to Morrison

"Not really," he replied with the faintest ghost of a smile. "I'm showing this thing the proper respect, that's all."

"Well no offence, man," Ox shot back, "but so far we found nuthin'."

"We will, and soon."

"What makes you so sure?" Rainwater said.

"Because I know it now. I know where to look. I know how to find it. You will all get to see her soon enough."

Morrison stretched, looked at Rainwater and Ox in turn, and then flicked his cigarette butt over the side.

"Well, I suppose I better get back to work,"

he said, and then headed back inside.

CHAPTER 29

Eighty-six miles away, Milton was watching the fish finder as his boat drifted through the crystal clear waters off the Californian coast. The initial excitement had turned to boredom, and the one quick drink had become five, which was leaving him fuzzy headed as he sweated in the sun. Melina walked over and sat on one of the sun loungers. He couldn't help but admire how good she looked in her bikini, and had to force himself to concentrate on the screen.

"See anything?" she asked as she stifled a yawn.

"No, not yet. We're in the right place though."

"Oh yeah?" She said with a smile. "How do you figure that out?"

"Gut feeling. Instinct. I don't know. I just feel it."

She stood and walked towards him, standing at his shoulder and watching the fuzzy radar display.

"So," she said, "how does this thing work?"

Trying as best he could to ignore the intoxicating perfume and coconut sun cream smell coming from her, Milton cleared his throat and explained.

"Well, the fish finder is essentially sonar. It fires a pulse from below the boat, which hits the ocean floor and comes back. Anything it passes on the way is recorded here on screen."

"And you can tell what all of these little dots are?" She asked, pointing to the masses of captured shapes on the screen.

"Not really, and in fairness, I don't need to. I don't need to know if it's a fish, dolphin or shark, what we're looking for is big enough to stand out like a sore thumb when we hit it."

"What then?"

He paused. It was a good question, and one he had been putting off discussing with her until the last possible moment. He took a deep breath, inhaling more of her sweet scent.

"I know I said I wouldn't, but I still want to use the shark cage."

"Milton-"

"Imagine if I could get in the water and film this thing from below the surface. It would make us famous."

"You can't do that." She said simply, taking a step away from him as if he carried some kind of contagious disease. "It's madness."

"Madness? You said to think outside the box, you said to make myself get noticed."

"Not by killing yourself."

"It's safe, the thing won't even know I'm there. I thought you would be happy that I was doing something positive."

In his mind, he had seen her overwhelmed by his bravery and commitment, which made the reality of her rejection harder to bear.

"Making a difference is fine, as is showing the network that you can do a good job. You would be crazy to get in the water with this thing out there. You saw what it did to that boat race. They said on the radio it is suspected of destroying a Russian submarine. It's too dangerous."

"I bet they said the same thing to Attenborough all those years ago and it didn't stop him. Besides, that sub was no doubt making all kinds of vibrations this thing probably saw as a threat. I'll be sitting in the water in my completely passive, vibration free cage, filming the thing as it goes by. I won't be in danger."

"You don't know that. Nobody knows what this thing is. How can you know you will be safe?"

"The cage is perfectly safe. The guy in the shop said it was—"

"The guy in the shop isn't the one going into the water." She interrupted.

They were silent for a moment, and Melina walked to the rail, staring at the water as it licked against the fibreglass hull of the boat.

"Look," she said quietly, "I know you are trying to better yourself, and I'm all for that. Just not like this. I... care about you despite everything that happened between us."

Milton's mind filled with hundreds of things he had rehearsed saying to Melina in response to such a statement. No sooner had he begun to consider the right one, when his attention was caught by the sonar screen.

"What is it, what's wrong?"

"It's here."

"How do you know?"

If Milton heard her, he didn't answer. Instead, he stared at the screen. Where it should have shown hundreds of shades of colour representing the multitude of life forms in the ocean, the screen was blank. Something had frightened everything away, and Milton had a good idea what it was. His stomach pulled into a tightly knotted ball as he stood and hurried across the deck.

"Help me with the cage. I'm going into the water."

CHAPTER 30

Unable to delay any further, Clara had directed Russo towards the Californian waters where she was sure the creature would be actively hunting. She walked through the winding interior of the boat, shadowed by the armed guard that had been assigned to her. She stopped at the door to Dexter's cabin and knocked on the door, waiting and eyeing her escort cautiously. Dexter opened the door and let her in. She entered and sat on the bed as he cleared his array of charts and paperwork which was strewn across the desk. He reached out to turn off the radio, when Clara grabbed his arm and shook her head. She motioned to the door, and Dexter nodded, turning the volume higher to mask their conversation.

"Please tell me you found us a way off this boat." She said, keeping her voice as low as she could.

"Sorry," Dexter replied, shaking his head. "They have this place locked tight. Whatever you did to piss them off certainly worked."

"What about if we stole one of the lifeboats?"

"Not possible. The deck is patrolled every twenty minutes, and the operations room has a permanent guard detail. You can't get near the boats without being spotted."

"Come on," She said with a desperate smile. "Give me something to hope for."

"Well, there could be something. I found a Zodiac in the engine room. Ten footer. We could get to it easily enough, it's getting it inflated and off the boat that will be our main problem."

"I wouldn't think it would have the range to get us to land anyway."

"Not from here, no." He agreed, then pausing to flick his eyes towards the door, leaned closer. "When we get to the location off the California coast where you think this thing is feeding, we could easily get to the beach and disappear into the crowd."

"Why do I get the feeling a spanner is about to be thrown into the works here?"

"Well, not a spanner as such, but a potential stumbling block. I can get to the boat, and I can get it on deck. The second I do though, I'm going to be spotted."

"Unless there's a distraction." She said quietly.

"Do you have an idea?"

"Maybe. How long would you need?"

"As long as you could give me. Ten minutes at least. What did you have in mind?"

"I'm not sure. We have a few hours to work it out, let me think on it. Just be ready to go."

"I have been ready to get off this boat since we arrived. Don't you worry, I'll be ready."

"Good. Until then, keep things relaxed and natural. I don't want these assholes getting a sniff of what we're about to do."

Milton's shark cage was bobbing in the water at the stern of the boat. Melina chewed her nails as she looked at the fish finder, hoping against hope to see the screen filled with signs that the marine life had returned, but it was still barren, and she cast a cautious eye out over the water, shielding her face against the sun. It was calm and looked perfectly tranquil, beautiful if not for the fact she was aware of what was out there. Milton walked on deck, zipping his blue wetsuit. If he was afraid, he showed no signs of it.

"Any sign of the creature?" he asked as he checked that his air tanks were operating correctly.

"Nothing. The fish finder still isn't picking anything up. Maybe it's gone."

"No, it's definitely out there. I can feel it."

"Milton, please, don't do this."

"Relax," he said, flashing a grin that was more confident than he actually felt. "I'll be perfectly safe. Pass me the underwater camera, would you?"

"Its heavy," she said as she handed it to him.

"It'll be fine once I get it in the water. Come on, help me into the cage."

He sat on the stern and lowered his legs over the side, then set the camera across his knees. He turned to her, and although he was managing almost to hide it, she could see he was as afraid as she was.

"This is it," he said, not quite able to manage a smile. "This is the moment that will change my life for the better."

"Milton, please, don't go." Melina said softly, placing a hand on his shoulder.

He didn't think he had ever seen her looking as beautiful as at that exact moment, framed by the golden hue of the sun. In the movies, he knew this would be the moment where he would profess his undying love for her, and they would break into a passionate kiss as the music swelled to a crescendo. This was real life, and although he would like nothing better than for that to happen, the reality was that he was sick with nerves and wanted to get in the cage before he changed his mind. He broke eye contact as he picked up the all in one helmet, which would enable him to speak with Melina during the dive.

"Okay, I'm ready. Once I'm inside, lower the cage to around thirty feet. The camera will feed the footage back in real time to the computer beside the fish finder. Just check and see if its recording would you?"

She did as he asked, the monitor fading into life and displaying a crystal clear image of the twin humps of Milton's knees and the ocean beyond.

"Picture quality is good." She said, flicking her eyes to the empty screen of the fish finder.

"You might want to grab those headphones too, so you can hear me once I get the helmet on."

She grabbed the wireless headset and put it on, half in a daze that they were actually going ahead with such an insane plan.

"Can you help me with this?" he said as he lowered the Perspex fronted helmet into place. Melina helped him to fasten the airtight seals, and now as she stepped back, he was looking at her through the fish bowl like mask. From within, he would have an unobstructed view of the ocean.

"Okay," he said, his radio muted voice coming now from her ear piece. "Can you hear me through the headphones okay?"

"Yeah, signal is clear."

"Okay," he said. She could hear how ragged his breathing had become, and his eyes flicked towards the massive expanse of open water around him.

"It's time. I'm going in. let me know if anything crops up on the fish finder. You will know about this thing before I do, so stay in touch."

Melina and Milton locked eyes, and it seemed there were no words that were valid for them to say. Melina broke eye contact, looking at the deck of the boat as Milton shuffled forwards, gripped the camera, and lowered himself into the water. He ducked under to test that his air supply was feeding through correctly, and resurfaced, adjusting his grip on the camera.

"Okay, everything is good here. Lower me down. Keep an eye on the fish finder. I need to know which direction to point the camera."

He pulled the lid of the cage closed and submerged.

Even though she fought it every step of the way, Melina activated the winch, lowering the cage into the water. Some nine hundred and fifty feet away, the tiny vibrations made by the cable as it lowered the cage into the water, reached the immense predator almost instantly. Intrigued by this new stimulus, the creature flicked its massive tail and set forth to investigate.

CHAPTER 31

Milton's world consisted of shades of blue. The water was colder than he expected, yet it was secondary to the heady mixture of terror and exhilaration that surged through him as he peered into the darkness. He had scuba dived off the Californian coast before, and knew the waters here were abundant with life as diverse as it was colourful. As he hovered in thirty feet of water below the boat, there wasn't a single fish to be seen. He peered through the bars, feeling more like a space explorer on a desolate planet rather than underwater.

"Everything okay?"

Melina's voice startled him, and he almost dropped the camera.

"Jesus, Mel, you almost gave me a heart attack."

"Sorry, too loud?"

"*Everything* sounds too loud down here."

"What do you see?"

Milton looked around again.

"Nothing," he said quietly. "Absolutely nothing. Anything on the fish finder?"

"No, just you. Maybe we should—"

She froze mid-sentence. The blank screen of the fish finder was starting to fill with colour. As Melina watched, she knew it was impossible, because whatever was being detected was wider than could fit into the display.

"Milton," she said quietly, her throat dry as she watched the screen continue to fill with colour, "it's coming."

The words had barely registered with Milton when he saw it for himself. The dark shade of the ocean grew lighter and it came out of the depths. It wasn't until then he truly appreciated the sheer scale of the creature. Its body was similar to a giant squid, in that it was long and tapered into an immense fluke. As it lazily approached the cage, Milton could see pectoral fins like that of a shark, the creature was also equipped with eight muscular tentacles, each one covered in suckers the size of a sewer drain cover. With nothing to compare it to, Milton could only gawp at both the beauty and scale as it slowly swam past the cage. As it passed, he could see the creature's mouth was partially open, revealing the tips of its backward facing serrated teeth. It was a hellish thing, an amalgamation of the entire ocean's most feared predators.

"Are you seeing this," he whispered as the creature passed, and the concussion wave from the flick of its tail was enough to rock the cage as it moved through the water.

"You bet I am, Jesus, Milton, you know what you have here? This is going to make you famous."

He didn't answer. Fame no longer seemed important. He realised now the cage in which he had so much faith in to protect him was woefully inadequate. In fact, as he looked at the creature's mouth, he was pretty sure it could swallow both him and the cage without bothering to chew. There was no reference, nothing he could compare it to that could help him process the enormity of the creature as it swam in slow, wary circles below the cage. Seeming to lose interest in Milton and the cage, the creature went on its way, disappearing into the murky depths.

"Okay, Mel, haul me up. Let's get the hell out of here."

Melina activated the winch, and began to pull the cage back to the surface.

Milton was excited to get back to dry land, and thought the network might even break off from its regular programming to present his footage in some kind of special newsflash. He—

There was only a split second to register the blur of movement coming from his right hand side. The creature slammed into the cage at full speed, sending the steel framed structure swinging wildly on its supports, as the creature passed the underside of the boat. The concussion wave hit Milton with the same force as if he had been hit by a speeding vehicle, and his body slammed into the unforgiving steel, knocking the wind out of him as he drifted towards the cage floor.

On the surface, Melina screamed as the boat was dragged along by the huge wake left by the creature, then turned in a lazy half circle and came to a halt. She shut down the winch and staggered to the monitor on rubber legs that felt ready to give out on her at any time, certain Milton must be dead. She watched the shaky film footage from the camera, which now lay on the floor of the cage. She could see Milton floating in the water, and in the background, the creature as it emerged from the depths like some hellish beast. She watched as it slowly approached the cage, pushing against it with its snout before turning away. It came again, its curiosity still piqued.

Instead of nudging the cage with its snout, this time the creature opened its mouth and bit down on the steel. The pressure of the creature's bite deformed the cage with ease, crumpling the framework as it tried to decide if it was edible.

Melina screamed as she watched the creature take its prize and change direction, dragging the boat along the surface of the water by the winch line. Seawater exploded and drenched Melina as the yacht was pulled sideways through the ocean. She was frantically trying to operate the winch controls, knowing that if the creature decided to go deep, it would drag both her and the boat with it. She managed to pull the release lever to the winch cable, and although the boat stopped its sideward motion, the reel was feeding out at pace as the creature took Milton further into the deep. She ran to the wheelhouse and snatched up the radio.

"Coast Guard, please, someone help me. It's attacking us." She screamed as she cycled through the channels on the radio, not even sure how to operate it or if anyone could hear her. She glanced over her shoulder at the winch, which was still feeding out.

"This is the Coast Guard. Confirm location."

"I don't know where I am, just fucking help me! It's attacking us!"

"Calm down miss," came the static charged voice from the other side of the radio. "Please tell us where you are and we will get someone to you. Are you presently in danger?"

She gave up and ran back out on deck. She was powerless to do anything but watch as the winch reel got closer to the end.

***

Milton opened his eyes, blinking away the blood that poured down his forehead. Pain shot through his body and it took him a few seconds to understand what was happening. Water was squirting in a fine mist through a hairline crack in his facemask, but he was otherwise okay. The creature's jaws had crushed the framework of the cage, and by some miracle, he had avoided being crushed by the creature. He was trapped in the bottom corner of the structure, inches away from the creature's mouth and those teeth that were as long as his forearm. There was no escape. He felt the direction change as the creature went deeper, and he knew what he had to do.

Melina stared at the winch reel, which had now almost completely emptied. She knew when it reached its end, the boat would be dragged along the water until it capsized or was pulled apart. She wasn't a strong swimmer, and it hit her that she was probably going to die.

"Melina."

She could barely hear him, his voice distant and weak in her ear.

"Milton…" It was all she could manage before she started to cry.

"You have to cut me loose."

"I can't do that, I won't do that."

"You have to. Release the cable. Cut me loose before you get pulled under."

"You know what happens if I do that. You'll die."

"It's too late to do anything about that now." He mumbled, his voice starting to break as he went out of range. "Get the footage to the network, make sure they see it, and make sure they know…"

"Milton, I—"

"Please. Cut me loose. Cut me loose and get the hell out of here."

She stood and poised her thumb over the controls. She would have given anything then, anything at all not to be in control of Milton's fate, but she knew no matter how much she tried to deny it, he was already lost. She couldn't hear him anymore in her headset, the line now filled with a static hiss.

"I love you, Milton." She whispered, and then pushed the button.

The winch cable was set free and was dragged into the water. Her world that had been a cauldron of noise and violence was now silent. Trembling and exhausted, she fell to her knees and started to sob. At some point, they became screams.

CHAPTER 32

First officer Pendleton raced through the corridors of the *Victorious*, heading for the command centre. Russo and Andrews were poring over charts as the young officer entered.

"Sir," the man said, a single sheet of paper clutched in his hands.

"Not now, Pendleton," Russo said without looking up. "As you can see, I'm busy."

"Sir, you definitely want to hear this."

Russo and Andrews looked at the officer, who cleared his throat and continued.

"We just intercepted a transmission to the Coast Guard from a boat claiming they had been attacked by the creature."

"Where?" Russo said, giving Pendleton his full attention. The officer handed over the sheet of paper.

"Six miles from here. Another vessel is on the scene and assisting."

Russo handed the paper containing the coordinates to Andrews.

"Give this to the captain. Tell him to get us to that location as fast as he can."

Andrews did as he was asked, leaving Russo and the officer alone.

"What else do we know about this attack?" Russo asked.

"Not much right now, sir. Seems it was some kind of news crew who were looking for this thing and got more than they bargained for. It was hard to tell, the woman who called it in sounded pretty hysterical."

"Keep me informed on any new developments as you get them."

"Yes sir," Pendleton said as he turned and headed towards the door.

"One more thing, Pendleton. The boat that is assisting on scene. Do we know anything about that?"

"It's a crabber. Four man crew."

"Do we know the name of the boat?"

"Yes sir, it's the Lisa Marie."

Russo stared at the charts, and in a sudden fit of rage, swept them off the table to the floor.

Mackay and Rainwater had helped Melina onto the *Lisa Marie*. Despite trying to find out what had happened, she wasn't able to relay the story with any coherence. The Coast Guard helicopter had arrived and airlifted her to safety, advising Mackay they would send out a crew to pick up her boat, and they were to wait with it. They watched as the bright orange helicopter grew smaller as it distanced itself from them.

"I think we should get out of here and go home." Rainwater said as the sound of the helicopter faded.

"Coast Guard told us to stay with the boat," Mackay said.

"I mean after they have come and picked it up. This has gone too far."

"You sure about that? If you call it quits now, you can't be changing your mind later. This is a one-time deal. I won't be doing this again." Mackay said.

"I understand, and I get it now. I was stupid to come out here and put you all in danger. I think we should call it off."

"It's about bloody time," Ox said, his eyes scanning the water. "Whatever this is, its way too big for us."

"No." Morrison said.

He was standing at the stern of the boat, staring out into the ocean.

"What do you mean no?" Ox said, looking from Morrison to Rainwater for some kind of backup.

"That fish finder on the other boat."

"What about it?"

"The screen is empty."

"So?" Ox said.

"So that means something has scared away the fish. Anyone want to hazard a guess what it could be?"

"Are you saying this thing is close?" Ox said, backing away from the edge.

"Oh yes, it's very, very close now."

Rainwater wasn't sure what disturbed him most, the fact the creature they had been looking for was in the vicinity, or that

Morrison looked not only completely unafraid, but ever so slightly unhinged.

"Let's leave it be. If the lad says he has had enough, that's good enough for me." Mackay said, trying his best to be assertive.

Morrison widened his grin, and this time Rainwater saw a man that wasn't just unhinged, but one who could well be insane.

"We came all this way," Morrison said, Reaching into his jacket and pulling out a grenade.

"Let's at least have a look at her," he said as he pulled the pin.

"No!" Rainwater shouted, but it was too late.

The grenade was already arcing through the air, away from the boat and into the ocean. There were a few seconds of utter silence, and then the ocean exploded, sending an eruption of spray ten feet into the air.

"You dumb son of a bitch," Mackay hissed, glaring at Morrison, who simply smiled as he concentrated on the water.

"You boys might want to pay attention and take a second to see exactly what we're dealing with here."

There was no more argument, and everyone looked at the spot where the grenade had exploded. Rainwater didn't know how long had passed. It could have been seconds, hours, or even days. Everything around him had come to a standstill. He was incredibly aware of his surroundings, more than at any other time in his life. The knot in his stomach, the dull creaking of the hull of the Lisa *Marie* as it bobbed in the water, the dry sensation in his throat, the sweat on his brow. All of it seemed so clear, so vivid. It was then that it happened, and it took all of his effort to keep from screaming outright.

To call it a wake would be a gross injustice. It was more a wave, a mountainous displacement of ocean rolling towards the impact point.

"Holy mother of God," Mackay muttered under his breath as the creature broke the surface of the water and he finally saw it with his own eyes.

The creature's slick grey body glistened in the afternoon sun as it swam towards where the grenade had impacted. Its scale was incomprehensible. A flicker of a tentacle breached the surface of the water as the giant creature passed less than thirty feet from the boat. The wake slammed against the *Lisa Marie*, pushing both it and Melina's boat some ten feet back in a lazy half circle.

When Rainwater had first encountered the beast, it had been too dark and too quick an incident to make out any detail. He had seen no more than a flash of skin through the rain before it had slammed into the *Red Gold*. Now, under the blazing sunlight and amid the crystal clear waters, he could see well enough. Part of him was filled with a mesmerised wonder, the rest a deep, sick terror. The creature angled towards the boat and dived back under the surface of the water. Nobody spoke as the creature passed directly underneath them.

"We can't kill that, no way, it's not possible." Ox whispered, wringing his hands.

"It's beautiful," Morrison said quietly as he watched the creature dive deeper and out of sight.

Collectively, held breaths were exhaled, and each of the crewmembers looked at his colleagues with utter disbelief. Morrison was the only exception. He was still staring at the water, a half smile etched onto his lips.

"I need a drink," Mackay said.

"Me too," Ox agreed as he followed Mackay towards the inner deck.

"I'll join you." Rainwater added.

Morrison waited until they were gone, then with a sigh, took out his tobacco pouch and started to roll a cigarette. Just a few miles away, The *Victorious* was bearing down on their position.

CHAPTER 33

Dexter knew exactly where the small inflatable speedboat known as the Zodiac was stored, but with an entrance at either side of the engine room, anybody could walk in and catch him in the act of stealing it. The network of pipes offered him ample places in which to hide, however, the sheer noise emanating from the room would make it next to impossible to hear anyone approach.

He could see the storage locker ahead that contained the rolled inflatable raft and the lightweight outboard motor. He paused and checked his watch, hoping Clara had managed to figure out the distraction as she promised.

The plan was simple enough. She would trigger the fire alarm, which would mandate an evacuation of the boat. They were now tantalizingly close to the coast and their escape route.

At the same time, Dexter was waiting with the Zodiac, Clara was psyching herself up to put her part of the plan into action. She hoped in the confusion whilst everyone else was waiting in line for the rowboats, she and Dexter would be in the motor fitted zodiac, which would enable them to easily outrun Russo, Andrews, and their crew, and get to shore.

The stakes couldn't be higher. They would either escape or not, win or lose, and maybe, just maybe live or die. It really could be so extreme. She had already managed to lose her escort by complaining loudly to Russo that she refused to work under such circumstances. To her surprise, he had agreed, and the security detail had disappeared as quickly as it had arrived. Now all that remained was to put the plan into action. Clara took a deep breath and set off the fire alarm, firing three distress flares into the air for good measure. Instantly, the ship was filled with the high-pitched wail of the alarm, which triggered Clara into action. She began to make her way back through the ship towards the stern, where if all went to plan, Dexter should be waiting with the Zodiac. She was pleased to see, as she made her way through the narrow corridors that the plan was working perfectly. The *Victorious* had come to a halt, and armed guards hurried past without paying the slightest attention to her as they headed towards the lifeboat stations at the front of the boat. She pushed her way through the stern door, and felt a huge sense of relief as she saw Dexter in front of her. The relief lasted no more than a split second, as her eyes immediately fell to the gun pointed at Dexter's head by Russo, who glared at Clara with a twisted half smile on his lips.

"You stupid, stupid bitch."

"What the hell do you think you are doing?" Clara said.

"I could ask you the same," Russo fired back, pushing the gun harder against Dexter's head. "Just where did you plan on going?"

"Away from here. I don't want anything to do with this. Not anymore."

"There was really no need for this little display. You could have left when we next docked. This is all so… dramatic."

She looked Russo in the eye, trying to ignore the gun in his hand.

"Come on, let's cut the bullshit. We both know that would never have happened. You can't risk me telling people about Project Blue."

Russo began to laugh, and the sound made Clara flush cold.

"Oh, it seems somebody has been watching too many movies. True enough, you might go spill your guts, but who will believe it?"

"The press will."

"And when they come to look for evidence they will find it doesn't exist." He shot back.

"This thing we're looking for is a pretty big piece of evidence if you ask me."

Russo smiled, but his eyes remained without humour.

"So what happens now?" she asked.

"That, as they say, is the million dollar question. Where do we go from here?"

The stern door opened, and Andrews rushed out. He did a quick double take as he saw what was unfolding, and hesitated.

"What is it, Andrews?" Russo asked.

"We have it on sonar."

Clara looked at Andrews then back at Russo.

"You're still interested aren't you, Dr Thompson? You still want to know what it is."

She declined to answer, because Russo had read her perfectly and she hated him for it. He knew it too, because he widened his slick, predatory smile as he turned towards Andrews.

"Get the men back on board and follow our target. Keep your distance. We don't want to spook it."

"Got it," Andrews stammered, unable to retreat quickly enough from the standoff.

"What do you say, Clara? Doesn't the chance to study a unique design of evolution stir you? Does the opportunity to see something unseen by man not entice you?"

"When you are pointing a gun at my assistant, the answer is no." She said, forcing herself to lock eyes with him.

"Touché," he said simply as he lowered the gun and shoved Dexter towards Clara. "Despite what you might think, I'm not a monster. I'm here to do a job. As are you."

Dexter rubbed at his temple as Clara glared at Russo.

"Take this as a warning," he said, tucking the weapon into his pocket and pulling out a roll of mints. "No more stupidity. I see no reason why we can't all get along and do our jobs then go back to our civilian lives."

"We both know that's bullshit. You have no intention of ever letting the two of us off this boat again."

Russo popped a mint into his mouth and shrugged. "You really shouldn't watch so many movies. Once my mission is done, it will be buried in red tape and hidden away. You might leave here and stir the pot, but you will never have a big enough spoon. What I can't have happen, is you spilling your guts whilst the mission is still in progress."

"Let me guess, national security?" she spat, feeling the colour flush in her cheeks.

"Actually, no. Professional pride. I have a certain reputation. When I say I will complete a task, I follow it through. This is no different. There's nothing personal, nothing against you or your assistant here. Just a desire to complete the job I was assigned without undue problems. I'm sure you can understand that."

"And what happens to us?"

"That is entirely up to you. If you do as I ask, you will go back into the world and do whatever it is you do. I have no desire to harm you."

"What if I decide to make trouble?"

"I hope we don't have to deal with that. After all, nobody likes a troublemaker. Now, it seems our elusive fish has surfaced, and we all have work to do."

"I hope this isn't some bullshit ruse to get me onside." She said quietly.

"And I hope you don't make me regret leaving your assistants brain inside his skull."

Russo countered as he walked towards the hatch door. The *Victorious* surged to life, angling away in pursuit of the creature.

"There is something you should know about me, Miss Thompson, and that will make our time together more bearable." He said as he drew level with them.

"What's that?"

"No matter how you think you have fooled me, no matter how smart you think you are, I'll always be one step ahead. I always have a plan."

"One day, someone's going to surprise you." She said as the boat picked up speed, whipping her hair about her face.

"I doubt it."

He grinned and walked towards the door, leaving Clara and Dexter alone to watch the tantalising safety of the coastline drift away as they headed out to sea.

CHAPTER 34

Ever since retirement, Paul Milla had wanted to swim with sharks. It had grown from a half-baked idea when he first saw a documentary on the Discovery Channel, to an obsession that had been financially out of reach until earlier that year. A supervisor in the warehouse where he worked had drunk a few too many lunchtime beers and run him down in a forklift truck. He had suffered shattered ribs, crushed vertebrae, and a broken leg. The doctors told him from the start that he would make a full recovery, even if the chances of him going back to work were slim.

It was only later, deep into his gruelling rehabilitation, when he was trying to figure out how he would be able to pay for the house and feed his family, when a word popped into his head that could solve all his problems.

Compensation.

He took some legal advice, more out of curiosity than with any intention of making a claim. When his legal team told him he could be looking at a hefty settlement and his wife chipped in to convince him it was money that he deserved, he reluctantly filed the claim, and was astounded with the outcome. He came out of it with a seventy-five grand pay out. The supervisor who had run him down did a hundred hours unpaid work for the community. Good deal.

Booking the trip to California was pretty much the first thing he had done when the cash landed in his bank, and he was now moments away from actually achieving his dream.

"Are you sure this is a good idea, honey?"

"We've already been through this. It's perfectly safe. The sharks won't be able to get anywhere near me. I'll be fine."

He looked at the man who would be responsible for overseeing the dive – a bronzed, blond haired, blue-eyed Australian named Greg Michaels, who was waiting patiently in his wetsuit for the Milla's to finish their dispute. With his wife for the time being silenced, Paul forced his body into the charcoal grey wetsuit, hiding his scar covered back from the heat of the sun.

"You ready there, mate?" Greg asked, making a few final checks to the cage.

"Absolutely, I've been ready for this my entire life. What if the sharks don't show?" he asked as he zipped up his wetsuit.

"Oh, they'll show. Seen a few big ones out already earlier this morning."

"I guess for you it's no real thrill anymore is it?"

"It's always a thrill, mate, although with over a thousand dives under my belt, it takes something a little bit different to get my blood pumping."

"Like what?"

"You ever heard of free diving?"

"No, what's that?"

"Well, it's pretty much the same as going in the cage, only without the cage." Greg said with a grin.

Paul glanced over to his wife, who was now snoozing, iPod earphones wedged in her ears as she soaked up the California sun.

"Could someone like me do that? I mean swim outside the cage?"

"I wouldn't advise it as a first timer. Trust me, you'll get enough of a thrill from inside, especially if one of those big buggers from this morning come to take a look."

"How big?"

"Sixteen footer. Came right to the cage to take the bait."

"But to be outside the cage..."

"No sense in running before you can walk, buddy. Maybe get this one done first and we can look at that next time."

"I can pay. Whatever it takes."

"It's not about the money, mate, it's more about the safety aspect."

"I thought you said it was perfectly safe?"

"Inside the cage it is. Outside, it's a whole new ball game. These things are predators, Mr Milla. Remorseless killing machines. Sometimes what happens is that they frenzy at the meat we put in the water to draw them in and the ocean gets cloudy with blood and chunks of flesh. Sometimes when that happens, a shark could mistake someone outside the cage for a floating piece of meat, which, I suppose is what you are. I had an eight foot tiger shark take a bite out of my forearm once, let me tell you, I almost shit my wetsuit."

Paul looked at Greg's unscarred tanned forearms, raising his eyebrows. As if reading his thoughts, Greg laughed.

"Chainmail wetsuit. It still hurts when they take a nip, but it makes sure you come back out of the water with all the limbs you went in with."

"I want to do it."

"Maybe next time, let's do the cage for now and see how you like it. Sometimes when you're down there, it's not what people expect."

Paul looked at the cage. Ten minutes earlier he couldn't wait to step inside, now after Greg's story, it all seemed too safe. Too pedestrian.

"I want my first experience of this to be the best it can be."

"The cage is a pretty amazing experience, mate."

"I'm sure it is, but I want more. I'll give you an extra two thousand to take me down outside of the cage."

Greg shook his head. "Sorry. Can't do it."

"Three grand." Paul pushed, a thin ghost of a smile starting to form on his lips. Greg squirmed where he sat on the transom.

"I really can't. I'm responsible for you out here and it wouldn't be ethical."

"Five grand, and I'll sign a disclaimer absolving you from all responsibility." Paul said, holding out a hand ready for Greg to shake.

Greg squirmed and looked at the cage, then at Paul's outstretched hand before reluctantly shaking it.

"Fine. Three things. First, I'll need to draw up that disclaimer before we go anywhere. Second, when we're there, you do exactly as I do. You watch me like a hawk. Where I move, you move."

"Got it."

"Three. Don't be a hero. These are wild animals, and if you screw around trying to touch them, you're likely to get yourself killed. That's something I don't want to have to deal with."

"Me either," Paul agreed, feeling the rush of excitement at what he was about to do.

"Okay, wait here." Greg said, heading below deck. Paul waited, looking out over the glass smooth ocean and gorgeous, cloudless sky. It was a perfect day. Greg returned and handed Paul the chainmail suit.

"Put this on."

"It's heavy," Paul replied as he dropped it to the floor and started to struggle into it. "Aren't you wearing one?"

Greg shook his head. "Only got that one, and since you are paying so much for this, I guess you better be the one to wear it."

Paul paused, and looked Greg in the eye. "Isn't that dangerous?"

"Only if you don't do exactly as I say. We're only going there to observe. No interaction. As long as you do as I do, we'll be fine."

Paul nodded and continued to climb into the steel mesh wetsuit.

"Oh, one more thing. Don't think because you are wearing that suit that these things can't hurt you. They might not be able to get through it, but they can still mangle you pretty badly. Are you sure you want to do this?"

Paul hesitated. For a split second, there was doubt. The cage would be safer, but he was sick of safe. He had lived his entire life safe. He wanted a real thrill, a genuine experience he could tell his friends about back home and watch them look on in envy. He could go in the cage anytime. This truly was a unique opportunity.

"I'm sure. Let's do it."

"Okay, let's get to it and see if we can draw in some sharks."

The *Victorious* cut through the ocean, racing in pursuit of the creature. In the control room, Andrews stood at the shoulder of the radar operator, watching as they closed on the signal. Russo walked in, striding over to the console.

"Give me the latest," he snapped as he squinted at the radar screen.

"We have it on screen, although we're struggling to keep up. It's fast."

"Why is it in such a hurry?"

"We think it's hunting, which is good for us."

"Oh, and why is that?"

"Because if it's occupied with trying to feed, it's not paying attention to the sound of our boat and trying to attack us."

"I see," Russo said, showing the smallest flicker of uncertainty. "Well, speed up, I don't want us to lose this thing now that we have it."

"This is as fast as we can go. I have it under control." Andrews said, giving Russo a sour look.

"What's the matter with you?"

"You know exactly what it is. What was all that business out on deck?"

"Don't worry about that, I was just setting some ground rules."

"With a pistol? They're civilians."

Russo turned to face Andrews. "It's obvious you have something to say, so spit it out."

To Russo's surprise, Andrews met his gaze. "You need to keep me in the loop on what's happening here."

"I have no idea what you mean," Russo said, offering a dry smile.

"I thought you were going to talk to her, not put a gun to her damn head."

"It wasn't to her head, it was her assistant, and in my experience, a gun often drives the point home better than words."

"Just remember, this is my trip. My project. You can't freeze me out and expect me to go along with it."

Russo laughed, drawing a few secretive glances from the crew.

"Don't be so naive. Do you really think you are in charge of anything here?"

"It's my project," he repeated. "You wouldn't know about this thing if it wasn't for me."

"Really?" Russo said, extending his grin. "I think you give yourself way too much credit. For the sake of clarity, I'll tell you exactly how this operation runs. This is *my* operation. Funded by *my* superiors who asked *me* personally to oversee this entire endeavour. Despite whatever you may think, we aren't equals here. You work for me, as does everyone else on board this ship. True, my methods are unorthodox, but they get results. If you have a problem with that, I might suggest you retire to your cabin until this is all over."

"This was supposed to be a discovery mission, not a chance for you to flex your muscles."

Russo smiled and shook his head. "You really do believe that, don't you?"

Andrews didn't reply, and instead concentrated on calming the rage that was bubbling in the pit of his stomach.

"Just as I thought. Look, I don't want to clash with you. Truth is that I can use you to help me to make sure this operation runs smoothly. I don't need to remind you that this project has cost a hell of a lot of money, and taking into account this misunderstanding about the power structure, it is, according to the paperwork at least, your idea."

"So, what you are saying is if this thing all goes belly up, it's me who will be dragged over the coals?"

Russo didn't answer. His smug expression said it for him.

"You really saw me coming with this didn't you, Russo?" Andrews said, trying to ignore the sick feeling in his stomach. "I was a ready-made scapegoat for you to do whatever the hell you want out here without having to take any responsibility for it."

"Don't worry," Russo said, his smug grin still in place, "you still have one thing going in your favour."

"Oh really, and what's that?"

"Me." Russo said, finally losing his wide, slick grin. "As you know by now, I always win. Keep that in mind, and both of us will come out of this fine. Choose not to, and I can't guarantee what that might mean for you and your career."

"You don't scare me. I don't appreciate threats."

"It's no threat, just an observation."

Russo held out a hand to Andrews, the gold ring on his finger shimmering in the gloom. "Now, can I count on you?"

Andrews had always been a good judge of character, but as he tried to penetrate that dark, emotionless gaze, he found in this instance, Russo was unreadable.

Better the devil you know

As much as he hated himself for it, he reluctantly shook hands with Russo.

"Good, I'm glad we resolved that little misunderstanding. Now, let's get back to tracking our fish, shall we?" he added, turning back to the radar.

Andrews joined him in looking at the screen, however he wasn't really watching. His brain was still overloaded with information, and if the instincts he had learned to trust over the years were right, he needed to tread very carefully.

CHAPTER 35

Paul peered into the gloom, clinging to the outside of the shark cage, feet kicking rhythmically as he looked at the abundance of sea life. As impressive as the uncountable species of fish were, he was really only waiting for the sharks to show. He glanced through the cage towards Greg, who met his gaze across the water. He held up a thumb to Paul, who responded with the same gesture. Greg pointed out into the ocean.

Paul felt a surge of adrenaline as the eight-foot tiger shark veered towards the side of beef on the side of the cage and took a cautious bite, sending tiny morsels of flesh drifting into the depths.

Paul was elated, thrilled, humbled, and a little frightened. At that moment in time, there was nowhere in the world he would rather be. As he watched, more sharks came, appearing like phantoms out of the deep blue depths and taking turns at attacking the carcass.

Greg had made his way around the cage, was now beside Paul, and pointed down. Milla looked and felt his heart leap into his throat.

The eighteen-foot great white shark circled in fifty feet of water. With a body designed by nature to be streamlined and efficient, the predator glided with grace, steering with its pectoral fins. It sensed other sharks in the area, but none big enough to pose a threat. With fearless inquisitively, it angled towards the cage.

Paul tightened his grip on the bars and was incredibly aware of how small and insignificant he was in the expanse of open ocean around him. Greg put a hand on his shoulder and gave the thumbs up. His eyes were relaxed and unconcerned, and that in turn helped him to relax. They watched as the shark angled past them, scattering its smaller cousins as it made towards the carcass. Paul realised he could have reached out and touched the creature as it passed him, its size and beauty awe-inspiring. He glanced at Greg, who also seemed to appreciate the sheer size and majesty of the creature as it attacked the carcass, its jaws hyperextending and eyes rolling back as it took a huge bite, shaking its massive head from side to side, and in turn rattling the cage as it tried to tear away its prize.

Breathing in ragged gasps through his regulator, Paul could only stare and appreciate the simplicity of the creature, and how in the grand scheme of things, he was such a small and insignificant part of the food chain. It was an incredibly humbling experience. As they watched, the shark broke away from the carcass and accelerated into the darkness. Paul looked over at Greg, and was alarmed by his expression. The earlier confidence he had been able to see in the Australian's eyes was now gone, replaced by a worrying uncertainty. Paul and Greg looked around the ocean. It was only then he realised what was wrong.

The ocean around which had moments ago been teeming with life, was now completely deserted.

They were alone.

Russo and Andrews watched the radar as the creature changed course.

"What happened?" Russo said, looking at Andrews for answers.

"Looks like it might be hunting. A whale maybe."

"Get Thompson up here. I want her opinion on this."

Andrews nodded and activated the loudhailer, requesting Clara's attendance. As his amplified words echoed around the ship, Andrews watched Russo beckon one of the soldiers by the door towards him. The blond haired, square jawed, giant saluted and stood to attention.

"Mito, ready the device."

"Right away, sir"

"What device?" Andrews asked.

"For once, I'm not going to keep you in the dark on this one. Come with me and I'll show you how we're going to tag this creature." Russo widened his grin as he said it, and then walked towards the door, pausing at the threshold.

"You there, on the radar."

"Yes sir?" the operator said, removing one bulky earphone from the side of his head.

"Make sure you don't lose that signal. If anything unusual happens, I want to know. Call me directly. Miss Thompson will be here shortly, tell her to wait here until we come back."

"Yes sir," the operator replied, turning back to his console.

Russo headed out of the door, making his way down into the ship as Andrews followed with Mito bringing up the rear.

"When I was a boy," he said over his shoulder as he walked, "there was a small pond near where I used to live. Every year, frogs would spawn there and in summertime, the pond would be crawling with them. There was a kid I used to know by the name of Francis. He would ditch classes then spend pretty much every day smoking or reading smutty magazines there."

Russo walked past the cabins, and past the door to the engine room.

"I used to spend a lot of time there too, but my reasons were different. I enjoyed the quiet away from my classmates. Francis, however, was a bully. He used to make life hell for the other kids, yet, for whatever reason, he never tried it with me. I was already taller than he was, and had a reputation of someone not to be messed with, so we existed in the same circles content to keep out of the way of each other. One day, he walked over to where I was sitting. I knew he was up to something because he had a stupid grin on his face. For a moment, I thought he had finally decided he wanted to try his luck and add me to his bully list. I wasn't afraid of him, I was just curious as to what he wanted.

"Hey, Russo, check this out," he said, and held up a bunch of firecrackers tied together around the middle. I watched as he put them inside one of those plastic zip bags and weighted it with stones, and I knew right away what he was intending to do. I watched as he lit the fuse wires, pressed the plastic seal closed and tossed the bag into the pond. It sank straight away, and for a while, nothing happened. I was sure it must have extinguished, or maybe the bag had sprung a leak. I was about to say as much when the water exploded, sending dirt and reeds raining down on us. We watched and waited. A few seconds later, they started to float to the surface. Frogs. Fish. All dead. There were way more than you could ever imagine for such a small body of water. Francis chuckled and cheered as more and more dead animals surfaced. I just watched and tried to decide how I felt about it."

Russo stopped at a steel door marked with a red and white 'restricted' sign, and turned towards Andrews, a wide grin etched onto his face.

"That's what I intend to do to our fish."

"You want to kill it?"

"No, of course not, that would be pointless."

He opened the door and stood back to allow Andrews to see inside.

"I just want to make it float to the surface."

CHAPTER 36

Greg stared into the expanse of deserted ocean. His gut said to get to the surface, his wallet said he needed the payday from this trip. Bills don't pay themselves and neither do gambling debts, and he already owed Victor Malone a ton of money. This charter would at least get the heavies off his back for a few weeks and if that meant babysitting another pushy prick who wanted to get a thrill from swimming with the sharks, so be it. He glanced towards his meal ticket, and thought it was a good thing the sharks didn't decide to take a bite out of the cage or the guy would have likely shit his wetsuit.

Something caught Greg's eye, and he turned back towards the gloom. His first thought was that it was a whale. However, as more of the creature appeared from out of the murky ocean that idea faded away. He felt fingertips dig into his arm as Paul also saw what was approaching. The pair could only stare as the creature drifted towards the cage.

The T7500 resembled a miniature snub-nosed missile, which, in effect it was. Andrews looked over the green painted unit as Russo looked on.

"Well, what do you think?"

Andrews didn't answer. Russo seemed keen to explain anyway as Mito continued to prepare the weapon.

"This is my answer to the school bully firework."

"What does it do?"

"Before you start to panic, don't. This isn't an explosive device, not as such. This is strictly short range."

"How short?"

"Within a thousand feet for best results."

"That seems a little *too* close."

"There is a reason for having such a short range. It doesn't explode on contact like a conventional missile or torpedo, but in proximity to its target. The explosion launches a concussion wave that will be powerful enough to stun this big son of a bitch. After that, we tag our fish with a tracking device. Once we do that, the hard part is done. We can just keep our distance and know where it is at all times."

"How do we launch the torpedo from here?"

"Traditionally, the weapon would be fired from a hand held rocket launcher, however, for this mission we've rigged an underwater frame, which will enable us to fire it remotely from the boat."

"What if you miss?"

"As unlikely as it is that we would miss, we do have a reserve unit, however, we would want to be certain we hit our target with this weapon, as the backup isn't yet fitted for underwater operation."

"This concussion wave, it would have to be powerful to stun something so big."

Russo nodded. "Oh, don't worry about that. The T7 might look small, but it packs a hell of a punch."

Andrews ran a hand across the smooth surface of the weapon.

"What about the other things this concussion wave of yours hits?" he said, glancing towards Russo.

"You mean the fish?" Russo snorted. "A few go belly up. No big deal."

"I was actually thinking about the boat."

"We might feel a little disturbance, but most of the damage will be done under the water. The blast wave will be directed away from us."

"This sounds dangerous. What if you trigger a tsunami or something?"

Russo snorted and shook his head. "That's highly improbable."

"But not entirely impossible, right?"

"I said it's improbable. We know what we're doing."

Andrews thought about arguing, but knew it was pointless. Instead, he turned his attention back to the missile.

"I have level three clearance, and I can't say I have ever heard of this type of weapon before."

"I'm not surprised at only level three clearance," Russo scoffed, popping a mint into his mouth. "This is strictly off the books. A prototype."

"So it's untested?"

"Of course not," He replied with a shake of the head. "We've tested less powerful versions of it, but we needed to up the potency if you will, to ensure that we knock this thing silly for long enough to tag it."

"And who made that call?" Andrews asked. "Who decided how powerful a blast would be needed to do what you intended without killing the thing? Thompson has only been a part of this for a few days. I can't imagine she had anything to do with this."

"Don't be so naïve," Russo said. "You really think the Thompson woman is the only source of information we have? She is one of a few experts I have working on this project. Besides, it's not really that hard. We can estimate its weight based on its length, then from that, the size of concussion wave needed to put it to sleep for a few minutes."

"It sounds like you have it all figured out."

"I do. That's why I'm so good at my job."

Andrews looked Russo in the eye.

"Let me ask you something, completely off book."

"Go on," Russo said with a thin, arrogant smile.

"Is there a limit?"

"To what?"

"How far you will go to win even if people get hurt, even if they die?"

Russo shrugged his shoulders. "People get hurt and die every day."

"Does that include you? Me? The crew? Dr Thompson? Are we potential statistics in all this?"

"If you're asking if you are expendable, the answer is no. As long as you do as I say, we will all get along fine. It's when people start to think for themselves that things tend to get ugly."

Before Russo could say anymore, his phone began to vibrate. He pulled it out of his pocket and answered.

"Russo." he barked into the headset. Andrews watched as Russo listened. "Got it, I'll be right there," he said, before disconnecting the call.

"Our fish is close, but there's a damn boat on the water." He turned to Mito, who was busy making final adjustments to the unit.

"I want this thing in the water right now. It's time to get to work."

"Yes sir," Mito said, as Russo swept past and out of the room, heading back upstairs. Andrews took a last look at the missile and followed, jogging to catch up.

CHAPTER 37

The creature propelled itself forward. Greg watched in awe as its greenish grey body passed him, and so large was the creature, it filled his field of vision for what felt like an age. He saw a sliver of sharp teeth in the partially open jaw, as the vast animal snagged the side of beef away with a single, effortless bite. He knew he should check on his client, but was so mesmerised by the giant yards away from him, he couldn't bring himself to tear his eyes away from it. The creature nudged the cage as it passed, and for a split second, Greg lost his grip, snatching twice at the bars before managing to restore his hold. It was then he saw the great white ascend from below. It was big, at least an eighteen footer. Even it looked tiny in comparison to the immense creature. The white had been drawn in by the bloody carcass, and unlike its brethren, had not fled from the creature. It was only when Greg saw the other sharks appearing out of the darkness that he thought he understood what was happening. Hunters in their own right, the sharks were ready to respond to the new threat by challenging its supremacy.

It was at that precise second that fear replaced the thrill, and Greg turned towards his client, who was still staring wide eyed at the creature. It seemed he hadn't noticed the sharks, which Greg thought could be a good thing. He shook Paul by the shoulder, snapping him to attention. His intention had been to give the instruction to ascend, yet when he looked towards the surface, the path was blocked by great whites, which were circling and waiting to attack. As experienced as he was, he would never risk swimming to the surface, especially as the whites looked ready to attack at any given moment. Instead, he pointed to the cage, swimming to the roof and pulling open the hatch. Paul had noticed the sharks now too, and his eyes flicked wildly between the giant creature and its potential attackers. Greg banged on the cage to get Paul's attention, watching as one of the whites cautiously darted closer to the creature, then retreated. He banged his fist on the cage roof again, and although Paul briefly looked at him, he didn't move. He released his grip on the door and moved towards the edge of the cage roof, grabbing Paul by the shoulder and finally getting his attention. Perhaps it was the fear or desperation in his eyes, or the gravity of the situation finally hitting home which forced him into action. He inched his way up the side of the cage between frightened glances at the gathering sharks. Greg dragged him the rest of the way, yanked open the hatch and shoved Paul inside. He followed and pulled the door closed, and not a moment too soon. One of the larger whites, a twenty-two foot male, charged towards the creature and snapped at one of its tentacles. The reaction was devastating. The creature lunged for the shark, shearing away a huge flap of its underbelly in a single bite. As the great white convulsed and sank into the depths, its brethren as one began to attack.

The *Victorious* came to a halt, bobbing and rolling with the tides as Russo made it back into the command station.

"Why have we stopped?" He barked.

"I told him to. There's a boat out there on the water." Clara snapped back, glaring at Russo before turning her attention back to the radar.

"Who gives you the right to-"

"Shut up and look at this."

Russo strode over to Clara, looking out of the window at the boat bobbing on the water, then at the radar. He could see the creature represented by a green smudge on the screen and surrounded by numerous other signals.

"What am I looking at here?" Russo asked.

"It might not look like it, but that's one hell of a battle going on."

"What kind of battle?" Russo snapped.

"Sharks. They're moving too fast to be whales."

"Surely they wouldn't be so stupid as to attack this fish of ours."

Clara flicked a gaze at Russo that would sour milk, and then turned back to the screen.

"Fortunately, nature doesn't give a shit about your orders or plans. All it cares about is redressing the balance this thing has shifted when it appeared."

"You told me sharks are rogue. You said they don't hunt in packs."

"That's true. Unlike whales, they aren't social creatures. Faced with such a unique threat, it's conceivable they are working together to take this thing down. You have to imagine that sharks are natural predators. Although they won't always attack something bigger than they are, they also don't have any concept of what we would call fear. If anything, they're inherently curious. My best guess is that the owners of that boat are in a shark cage right now, and the bait has drawn in not just our fish, but also sharks from all around. It was only a matter of time before the two species clashed."

"This is perfect, we couldn't have asked for a better opportunity." Russo said as he beckoned one of the soldiers by the door towards him.

"Go and tell Mito I want the device in the water and ready to launch right now. Have him call me when it's ready."

"What device? What's going on?"

"None of your concern, Dr Thompson. Just the next vital step in our mission."

"What device?" she repeated.

Russo looked wired, pacing around the deck with a wild look in his eye.

"How far to the target?" he asked the radar operator, ignoring Clara's pleas.

"Seven hundred feet, sir," the man replied.

"Good. Hold station and keep the distance constant, I don't want to mess this up."

"You brought me here to help, so I suggest you tell me what you have planned."

"I don't have time for that. Andrews looks like he's positively bursting to fill you in, so I'll let him do it. I have work to do."

He strode away, leaving Andrews and Clara in the control room.

"What's he planning?"

"He has this missile… it's like a concussion grenade designed for underwater. He wants to knock it out."

"He can't," Clara said, her eyes wide as she stared at Andrews. "You have to stop him. Doesn't he know there are people in the water?"

"Of course he knows, but you know as well as I do, he has his own agenda."

"Then maybe it's time you grew some balls and stopped him before he kills someone."

The words hurt Andrews more than he expected, and he realised Clara was right.

"Hail the boat on the radio," he said as he jogged towards the door. "Tell them to get those people out of the water now, under instruction from the United States government."

"We already tried, they aren't responding."

"Then try again. Keep trying until you get through."

"Where are you going?"

"I'm going to stop Russo from putting that thing in the water."

CHAPTER 38

The ocean was a churning mass of activity littered with bloody clumps of shark as the creature decimated wave after wave of its attackers. Most of the bigger pieces sank into the depths, but some of the smaller morsels bobbed and floated, and were pushed around by the currents as the gargantuan creature repelled attack after attack. To Paul, the great white had always represented to him the pinnacle of single minded ruthlessness, an unmatched perfect predatory machine, and yet although they had attacked en masse, the immense beast was more than a capable match.

Paul saw a twelve-foot white get bitten completely in half by the giant monster, only to have the other sharks nip and tear at its body as it spiralled into the depths. Now, of the hundred plus sharks that had instigated the attack, less than a dozen remained, which were systematically attacking the creature in turn before retreating out of range. Two tried to attack the creature's body, but even their hyperextended jaws couldn't maintain a grip. Instead, they were now focussed on the array of tentacles and flippers in the hope of disabling the creature. In retaliation, the giant snapped at one of the whites – an eighteen-foot male, shearing away a huge section of its underbelly. The shark twitched and swam erratically away from the creature, leaving a cloud of blood and entrails behind. The creature gave chase as the remaining whites, realizing the attack had failed, fled into the ocean. The crippled shark tried to swim over the cage and became tangled in the winch mechanism. It thrashed and rolled on top of the steel structure, desperately trying to free itself. Already mortally wounded, the creature was too weak to escape. Greg and Paul cowered as hot entrails spewed out of the wounded underbelly and filled the cage. Through the blood, they saw the creature as it approached its incapacitated prey.

"Get that thing in the water," Russo barked as he strode out on deck. Mito did as he was told, operating the winch to lower the weapon towards the water. Russo picked up the remote control as Andrews rushed through the outer door.

"What the hell are you doing here? You are supposed to be mon-"

"You have to stop." Andrews blurted.

"Why on earth would I do that?"

"Because there are people out there, civilians." Andrews shot back, pointing at the shimmering white boat across the water.

"I see that. Fortunately, this is going under the water. Those people might feel a little bump, but they won't be affected."

"Don't try it, Russo. You know well enough whoever that boat belongs to is in the water. The concussion blast could kill them."

"Do you see that, Andrews?" Russo said, pointing to the frothing ocean ahead, which was littered with fleshy chunks.

"That is our creature feeding on those sharks. This is our best opportunity to stun and tag it."

"What about the people?"

"Grow up, Andrews! We both know anyone in the water amongst all that carnage is likely already dead. I refuse to jeopardise a multimillion dollar mission because a couple of tourists picked the wrong spot to go fishing."

"Package is in the water, sir," Mito said, giving Andrews a cold glare.

"Good. Prepare for launch."

"Didn't you hear me? We need to get those people out of there before you do anything. You have to see reason."

"And how exactly do you propose we do that? Are *you* willing to swim down and help them out?"

Andrews answered with silence, and looked at the deck.

"Just what I thought. If you don't think two potential casualties is a fair price to complete this mission, I misjudged you."

"Tell that to their families, Russo. What if it was you?"

Russo shook his head and snorted. "Please, don't bother to try to appeal to my human nature."

Andrews took a quick step forward, snatched the remote controller from Russo, and held it out over the side of the boat. In the same instant, Russo pulled out his gun and aimed it at Andrews's face.

"Back off, I'll drop it, I swear."

Russo smiled, his hand unwavering. "Well, this is an interesting development. It seems you may have a backbone after all, Andrews."

"Look, I'm not trying to stop you, I just can't let you do this until those people are out of the water."

"Even if they're already dead?"

"Yeah."

"I see," Russo said, offering a small smile.

"The way I see it," Andrews said, "is that you don't really have a choice here. I know this mission is important to you. Get those people out of the water, and I'll give you back the control."

"You're sweating." Russo replied, his gaze unwavering.

"It's hot. What do you say?"

"We could do it your way and risk losing time and possibly our only chance to tag this creature. Or you can give me the controls and pretend this entire situation never happened."

Andrews shook his head. "I can't do that."

"The other alternative is I can shoot you in the head right now."

"Then you'd lose the controls."

Russo grinned, and Andrews felt a stab of fear tingle down his spine.

"True," he said as he adjusted his grip on the gun. "I could ask Mito to get the backup unit and it would be business as usual."

"You can't bluff me. I know this business too well. You seem to forget that. You already told me the other unit isn't modified for underwater use."

"It isn't, but that's irrelevant. I'm talking about a reserve control unit, not the weapon itself."

"You wouldn't have a gun on me if you had a second controller. I know you better than you think."

"I have a gun on you as a matter of principal, and I would shoot you without hesitation just for the fact that you tried to do something so stupid."

"I don't believe you."

"Go right ahead. Drop the control overboard. See what happens."

"Are you really willing to kill another government agent over a fish?"

"Are you really prepared to give your life for people who you have never met, who are probably dead already? The longer you delay the more chance our fish has of escaping. Now please, hand over the control. I won't ask again."

Andrews looked at his hand, and realised that a few pounds of pressure either released by him or applied by Russo, would probably result in him losing his life. For as much as he had grown to hate Russo, he did have a point. There was no reason for him to protect these people who he didn't know. He had his own life, a good job with good benefits, and even if this particular mission was going all kinds of wrong, the sooner it was over, the sooner he could get back to the real world. He held the control out to Russo, who lowered the gun.

"See? I knew you'd see things my way. People always do."

He turned to Mito. "Is it ready to launch?"

"Yes sir."

"Well, let's see if our toy works."

CHAPTER 39

The great beast readied itself to attack its crippled foe, and yet remained cautious. It could sense the cage and the two other heartbeats within. Although it had previously swallowed the shark cage containing Milton, the steel had cut the insides of the creatures stomach as it was swallowed, causing it to regurgitate its meal. Much like the sharks that had attacked it, the creature's entire stomach was expelled from its mouth like a balloon, pushing out the unwanted steel frame and with it, partially digested lumps of blubber and flesh. It was a painful and uncomfortable process, and one that the creature was not in a hurry to repeat.

It was cautious, and kept its distance from the cage, waiting for the creatures within it to die. Greg had seen similar behaviour in sharks, and knew that attack was imminent. In that instant, he forgot all about gambling debts and the suspected affair his fiancé may or may not be having - all that mattered was survival. He turned towards Paul, who was still clinging to the bars and staring at the circling beast. He then turned his attention to the hatch, which was pinned closed by the dead great shark. He saw a flicker of movement and glanced at Paul who was backing himself against the cage, his eyes wide as they peered through his mask. Greg whipped his head around in time to see the creature accelerating towards them. He knew they wouldn't survive, there was no way they could. He bit hard on his regulator and hoped it would be quick, and that he wouldn't feel the agonising pain as his flesh was punctured by the beast's jaws. Greg closed his eyes, waiting for the black warmth of the bite, which would signal the end of his life.

The creature opened its mouth to bite down on the cage when it registered the signal coming from behind. Enraged that another animal was challenging its dominance, the creature abandoned its meal, and turned to face its attacker head on. The snub-nosed T7500 missile sped through the water, guided from the surface towards its target by Russo, who could see everything unfolding from the nose mounted camera

He could see the creature on screen as it closed in, opening its mouth to bite down on the missile a split second before the proximity sensor triggered the detonation.

Greg had managed to force enough of the hatch open against the dead weight of the shark's corpse when the concussion wave hit. The shockwave rocked the cage violently, snapping his hand – which was trapped between cage and hatch- like kindling. With no protection from the blast, Paul was slammed against inner wall of the cage, his head smashing against the bars as he was flung like a ragdoll. With his mangled hand trapped in the hatch and the full weight of the shark's body pinning it down, Greg hung helplessly, trying to shake away the ringing in his ears as he peered through his cracked facemask. Something caught his eye. He looked around as multiple species of dead fish began to float to the surface. All sizes, all varieties. He saw a dolphin, floating vertically past the cage rotating in a graceful arc as it climbed. The ocean had gone from battleground to a macabre showcase of the dead, as species after species floated to the surface.

He had heard about this before. Some people used to fish this way back before it was made illegal. Blast fishing where dynamite would be tossed into the water would cause the stunned fish's swim bladders to rupture, resulting in a horrible, painful death. Although he could see a huge number of animals floating to the surface, he knew it could have been worse, as many of the larger species of fish had already fled away from the carnage that had taken place. He shifted position where he hung by his arm, biting down hard on his regulator as pain jolted from his wrist. It was then that he saw the creature. It too was motionless and gently floating belly up towards the surface, its tentacles splayed out and drifting in the current. Again, he was mesmerised by the sheer scale of the animal. It was completely unlike anything else he had ever seen before, and fear aside, he appreciated its majesty.

***

On the surface, there was initially no indication of the huge undersea explosion. The *Victorious* bobbed gently on the shimmering ocean, Russo staring at the waves as Mito prepared the barbed harpoon tracker. A few smaller fish appeared on the surface, then the dolphin, which had pirouetted past the cage. Russo smiled as memories of the pond full of frogs came back to him. He could see the colour of the water grow from dark to light, and knew their target was about to surface. The water parted, and so large was the animal that it at first appeared as if a new island was growing out of the ocean. Even Russo, who knew what to expect, drew breath as the giant breached a hundred and fifty feet ahead of the boat, floating half on its side, its tentacles limply bobbing with the tide.

"Mito, call the wheelhouse, tell them to get broadside. I don't want to miss this shot."

In the cage, Greg struggled to free himself. His ears were still ringing from the explosion, and salt water dripped into his eyes from the hairline crack in his facemask, but he was otherwise in reasonable shape. He stopped flailing and checked the gauge on his trapped right hand, confirming his fears. The small wristwatch like device told him the air tank on his back was running dangerously close to empty. He estimated he had less than fifteen minutes of air left before he would drown. The thought of death renewed his energy, he redoubled his efforts, alternating between trying to yank his arm free, and getting enough advantage to displace the shark corpse, neither of which seemed to be doing anything but sending explosive jolts of paint through his broken wrist. He began to suck air greedily from the regulator, knowing every breath was precious, but still unable to help himself. On the floor of the cage, Paul didn't stir, and had slumped to the side, a steady cloud of blood mushrooming from the wound in the back of his head. Faced with the fact he was never going to be able to move the dead shark that was pinning the lid of the cage closed, Greg knew he would have to make a drastic choice. The floor of the cage was also hinged in case of emergency, and he knew it was his one and only way out. First, he had to free himself. He looked at his mangled hand, and realised what he needed to do.

How much do you want to live?

He asked himself as he twisted and tugged at his arm.

How far will you go to survive?

It was then that absolute clarity came to him and he stopped struggling. It was extreme, and he knew he would have to do it quickly before his air supply ran out. Despite the urgency, there were a lot of questions he didn't have the answer to.

Could he go through with it?

Could he withstand the pain, and if he did, could he get to a doctor in time?

What if he passed out halfway through?

Answers or no answers, it didn't matter. There was no other choice. Taking a deep breath of precious air, he unsheathed the hunting knife from his diving belt, the blade warping the light as he held it to his face. It was a good knife. Sharp too. He hoped it wouldn't hurt, maybe if enough numbness had set in…

No.

Enough delays. He had a job to do, and every second was precious.

Pleasedonthurtpleasedonthurtpleasedonthurt

He repeated it over and over in his head, praying he would have the strength to do what needed to be done. As he began to hack through the soft flesh of his wrist, prying bone away from bone, shearing tendon and flesh, brilliant, white hot agony surged through his body, and he bit on the regulator hard enough to fracture two teeth. As he carved away at his wrist through a cloud of blood, tears streaming down his face and mingling with the salt water that had already penetrated the mask, another question came to him.

What happens if the creature wakes up?

Back on the surface, the *Victorious* was now alongside the creature, which was bobbing on the surface a hundred yards from the boat. Russo readied the harpoon.

"Mito, are we ready to fire?"

"Yes sir."

Russo lifted the weapon into position, nestling it on his shoulder in the same way a rocket launcher might be aimed. He peered through the sights, bringing the mottled grey flesh of the creature into focus and positioned his finger over the trigger. To ensure maximum chance of the dart staying attached to the creature, Russo wanted to tag it somewhere between the eye and the first giant dorsal fin. Further down the body would risk the device being detached by a wayward swipe of the tentacle or encounter with another creature. Despite the sheer scale of the animal, his target area was relatively small. He took a deep breath and prepared to fire. Before he could launch the harpoon, a streak of colour flashed across his field of vision. He blinked and lowered the weapon in time to see the *Lisa Marie*, which had pulled broadside with the *Victorious* and blocked Russo's shot. On deck, Rainwater, Bo, Mackay, and Morrison stood facing Russo.

"Move, get out of the way!" Russo yelled, the veins in his neck bulging.

"I don't think so," Rainwater called back. "There are people in the water. It's too dangerous."

"You're obstructing a government official in his line of duty to-"

"Save the bullshit, pal," Mackay yelled. "We ain't moving till we get those people out of the water."

Rainwater found it hard to suppress his smile at how flustered Russo had become.

"If you don't move I have the authority to-"

"What are you gonna do? Have me discharged again?" Mackay interjected, spitting on deck as he glared at Russo.

"I know you!" Russo said, staring at Mackay.

"Yeah, I punched you in the mouth a few years back, remember?"

"Don't you realise you're interfering with government business? This could be seen as terrorism!"

Rainwater laughed, unable to help himself for the sheer absurdity of Russo's statement.

"You're the son of the fisherman aren't you? The one this thing killed."

"That's right," Rainwater said, forcing himself not to break eye contact.

"And yet, you surround yourself with these... people... and protect it. I wonder if your father would be proud."

"Don't listen to him, lad," Mackay interjected. "He's trying to get inside that head o' yours. All these government types are the same. This asshole would tell you anything."

Russo grinned, a slab of brilliant white that seemed stretched a tad too far across his lips.

"Don't try to push me, you know first-hand how far I will go to get what I want."

"That sounds like a threat." Mackay said.

"It is. Move now, or I'll be forced to take action."

"Unless you can shoot that thing around corners, I'd say we hold all the cards." Rainwater said.

"Not exactly," Russo shot back, then gave another greasy smile.

A single rapport of gunfire shattered the still air. Rainwater was aware of it a split second before he felt the sticky warmth of blood and bone as it spattered all over his face. He blinked once, exhaled, blinked again. Ox staggered forward, the upper portion of his skull now missing. The engineer fell, his chest slamming into the rail of the boat, the remains of his head hanging over the edge of the water. There was absolute silence for what felt like an age, which in reality was only seconds. It was only then that Rainwater started to piece together what had happened.

Morrison's gun was still smoking from the barrel where he had pressed it into Ox's head a split second before he had fired.

Despite his own close call, Rainwater had never seen actual death first hand before. He saw it plenty on movies or on the news, but none of it prepared him for it happening right in front of him. He could smell the smoke and blood, he could hear the sound of Ox's brains as they dripped into the sea. He could see the calm indifference in Morrison's eyes as he turned the weapon on him and Mackay. Most of all, he could hear Russo. He was laughing.

"Like I have said a hundred times already, I always have a plan." Russo let his eyes linger on Rainwater, his expression almost goading a response. All Rainwater could concentrate on was the bottomless black hole of the gun barrel which was aimed at his head. He risked a glance at Mackay, a brief flick of the eyes. It seemed the fear that surged through Rainwater had manifested itself as fury in him, and he glared at Morrison with little evidence of fear.

"I'll fuckin' kill you for this," he hissed, and managed a smile that was every bit as wide and sick looking as Russo's.

Morrison didn't seem overly concerned, instead he shrugged and trained the gun on Mackay.

"I'm sure you intend to do just that. Right now, I have to insist you move the boat forward like Mr Russo asked."

"Mr Russo?" Mackay said, still not quite able to drop the grin. "So you are some sort of stooge? His little boat bitch is that it?"

Morrison shrugged. "Don't be like that. This is business. I do whatever the money pays me to do. Come on, Mac, you knew I was a mercenary when you hired me. It was bad luck for you that he got to me first. Why do you think I made a point of getting in touch with you again? Who else would you have turned to for something like this?"

"Mercenary maybe. I never had you pegged as someone who would stab a friend in the back."

"I can't believe you're surprised. You know what I am. What I do. Surely, you saw this coming. Now please, move the boat forward. Despite what you might think, I really don't want to shoot you, even if it's just for old times' sake."

"Aye, we have history alright. That's why I don't think you'll do it. Not for money."

Morrison snorted, shaking his head and smiling. "You always did know me too well, Mac. You were always a good judge of character."

Still smiling, he turned the gun on Rainwater.

"Now move this fucking boat before I spray this little shit's brains all over the deck."

Somehow, he hadn't passed out. Maybe it was the adrenaline or the desire to survive. Whatever the reason, Greg was still conscious. It had been close. The soft tissues weren't too bad, but the nerves felt charged with millions of vaults of electricity, as he had sliced through them. Even so, he was still woozy. The knife grinding against bone as he separated his wrist had sounded incredibly loud in his head, and he had to count backwards from ten to keep conscious. Knife blade trembling, he cut through the last of the gristle and was at last free, sinking to the bottom of the cage and leaving a mushrooming cloud of blood behind as if he were some kind of bizarre distress flare. The relief lasted only for seconds until the pain found him, bringing his nerve endings alive with fierce agony. He clutched his bleeding stump to his chest, and sank towards Paul.

Even though the thought horrified him, Greg half hoped he was dead. At least then, he could take his air tanks. However, although his breathing was shallow he was still alive. He didn't have the strength to both lift the emergency escape hatch and keep a tight enough grip to be confident that he wouldn't slip and lose him to the depths. Plus, there was the matter of his own air supply. As tough a decision as it was, there really was no other choice but to go to the surface alone and get some help. He turned towards the hatch handle, and froze.

Ahead of him in the murk, the creature bobbed on its back, its massive jaws partially open. As Greg looked on, its car tyre sized eye flicked open.

Rainwater knew he was about to die. He had always suspected Mackay was a little bit unhinged, but he would never have predicted the response to Morrison's threat. Rather than do as he was asked, Mackay simply stood his ground and laughed. If it was a bluff, it was the best one Rainwater had ever seen. He only wished Morrison had been unsettled by it, but the gun never wavered, nor did his icy stare.

"Don't test me. You know I'll do it."

Mackay must have seen something in Morrison's eyes, or maybe got a sense of the danger he presented, because he shifted his weight, and all at once seemed a little less sure of himself. Rainwater was about to tell Mackay to do as Morrison said, as it wasn't worth getting killed over, when he saw the flicker of movement on the water.

Still woozy from the explosion, the creature had come to in a rage, and attacked the closest thing to it, which happened to be the *Lisa Marie*. Rainwater saw it coming, and was instantly transported back in time. Instead of the sun-baked deck of the *Lisa Marie*, he was in the dark aboard the *Red Gold*, watching the wake come towards him. He blinked, and was back in the present. Neither Morrison nor Mackay had noticed it. They were still trying to stare each other down. It was Russo who broke the silence, and the three words he bellowed was enough to herald in the chaos.

"Here it comes!"

Morrison and Mackay saw the wake just a split second before the boat lurched out of the water.

CHAPTER 40

Russo was twelve years old the last time he was ever truly afraid. It was as his mother lay dying from the cancer that had eaten her alive, and he had first realised he was soon to be an orphan. His father had walked out on them when Russo was a baby, and as he looked down on his broken mother, he had been overcome with an immensely powerful sadness.

"James," she had whispered from her deathbed as she reached out a trembling, skeletal hand.

He had taken it, fearful her bones could snap if he held her too tightly. The room was quiet apart from the muted sobs of his sister.

"I'll be gone soon," she wheezed, "don't ever let anyone tell you can't be who you want to be. You can be whatever you want to."

She had smiled, a flesh covered skeleton with sunken eyes. He could see the defeat in them as much as he could smell the death on her.

"I love you, always remember that."

She looked at him, her watery eyes full of expectation.

My God, she wants a reply.

Russo couldn't understand why it was so hard to formulate simple words. Try as he might, he couldn't say them. Instead, he simply stared, wishing she would hurry up and die so he wouldn't have to say those three words that were so alien to him. He had pulled his hand free of her grip and left the room, not looking back. He wasn't there when she died, and even though he was sad, it was a distant sadness. It was then he had felt fear, simply because the sorrow was absent, leaving an empty void in its place.

It was that same fear which came over him now, as he saw the creature slam into the *Lisa Marie*, sending Mackay, Rainwater, and Morrison crashing to the deck. Morrison's weapon fired as he fell, the bullet cutting the air past Russo's ear with an audible *wsssssssss*. Russo flinched, watching as the giant creature angled away from the boat, launching a thirty-foot wall of spray in its wake. The creature moved away from the *Lisa Marie*, which was already listing from the impact. The commotion brought the crew of the *Victorious* out on deck, each of them trying to get a glimpse of the creature. Andrews pushed through the crowd towards Russo.

"What the hell's going on?" He roared.

"They blocked my shot, and now it's pissed." He replied as calmly as if he were discussing an event in the news.

"You have to help them," Clara interjected, unable to stop staring at the wake left by the agitated creature as it started to turn back towards the boat.

"Not until I get my shot," Russo said again, showing her the barbed harpoon as if to emphasise his point.

Murmurs from those on deck pulled Russo's attention back to the water, just in time to see the creature smash broadside into the boat a second time, making deck boards explode as it was spun around, the resulting wake slewing the *Victorious* aside and furthering the distance between it and the *Lisa Marie*. Already wounded, the fishing boat began to slide slowly into the ocean, its bow lifting out of the water as its stern sank. The crew scrambled to stay above the waterline as the creature retreated again, pausing to snag Ox's body where it bobbed on the surface, swallowing it in a singular bite as it once again raced away and readied a new attack.

"If you don't help them, they'll die," Clara said, and Russo turned to her. All eyes were on him, and he grinned.

"Not until I get my shot."

"They're innocent people!" She screamed.

"Innocent? Those people interfered in a government operation. They don't deserve my help."

"That's not for you to decide, they need to be tried in a court."

Russo's grin faltered for a second, and then he shrugged.

"Either way, nobody steps foot on this boat until I get my shot."

"Then do it, take the damn shot and help them!" she said again, watching as the creature prepared to attack.

"I can't risk missing. If they hadn't interfered, none of this would have happened. They only have themselves to blame."

"Give me the harpoon." Clara said.

"What do you mean?"

"You say you will help them if you make this shot, then give it to me. I'll make sure it hits the target. You get those people out of the water."

"You better not be lying to me."

"Hurry up and hand me the damn harpoon." She said, glaring at Russo.

He did as she asked, and was about to instruct her on how to operate it when she deftly swung it onto her shoulder, adjusted her aim and readied to fire.

"You've done this before," Russo said, genuinely impressed.

"Don't talk to me. Just get those people out of the water before I change my mind."

Russo turned to Mito and nodded, and the officer ran to the lifeboat station. Clara aimed at the water, allowing her breathing to calm, making sure her feet were spread evenly as she watched the beast circle.

"No games," Russo hissed over her shoulder, the smell of his minty breath close to her face. "If you miss or try to screw me, I won't be responsible for what happens."

She could feel the eyes of everyone on deck boring into her and tried her best to ignore it. The sun was hot on her neck and a trickle of sweat ran down the inside of her nose. She adjusted her aim slightly, paused and spoke to Russo.

"I'm, ready. You'd better stick to your word."

"That all depends on you."

She ignored him, readying herself as the creature charged, looking to finish off the stricken boat, which was rapidly losing its fight to stay afloat.

She relaxed her shoulders and exhaled as the grey streak raced along below the surface. Sunlight glittered off the water, making it difficult to be sure where she was aiming. She squeezed the trigger, hoping against hope to land a fleshy spot on the creature somewhere the barbed harpoon could find purchase. She had expected a deafening roar of gunfire when she squeezed the trigger, but instead, the weapon fired with a hollow pneumatic *Whumph* as the harpoon speared into the water, burying itself in the soft flesh above the creature's eye. The harpoon sheared through tangled clusters of nerves, igniting pain receptors, which sent the charging beast into agonising spasms. Rearing away from the crippled *Lisa Marie*, the creature dived deep, trying to cool the searing pain of the dart in its flesh. Clara lowered the spent harpoon, then turned to watch Mito as he loaded its survivors into the lifeboat and winched it to the deck. Clara dropped the harpoon, trying to ignore Russo's oozing smile.

"Thank you," he said, clapping his hands together as Rainwater and Mackay were ushered towards Russo. Morrison followed, hands in pockets and smiling as he took his place beside Russo.

Rainwater watched as the bow of his father's boat sank beneath the waves, leaving only a field of debris to let anyone know it had ever existed.

"Mito, escort our new friends below decks and make sure they stay out of trouble."

"You can't do this, they didn't do anything." Clara said, glaring at Russo.

"Oh, don't worry. You're joining them."

"You need me."

"I did," he said, grinning as he opened a fresh pack of mints and popped one into his mouth, "until you tagged the creature. Mr Morrison will be taking over your duties from now on."

Mito escorted them away, flanked by two soldiers with automatic weapons. Russo watched them go, and then took a deep breath. Everything was going exactly to plan.

"Okay," he said, clapping his hands together, "let's get back to work, shall we?"

CHAPTER 41

Greg managed to get out of the hatch and swam around the cage and to the surface. He burst from the water, tearing the regulator from his mouth and gulping in fresh air. For a moment, euphoria replaced the pain.

"Mrs Milla!" he screamed, clinging on to the winch cable with his remaining hand.

Her moon face appeared over the edge of the boat, eyes wide with panic.

"I didn't know what to do, I didn't know how to pull the cage up, then that thing showed up and attacked the other boat..." she stammered, then saw his ravaged arm.

"Where's Paul? Please, tell me he's not dead, oh God, oh, God, it got him didn't it? That thing ate him..." her words became incoherent babble, which in turn became sobs.

"Mrs Milla," he said, trying his best to keep calm. "He's fine. He's injured but fine. You need to help me out of the water. I'm hurt and can't do it by myself."

"I can't cope if he's dead, I told him not to do this, but he insisted, he's stubborn, you see."

"If you don't shut up and listen to me, he'll die." Greg snapped. "Please, I need to raise the cage and get him some help. I need you to help me."

He spoke slowly, trying to coax the hysterical woman into action.

"What if it comes back," she whispered, looking out to sea at the departing *Victorious*. "See? Even they've left us."

"Mrs Milla, you see the controls for the winch?"

"Yes, I already tried, when that thing surfaced, I tried. Oh God, what are we going to do..." she was about to lose it again, and though he felt like a heartless bastard for doing it, he shouted at her again.

"Stop it. I need you to focus. Do you see the controls?"

"I already told you I tried it!" She wailed. "The button doesn't work."

"At the bottom of the winch panel, there's a toggle switch. Do you see it?"

She walked over to the controls.

"Yes, yes I see it."

"That's the winch lock, press it and—"

The winch started to move as she sprang into action and activated the controls. Greg let the cable slide through his hand and watched the cage come to the surface complete with the remains of the dead shark. His feet touched the sharks flesh, and started to lift him out of the water. Straddling either side of the corpse, he was raised out of the water enough to hop on board the boat, his stumpy wrist spilling precious blood all over the bright, clean deck boards.

"First aid kit..." he said, pointing towards the wheelhouse as he held his wounded arm in the air.

She hurried off, doing as she was told. Greg looked at the cage, which was now half out of the water. With the extra load of the shark, it was too heavy to pull out all the way. Inside the cage, Paul floated face down at the bottom. Greg stopped the winch, and lowered it so it was level with the transom of the boat. "Help me with this," he said as he leaned into the body of the shark.

"Is it..."

"It's dead," He grunted as he put his shoulder to the shark's body, shoving with everything he could muster. "Now please, help me push it off the door so I can get him out of the water."

Despite his concern that he would have to coerce Mrs Milla into helping, the sight of her husband floating in the cage spurred her on, and she drove her shoulder into the shark carcass, gritting her teeth as she shoved. At first, the dead fish held in place, then it was moving, sliding off the cage and into the water where it sank out of sight.

"Okay," he said, trying to catch his breath. "Get some bandages ready for my arm whilst I swing the cage onto the boat."

Pale faced, Mrs Milla did as she was asked, watching her husband's body bob on the water as Paul manipulated the winch controls, first bringing the cage out of the water and swinging it over the edge of the deck, where he set it down. With his good arm, he grabbed the top of the cage, trying to tip it over.

"Mrs Milla..." he muttered as white spots began to dance across his vision.

She came immediately, helping him to lower the cage onto its side.

"Good, now call the Coast Guard whilst I help him." He said, scrambling through the top hatch. He absently wondered what had happened to his hand, and presumed it had fallen into the ocean when he had dislodged the shark.

"Will he be alright?" she asked, a pale faced ghost who was looking at him with expectation.

"I'll do my best to help him. Please, make that call. Tell them we need someone out here ASAP."

Mrs Milla disappeared into the wheelhouse, as Greg did the best he could with one hand to drag Paul out onto the deck. Whatever happened, he swore he was done with the ocean. He had treated it with respect and in response, it had chewed him up and spat him out.

"Hey, man, you with me?" he asked as he looked at Paul. He was murmuring, his eyes half closed. Blood streamed from his eyes and ears and pooled around the back of his head.

"We have some help on the way, just hang tight, okay?"

It took twenty-five minutes for the Coast Guard helicopter to arrive. By then, Paul Milla had already succumbed to his injuries. As the chopper drew closer, Greg sat on the blood-streaked deck, his roughly bandaged stump held upright to stem the blood flow. They had covered Paul with a towel, leaving his wife sobbing at his side as she held his hand. Greg glared out to sea, knowing somewhere in the deep, the huge creature that had ruined his life lived on.

CHAPTER 42

Rainwater, Mackay, and Clara were led through the bowels of the *Victorious*. Mito opened the door to the storage room and ushered them inside.

"How long are we expected to stay here?"

"Not for long," Mito said, shrugging his shoulders. "We're having rooms prepared for you, and this is the safest place to hold you for now."

"Hold us?"

"Yes."

"Why? What have we done?" Rainwater pressed.

"That's not for me to say."

With that, Mito closed the door and locked it, leaving the trio alone. Rainwater sat on the floor and leaned his head against the hull.

"Thanks for what you did, to help us I mean." He said, looking at Clara.

"It might have helped you, but it gave him what he wanted."

"How did you get involved in all this?" Mackay asked. "You shouldn't be mixing with a prick like Russo. He's dangerous."

She shrugged, sliding down the wall into a sitting position opposite Rainwater.

"I keep asking myself that same thing and I'll be damned if I can figure it out. I thought it was going to be some kind of scientific study of a new species. At the start, I mostly dealt with the other guy, Andrews. I thought he was in charge. Now it looks more and more like Russo is pulling his strings."

"So what are you, some kind of scientist?" Mackay asked.

"Marine biologist. They brought me out here to consult and help them to locate this thing."

"But why?" Rainwater said. "Why is the government so interested in this creature? I can understand the need to make sure the public are safe, why don't they kill it instead of going to all this trouble to tag it?"

"Fucked if I know, lad," Mackay grunted. "This whole situation seems screwed up to me."

"I know what he wants, and it has nothing to do with public safety."

Mackay and Rainwater both stared at Clara, who looked right back at them.

"Go on," Rainwater said.

"I had my suspicions he was up to no good, so I did some snooping. I found a folder full of stuff about something called Project Blue."

"What's that?"

"It seems they knew about this thing since ninety seven when they recorded its call on sonar. They've been looking for it ever since. Called it 'The Bloop'."

"I heard of that," Rainwater said. "They said it was a sound louder than anything ever recorded on earth. Didn't they recently explain it as an ice quake?"

"Of course they did. The public was getting too interested, so as they always do, they fabricated a story to stop people from asking questions."

"Why the gap? Why has this thing only surfaced now?" He asked.

"According to the documents, the government was desperate to find this creature without success when they first detected the signal. They'd almost given up until our friend Andrews came up with the same theory I did."

"And what theory is that?" Mackay said.

"That this creature has some kind of lair and had maybe gone into hibernation."

"For so long?"

"It's not as strange as it sounds. Sea currents move millions of tons of micro bacterial organisms around the ocean. It's entirely plausible that much like certain whales, this creature allowed the currents to pass through it, taking out the nutrients from the ocean and giving it a rudimentary form of sustenance. All it would need is a lair. Somewhere for it to remain undisturbed."

"Any idea what made it wake up, or why it went into hibernation in the first place?" Rainwater asked.

"I don't know why it would have gone into suspension, but I would have to be able to examine the creature in detail before I could give an answer. As far as it waking, I do have a theory. It seems just before it became active, a huge section of the Ross Ice Shelf fell into the ocean. I suspect our creature was holed up nearby when it happened, and the sound of the quake roused it. Like any animal, it will be looking to establish its territory and it will need to feed regularly. A creature of that size would need to take on a substantial amount of food to sustain it."

"I take it the micro critters won't cut it anymore?" Mackay asked.

Clara shook her head. "No, whilst it was inactive and conserving its energy, such a diet would suffice. Now it is active and burning millions of calories a day, it will need to feed more regularly."

"Morrison seemed to think it fed every couple of days." Rainwater said.

"Don't mention his name to me," Mackay growled. "I still have unfinished business with that bastard."

"Nevertheless, he was right," Clara said. "My guess is it feeds every fifty to sixty hours, supplemented by whatever else it can find along the way. It's a natural hunter, so those figures are guidelines more than fact. Before I came out here, I'd been looking into a spate of unexplained beaching's. Sea life of all varieties were veering out of their usual migratory patterns and literally swimming out of the ocean. My guess is they were trying to get away from our creature."

"I still don't get it," Rainwater said. "Why is the government so desperate to find this thing?"

"That's what Project Blue is. Russo's job is to find the creature and tag it with a tracker, which he has now done. It seems the government came to the same conclusion I did. Based on the creatures feeding pattern and the spate of beaching's, it must have a lair of some kind, a place where it dwells between feeds. The chances are it will be close to where it first went into hibernation, and would be secluded and large enough to house it comfortably."

"So this prick Russo finds its lair, then what? Does he kill it? If he does I'm not sure we should be trying to stop him." Mackay said, his eyes glinting in the gloom.

"That's the point," Clara shot back. "At first, I wanted to conserve this creature, to study it, now, I recognise it's just too dangerous to be allowed to exist. Not only has it played havoc with the entire marine ecosystem, it's a threat to our economy too. Fishing, shipping, transportation, undersea drilling. All of those things would all have to stop. Our oceans would be rendered pretty much unusable. I don't like to see animals harmed, but whatever this thing is, it shouldn't be here. It needs to be destroyed."

"And I take it our prick of a captor has other plans for it?"

Clara looked at Mackay and nodded. "Project Blue is an extension of a government initiative first trialled in the early seventies. The idea was to see if there was any gain from harnessing and using animal life as weapons of war. There were a few trials with wild lions that were taught to hunt enemy soldiers, and dolphins that were fitted with cameras and trained to swim off enemy coastlines and record naval movements and such. According to the records, it was too expensive and was shut down in nineteen eighty-three. When Andrews heard about the Bloop and was told of the potential scale of the creature, he immediately started to research Project Blue, which had been worked on by his father. It becomes a little hazy here as to what happened. Either way, it seems this is where Russo appeared on the scene. He had the connections high in the government to reopen Project Blue and be given control over it."

"Why bother?" Rainwater asked. "It was already a dead project by the sound of things."

"In the eighties it was. Since then, technology has come a long way, and Russo managed to convince someone way up the chain that he could pull this off. His plan is to find where this creature makes its lair, call in a huge support team who are waiting on standby. He wants to capture it, house it in captivity and if possible, clone it. One of these is devastating enough. Could you imagine an army of them?"

"Impossible, there isn't a place on earth that could hold it captive. Let alone the public reaction if people found out what was going on. Greenpeace for one would be all over this guy." Rainwater said.

"That's why he's so desperate to keep it under wraps. He knows if word got out, the entire project would be shelved. As to keeping it captive, it's not as impossible as you might think. I saw plans for a facility in Florida. It's all tied up in red tape and listed as a new multi-million dollar aquarium complex, which, in essence it will be. There's also a separate wing closed to the public with tanks more than big enough to house this thing."

"Sounds like a dumb move to me," Mackay said.

"No, actually it's brilliant." Rainwater said. "Where else to hide it but in plain sight? Nobody would ever really know as long as the area was big enough and completely closed off to the public. Easier to hide it there than in a specific custom made facility designed to house it."

"Exactly," Clara agreed. "Russo is pouring millions into this aquarium and has teams working round the clock to finish it. The outer structure is still being worked on, but documents in the folders I read point to the holding tank for the creature being just about ready."

"We need to tell someone, expose this for—"

"No time," Clara interjected. "This is happening now. By the time we tell anyone, this will be all over. Even if we exposed the facility in Florida, I have no doubts they can tie any investigation in enough red tape to last for years. They have all the bases covered."

"I think the both of you are missin' the point."

Clara and Rainwater looked at Mackay, who had a wry smile etched on his lips.

"What do you mean?" Rainwater asked.

"Well, it seems to me if the young lady here is locked in here with us, Russo must assume she knows about his little plan."

"He does." She said, watching the leathery fisherman.

"What makes either of you think any of us will get off this boat alive to be able to breathe a word of it?"

Rainwater felt cold fingers touch his spine at the simplicity of Mackay's words.

"You think they would go that far? Over a fish?" He asked.

"I do." Clara said, her throat dry as she said the words. "This Russo guy is willing to do anything to win. He has no boundaries. He's already seen one man killed to get what he wants. What makes you think he would stop?"

"Exactly," Mackay said, further stretching his grin as he looked at them in turn. "Look at what he has done already. He's already responsible for letting Ox die, as well as those people who were in the water when they tagged the fish. Do you really think he would lose any sleep if he decided to put a bullet in the heads of the three of us?" He snorted and rubbed at his stubble-fluffed cheeks. "No, I think the only reason we're still alive is because he's concentrating on finding our fish. Keeping his eyes on the prize as they say. Soon enough, his thoughts will come back to us, and he'll probably try to pander us with bullshit and keep us sweet, we all know what's coming eventually."

He held two fingers to his head and dropped his thumb, then grinned.

"The two of you need to face it, we're dead already. It just hasn't happened yet."

"We can fight." Rainwater said, triggering a dry chuckle from Mackay.

"Oh, I'm sure we could try, but I counted at least twelve men on deck, plus Russo and the other guy."

"Andrews, and my assistant, Dexter. Oh God, I hope he's alright." Clara said.

"Aye, Andrews," He repeated. "Most of em' are armed. Plus, this is their boat so we have no real means of escape. I like a gamble as much as the next man, but these odds are too steep for me."

"You can't give up," Rainwater said, holding the Scotsman's gaze.

"Oh, don't worry. I won't go down without fighting. I'll be doing all I can to take that bastard Morrison with me. I just don't want you to get all excited about some grand old escape plan that ain't gonna happen."

"Can we get word to your assistant? Get him to help us?"

"I don't see how," Clara said, shaking her head. "After we tried to get off the boat, they confined him to his room. Even if he did come looking for me, it's not like they're about to tell him where I am."

"Any ideas?" Rainwater asked Mackay.

"I suggest for now we wait here and see what happens. With a bit of luck, this bastard fish will eat him and put an end to this. Until then, it's a case of waiting to see if this damn crazy idea of theirs works."

CHAPTER 43

Ocean world Construction site
Florida coast
5:45am.

Tom Royston woke to the high-pitched tone of his alarm clock. The forty four year old foreman swung his legs out of bed and rubbed his eyes. The air conditioning unit growled under the window, which although irritating was better than having to face the stifling humidity. Ignoring the aches that had beset his body over the last few weeks, he stood, shuffling towards the bathroom. As he urinated, he wished he was back in England. He enjoyed the sun as much as anybody did, but this was unbearable. For five weeks, he had been overseeing construction of the giant lagoon part of the complex. As was the American way, it really was huge. Shifts of men were working in constant twelve-hour rotations, meaning the site was always a hive of activity. He was foreman for the seven to seven shift, and even though he hadn't looked outside, he knew by the golden bars of sunlight, which were trying to penetrate the curtains, it was going to be another scorcher.

He walked to the window, pulling open the curtains and letting in the intrusive sunlight. His view, such as it was, consisted of the skeletal construction in progress. Looming ahead was the giant dome of the lagoon complex, its intimidating steel framework shimmering in the heat. Working in such oppressive conditions was bad enough, however his contract also stated he had to live on site until construction was complete. He, along with the rest of the workforce, had been provided with temporary accommodation, and the money was good so he didn't complain. He turned his attention towards the workday and hoped the night shift had managed to meet their quota. They had been lagging of late, and it had been down to his dayshift to pick up their slack. Even so, it didn't really matter. The lagoon was ready for all intents and purposes. There was just a couple of weeks' worth of minor work to be done, then they could move on to the rest of the complex.

As he looked at the giant structure, he had to hand it to the Americans. When they got their teeth into a project, they always went big with it. It looked more like a football stadium from the outside than an aquarium and he wondered how much it must be costing the people who were bankrolling it.

Still, none of that was his problem. He had work to do, and pay to earn. With a sigh, he headed back to the bathroom and started to get ready to go to work.

Forty-five minutes later, he was making his way across the construction site, hardhat tucked under his arm. The heat was already borderline unbearable, and he was certain they were in for one hell of a day. As he approached the huge domed wall of the aquarium, he could see the night supervisor, Trautman, waiting for him. He was pacing by the door.

"What the hell are you doing here?" Tom asked, as he looked the portly Brooklyn native up and down.

"Overtime," he said, exhaling acrid cigarette smoke and rolling his narrow eyes at Royston.

"Overtime? For what? We're way ahead of schedule."

Trautman shrugged, "Damned if I know. All I was told is the people in charge want this project finished and quick. Until it's done, they are offering to pay the guys as many hours as they can put in."

"What's the rush?"

"They didn't say. All I know is they want the lagoon bowl finished and filled by Sunday."

"Next Sunday?"

"I wish. *This* Sunday."

"Today is Wednesday. We need at least a couple of weeks."

Trautman nodded. "I know, I told them the same. They said there's a bonus in it for us if we can get it done on time."

Tom nodded and looked at the imposing dome, grateful to be standing in its cooling shadow.

"I don't see why they're so desperate to get this thing finished. What's the rush?" Royston asked.

"I don't know, and frankly I don't care. I'm on overtime rate, so as long as they pay me to be here, I'll be here."

Tom nodded, squinting at the pristine blue sky.

"Well, in that case, I guess we better get back to work."

"I'll follow you in, I'm just going to finish this smoke." Trautman said, holding up the tempting looking cancer stick to Royston.

Resisting the urge to snatch it from his hand and smoke it, Tom put on his hard hat and went inside.

CHAPTER 44

The creature went deep, attempting to quell the searing pain where the barbed harpoon had struck. The *Victorious* followed at a distance, matching every move and change of direction the creature made.

"Do you still have him?" Russo asked.

Andrews lowered his headset.

"Signal is good and strong. We're right behind it."

"I wonder where it's heading?"

"Somewhere familiar. A territorial hotspot. Somewhere our fish likes to call home."

Both Andrews and Russo looked at Morrison, who was leaning on the wall, deftly rocking with the motion of the boat as he hand rolled a cigarette.

"What makes you so sure?" Andrews asked.

"Hunch," Morrison replied as he licked the edge of the cigarette paper and rolled it tight.

"This is a multimillion dollar mission," Andrews countered. "I think we need more than a hunch."

Morrison sighed and looked at Russo, then turned his attention to Andrews.

"Well, whilst you have been here hanging off Russo's dick, I've been tracking this thing. I've also been studying its feeding patterns. It's all there if you choose to look for it. Since it found its way into the world, our fish has been without challenge."

Despite the no smoking signs, Morrison popped the cigarette into his mouth and lit it, exhaling through his nostrils. Andrews looked about ready to protest when Morrison continued speaking.

"When the harpoon dart hit our fish, it got him just here."

Morrison pointed to the soft tissue above his eye. "It will have hurt. All those nerve endings will have come alive, and our fish here, he's not used to pain. He's used to being king of the seas. So he runs and we chase. According to the radar, he's gone deep, and my guess is to try to cool the burning. Our fish isn't used to it. It panics. What would you do in that situation?"

Andrews stammered as Morrison watched him.

"Let me help you out," he said, letting Andrews off the hook. "You'd go somewhere familiar. Somewhere you could go and lick your wounds. You'd go back to wherever you called home. That's where our fish is going, and we're gonna follow it."

"Do we have any idea where?" Andrews asked.

Russo looked to Morrison, who took a long drag of his cigarette. "Antarctica is my guess. Back to where it came from."

Andrews nodded, and Morrison grinned, taking another drag of his cigarette.

"Keep me informed." Russo said, as he headed below deck.

Andrews watched Morrison as he smoked.

"Let me ask you something," he said.

"Shoot."

"Do you think we can do it? Catch it? Clone it?"

"I don't know much about that," Morrison replied as he exhaled more acrid cigarette smoke. "All I do know is that this is a big, dangerous animal. If it wanted to, it could tear this boat apart and none of us would stand a chance. Then I remind myself it's just a fish, and if we use our brain and outsmart it, we can take it easily enough."

"What if you're wrong?"

Morrison shrugged, "If I'm wrong, I don't think it really matters. We won't live long enough to worry about it."

CHAPTER 45

Russo made his way below deck towards where his prisoners were held. Although he would rather not go to the trouble of getting his hands dirty, it was looking increasingly likely he would have to, especially with their insistence on interfering in the mission every chance they got. With the creature tagged, all that remained was to track the creature to its lair. Once the location was established, Russo would contact the 880-foot Navy battleship Titus.

Officially decommissioned in the mid-nineties, the records said the ship had been dismantled and sold for parts, however, the truth was it had never left dock. Its serial numbers had been changed, as had all its markings identifying its previous lineage. In essence, it was a ghost ship. Russo's department had spent a small fortune converting the boat to accommodate his needs. Its innards had been removed and remodelled, the aircraft hangers replaced with laboratories and rooms to house the 2,000 strong staff on board. The bulk of the remodelling and much of the multi-million dollar budget had been spent on the five hundred foot long holding tank designed to transport the creature. Located centrally in the hull, the corridor like enclosure was designed to hold the animal in place safely without allowing it the manoeuvrability to let it cause problems for the duration of its journey and overbalance the ship. At the bow, seawater was fed via pressurised tubes through the tank and out of rearward facing exit pipes, ensuring a constant flow of seawater allowed the creature to breathe. There had been some concerns over the stress, which may be caused to the creature under such conditions, each of which Russo had swept aside. Even if the creature didn't survive, he was still confident the cloning could still take place. His team were under instructions to take blood and tissue samples from the creature as soon as it was on board. He fished a fresh roll of mints out of his pocket, popped one in his mouth and entered the storage room.

"What the hell do you want?" Mackay said, spitting on the floor for good measure.

Russo simply smiled and sucked his mint, rolling it around his mouth.

"How long do you plan to hold us here?" Clara asked.

"That depends on the three of you." Russo replied, sitting on the lip of a wooden box filled with potatoes. "I've come here to offer you all a chance to fix this mess, and save us all any more of this unpleasantness."

He waited for an answer, and when none came, he continued. "I appreciate we've had a few disagreements."

"Disagreements? You had an innocent man shot." Mackay snapped.

"That was a mistake, I won't deny that. You left me with no choice."

"Yeah, Project Blue right?" Rainwater said.

Russo's smile faltered for a second.

"I'm surprised you know about that," He said to Rainwater whilst looking at Clara. "Although, maybe I shouldn't be."

"It's a mistake. You know it as well as we do." Clara said, forcing herself to meet his gaze.

"I thought you were all for conserving these creatures? Studying them for the benefit of science." He countered, reaffirming his grin. "You need to pick a side and stick to it, Miss Thompson."

"It's not about sides," Rainwater cut in, "it's about doing the right thing. This isn't something you can weaponise or control."

"You have it wrong. You see me as some kind of monster, hell bent on creating the next super weapon to feed my own ego. What about the other benefits? What if this creature has properties that can advance science? Cure diseases? Would you call me a monster then, or a visionary?"

"That's bullshit and you know it," Clara said, the colour rushing to her cheeks. "You don't care about advances in science, or the safety of us or anyone involved. All you care about is completing the mission."

"For someone who is supposed to examine evidence with an open mind, that's a pretty judgemental viewpoint."

"What did you expect?" She shouted, surprising both Mackay and Rainwater. "You put a gun to my head, you lock me in here, and you threaten me. I only came here to do a job, not risk my life."

"And yet here you are. I wonder if you know what side you are on."

"I don't have a side!" She screamed, glaring at Russo. "I'm a scientist, I thought I was going to be able to study a brand new species, I didn't expect to be treated like a prisoner."

"You aren't a prisoner." He shot back, for the second time, his smile faltering.

"Shoving us in here and locking the door says otherwise." Rainwater cut in.

"Look," he said holding his palms up and finding his greasy smile again, "we're going off track here. I came here to make peace, not point the finger."

"Tell that to Ox." Mackay grunted.

"I'm sorry about your friend, I'm afraid he was a -"

"Don't say casualty of war, or collateral damage or any of that shit," Mackay said, standing and taking a half step towards Russo. "As it is, I'm only a hair away from breaking those fucking shiny white teeth of yours."

"Take it easy," Rainwater said, hopping to his feet and standing between Mackay and Russo.

"You should listen to your friend." Russo said, his confidence restored now there was a physical barrier between him and Mackay. "You can either move into a nice cabin with a window and relax until this mission is over, after which, we will drop you back at port and let you go on your way, or you can stay here. All you need to do is sign disclaimers, confidentiality agreements bound by-"

"Forget it." Mackay said. "You're going down for this, Russo. You can shove your disclaimers up your arse."

"Do you speak for everyone?" Russo said, eyebrows raised as he looked at Rainwater and Clara in turn. Neither of them spoke, and so he sighed and shook his head. "So you'd all rather stay locked in here and face trial for interfering in government business? If that happens, believe me, I'll make sure you all rot in the worst hellhole on the planet. *That*, I can guarantee."

He looked at them again, waiting for a reaction. When none came, he sighed and shook his head.

"It seems I've done all I can. If you don't want my help, I'm afraid I have no choice but to have you arrested as soon as we return to port. I wish the outcome would have been different."

"We'll take our chances." Rainwater said. Stepping back alongside Mackay.

"Very well, you can't say I didn't try."

"You know this won't work, don't you?" Clara said as Russo walked towards the door.

"That question might concern me if I thought you had the slightest idea about our ability to complete this mission. We have everything under control."

"Are you sure about that? Are you absolutely certain you've taken everything into account?"

Russo hesitated, and then turned back towards Clara.

"Let me guess, you think we've missed something, some minor detail, some overlooked thing you have seen? Let me assure you, there are greater minds than yours working on this."

Clara flinched, and seeing the chink in her armour, Russo exploited it.

"Really?" he said, his grin growing wider. "Did you really, genuinely, think a multimillion dollar mission, vital to the national security of this country, would be dictated by the opinions and guidance of a mere marine biologist?"

Clara took a step back, as Russo continued to turn the screw.

"You were only here to verify our findings. We had our own people making the real decisions."

"Andrews said…"

"Andrews says whatever I tell him to say. Just like he thinks whatever I tell him to think, eats when I tell him to eat, and shits when I tell him to shit."

Russo's decimation of her had been astounding, deflating her confidence in just a few seconds. Mackay stepped forward, teeth gritted as he put a reassuring hand on her shoulder.

"Forget this prick," he said, glaring at Russo. "He might think he has all the answers, but there's one thing he hasn't allowed for."

"Oh really?" Russo said, growing more and more confident. "And what might the greatest brains on the planet have forgotten that the fisherman has remembered?"

Now it was Mackay's turn to grin, and the wildness in his eyes made Russo squirm a little.

"Out there. You fucks might have all the answers, gadgets, and high tech shit a simple fisherman like me can't understand, but you don't know the sea. I'll bet my arse you don't know these waters."

"Is that supposed to frighten me? Water is water. The *Victorious* is perfectly safe."

"Aye it is now," Mackay shot back. "Wait until we hit those cold Antarctic seas."

Russo squirmed, and his grin took on a fixed, elastic look. Just as Russo had done to Clara, so Mackay did to him, turning the screw without mercy.

"When you get out there, you'll have violent seas. Waves of forty feet at least, maybe as high as sixty. This smooth ride you are enjoying now will become a fuckin' rollercoaster. Temperature will be well below freezing. With the wind chill, it will feel like knives hacking at your bones. It will be so cold, you won't be able to feel your hands or feet. Our monster ploughs on of course. He doesn't care about the cold. This big old ship of yours, she ain't designed to be out here. See a big hull like this is prime for ice build-up. The spray thrown by the bow will freeze to the ship. What happens then is it starts to weigh you down. Steering don't work so well. Suddenly, this boat you are so sure of, starts getting tossed around by the waves like paper in a breeze. By now, all these braniacs you have on board are feeling sick. Every roll of the boat feels like it's gonna capsize her, every wave you crest feels like you are goin' nose first into the ocean.

"Your captain, as experienced as he might think he is, won't know what to do. Maybe a wave comes, a rogue eighty footer, catches you broadside. It hits with the force of a thousand freight trains. Already weighted with ice, the boat goes over. Up becomes down, left becomes right. The lights go out. You might hear screaming. You might feel icy water pouring in on you. You don't know where from. You don't know how to get out."

Mackay grinned, as everyone looked on and watched him in awe.

"Boat like this, heavy with ice will go down in maybe ten minutes. Less if the waves slam it again. This water, it's cold enough to take the breath away from even a gobshite like you. Within sixty seconds of being submerged, your core temperature will drop. Hypothermia sets in. A strong man might hang on for fifteen, twenty minutes. A scrawny shit like you won't make it more than five, if you manage to escape the vessel before it sinks that is. You'll be in the water, wind raging in your ears, body so numb with cold you won't be able to feel if you are still kicking to stay afloat. Come the end, you'll beg to die."

"You underestimate how strong I am," Russo said without conviction.

"Maybe," Mackay replied, "maybe not. You'll beg to die, because if the water don't get you, then our beastie is still out there and you can bet your arse it will come calling when it gets hungry."

"Then it looks like we'll all die together."

Russo didn't quite manage to sound as confident as he had hoped.

"Aye, maybe we will. Difference between you and me, is I know what to do to try to survive. You might not think so now you arrogant prick, but you'll need me before I need you, especially when those seas start to get rough."

Russo opened his mouth, and clamped it shut again. He looked at them all in turn, and then closed and locked the door.

"I hope that was a bluff," Clara said quietly.

"I only wish it was." Mackay replied.

Five miles ahead, the creature continued to head into colder waters as the *Victorious* gave chase.

CHAPTER 46

Royston wiped the sweat from his brow and looked out at the imposing lagoon below him. At an impressive two thousand feet in diameter, and the same at its deepest point, Royston was sure it had to be one of the biggest man made containment facilities in the world. It was an impressive sight. He watched as cranes lifted panelled sections into position, closing off the last few sunlight filled areas of the large domed roof. Jackhammers drilled, machinery growled as thousands of workmen scurried around. It truly was a thing of beauty, and looked even more impressive from his lofty position at the back of the structure. Trautman joined him, and for a moment, they simply watched.

"Looking good ain't it?" Trautman said.

"It is. I was worrying about finishing for Sunday, and here we are ahead of schedule."

"That's why I'm here actually. I just got word we need to start filling this thing tonight."

Royston turned towards Trautman. "It's not ready yet, tell them we can't."

"They weren't askin'," Trautman said with a sour grin. "Assholes said they want the pumps switched on by late this afternoon."

"That's not a problem in itself, the structure will be fine, but the filtration system is-"

"I know I know. No need to preach to the converted. I already told em' we don't have it online yet, plus the roof isn't finished and the thousand or so other minor jobs that still need to be done. Hell, you know what these assholes can be like. They didn't want to know. They insisted, so I told them we would go ahead and start pumping seawater into this place as long as they didn't hold us responsible if it all goes to shit."

"Are the pumps online? That was all assigned to you guys on second shift." Royston said.

"My guys got the job done. Those things are ready to go. We can start pumping seawater into this place as soon as we get everyone clear of the bowl."

"Why do you think they're in such a rush?"

"Who knows? As long as I get paid, I really don't give a shit." Trautman said, looking at his watch. "Do me a favour, get any of your people out of the bowl, we start the pumps in an hour. By late this afternoon, this place will be full of seawater. Let's hope those filtration systems work like it should, or repairing them is going to be a bitch."

"What do you suppose they plan to keep in here?" Royston asked.

"Couple of the guys have been wondering the same. I hear it could be whales, a family of them. Something about studying how they interact or some shit like that," Trautman said, shrugging his shoulders. "Whatever it is, it's none of my business. I just wanna get this job done and get out of this damn heat."

"I hear that." Royston agreed, because he too wanted away from the build. There was something off about it, something not quite right with how the entire thing was being run. The sooner he was on a flight back to England, the better. Something in his gut told him things were about to go bad. He unclipped the radio from his belt, patching in to his crews.

"Clear the bowl, I repeat, clear the bowl. We're filling her in an hour."

CHAPTER 47

Barraged by a vicious Antarctic storm, the *Victorious* ploughed ahead, somehow managing to stay afloat. The sky had turned to the colour of lead, and was already blasting sleet at the boat with increasing velocity.

"We have to call this off," Andrews said, staring at Russo who looked impassively out of the wheelhouse window, his view a bucking, rolling landscape of waves and snow.

"The path to paradise begins in hell."

"What is that, Shakespeare or something?" Andrews asked.

"Dante, and quite appropriate, don't you think?"

"Come on, Russo, you have it tagged. This storm is only going to get worse if we-"

"The storm doesn't interest me."

"We could all die!" Andrews said, garnering a few nervous glances from the crew. Russo saw it, and offered a cold smile.

"Are you afraid of a few waves and a little snow? I thought you Langley boys would be made of sterner stuff."

"Come on, this isn't about measuring dicks. We have people on board and this storm is only going to get worse. Look at these charts," he said, thrusting the papers towards Russo. "We're heading right into the middle of a category three storm. If you think this is bad, just wait until later."

"You feel free to panic if you must. I'm completely confident this vessel can handle anything the ocean can throw at it."

"Enough of the Americana bullshit. You think this storm cares about the history of this boat? You think it cares that you think we're indestructible?" He pointed to the officer piloting the boat, who looked completely out of his depth. "You really think this guy can steer us safely through these waters? Look at him!"

"And yet, you seem to be the only one complaining."

"That's because everyone else is too afraid to tell you how it is. If you want to throw your life away, then that's fine. You don't have the right to drag the rest of us along with you."

"You can get off at any time, it's not like we need you around here anyway."

"You're a god damn liability, Russo," Andrews said, striding across the wheelhouse and towards his quarters. Russo only grinned, then turned back to the dizzying, undulating seascape.

"Is that true?" he whispered next to the pilot's ear. "Is it true you're out of your depth?"

"Sir, I…" The young pilot stammered.

"It's okay. I just need to know if we need to get someone else to do this."

"Sir, I'm prepared to stay at the controls, but if there is someone more capable on board, I would be happy to step aside."

Russo stood and felt his stomach somersault as the boat crested a thirty-foot wave and smashed into the sea, sending a huge white wall of spray exploding into the air. He unhooked his radio from his belt and lifted it to his mouth.

"Mito, bring our guests. I need to speak to them."

Ten minutes later, Mackay, Rainwater and Clara stood in the wheelhouse, watched carefully by Mito and his men.

"Before you ask, it's a no." Mackay snapped.

"I want you to take the controls of this boat. I can make it worth your while." Russo said anyway.

"I bet you will. I'm still not interested."

"Even if I let you and your friends go?" Russo asked, eyebrows raised.

"Seems to me that's out of your hands now. By the looks of things, you'll be lucky to see dawn again."

"Which is why I want you to take over. You know these waters. You know how to navigate them safely."

"Not in conditions like these." Mackay said, finding a smile despite his stomach rolling as the boat slewed across the waves.

"Are you admitting you aren't good enough? Are you rejecting the challenge?" Russo asked, flicking his eyes to Clara then back to Mackay. The grizzled fisherman grinned.

"If you're trying to talk me into proving you wrong, it won't work. There's no way in hell I'm gonna bail you out of this one. You made the call to come into what looks to be the mother of all storms, and will have to deal with the consequences."

"You don't understand what I'm saying," Russo said. "This is just the edge of it. We're heading right into a category three, and it seems we're unequipped to deal with it."

Mackay's confident sneer faltered and he exchanged worried glances with Rainwater.

"You have to pull out. Get back to dock." Rainwater said.

"I can't do that."

"I don't think you get it," Mackay said, "there ain't' no safe way to navigate a category three storm. I told you what would happen, but you were too stubborn to listen."

"Just call it off, pick up the search in a few days." Rainwater cut back in.

Russo stood and stared, elastic grin etched onto his face. "I have a job to do. How can I go back to my superiors and tell them I was derailed by a storm."

"That won't matter," Mackay said, "because if you don't turn back, there's a good chance none of us will make it out of here alive."

"Take the controls. Guide us safely to my monster, and I'll guarantee you will be freed and all charges against you dropped."

"Fuck you," Mackay said, grinning at Russo.

Rainwater was sure Russo would break. Instead, he nodded and turned to the flustered captain who was struggling to control the ship.

"Do you have a name, son?" Russo asked.

"Jenkins, sir." He replied, as a twenty-foot wave smashed over the bow, smattering the windows with icy seawater.

"Stand down. You've taken us as far as you can."

"Sir, I—"

"That's an order, Jenkins. Relinquish the controls."

Jenkins did as he was told, leaving the boat without a pilot.

"Don't be an idiot, Russo, You need someone to steer the boat. If you don't hit the waves just right, we'll capsize." Rainwater said, glancing to the rolling seas outside.

"Tell your friend to do as I've asked."

"Nobody tells me what to do. Especially not you," Mackay said, holding Russo's gaze.

"Then it looks like we're in fate's hands."

The boat bucked and rolled, prompting Mito to step towards the controls.

"Don't you touch those!" Russo screamed, the veins bulging out of his neck. Mito shrank back, and like everyone else watched out of the window as the boat forged ahead without anyone to control it.

"Is this creature really worth it?" Clara said, trying to ignore the icy fear in her gut. "Is it worth our lives, *your* life?"

" This isn't just about the creature," Russo said, grinning as the boat was hit broadside by a wave and listed sickly to the right, before righting itself. "This is about orders. About seeing a job through to the end. This is about my reputation."

"All you'll be remembered for is failure, and getting a boat full of people killed." Rainwater said, balling his fists hard enough to leave tiny white crescents in his palms.

"No. I'll be remembered as the man who gave his all, including his life to try to complete his mission. I'm prepared for whatever comes. I wonder if you are too."

"I told you before. Death doesn't scare me. If it's my time, it's my time," He glared at Russo. "But unlike you, I have a duty to protect my friends. I'll pilot this boat for you, but I ain't taking it into a storm."

"You'll stay on course; otherwise, I'll have one of your friends thrown overboard. Remember, I only need you. Think about that."

Mackay walked towards the controls, and paused to glare at Russo. "I'll get you for this. I promise you that."

"Don't take it personally. We all have a job to do. Mine happens to be one of those dirty ones that nobody else seems to want."

Mackay paid no attention, instead staring out of the window as he took the controls.

"Are you a religious man, Russo?" Mackay asked as he steered into another giant wave.

"I went to church when I was a boy, why?"

"I suggest you start praying. Because from here on out, there are no guarantees."

"Get us safely through this storm and I'll make it worth your while."

"I don't want anything from you."

"Surely there's something you want? Something to make you more willing to give one hundred percent into keeping us alive?"

Mackay paused for a few seconds, then spoke almost too quietly to be heard.

"I want Morrison. Five minutes alone in a room with him."

"Interesting," Russo said with a grin. "Get us through the storm in one piece, and I'll let you have your little fist fight."

Mackay shook his head and shut off the engine.

"What the hell are you doing?" Russo said, glaring from Mackay to the controls and then to the tracking screen following the creature.

"You think I'd trust a slimy son of a bitch like you? I want my five minutes with Morrison now."

"The storm…"

"Storm isn't bad enough yet. Not here on its edge. Give me my five minutes, and I'll drive this boat of yours straight up this monster's arse. I can drop anchor here until we are done."

The wheelhouse was silent as the boat rocked and rolled and sleet barraged the windows. Russo held Mackay's gaze, then turned to Mito.

"Find Morrison. Organise a room. Let's get his over with."

Mito nodded and disappeared below deck. Three miles away, the violent storm was growing stronger.

CHAPTER 48

"This is crazy, you know that, right?" Rainwater said as he waited with Mackay. "This guy's a killer."

"I know what he is," Mackay said, watching as Morrison walked down the corridor towards him. "That doesn't change a damn thing."

"Don't you think you're out of your depth here? You can't beat this guy."

"We'll see."

Morrison stopped in the narrow corridor, looking Mackay up and down.

"I'm told you want to fight with me." He said, flicking his eyes to Russo. "And it seems our host has no problem with it."

"I don't," Russo said. "If he wants to get himself beaten to a pulp that's up to him."

"You hear that, Mac? This is the last chance you'll get to pull out." Morrison said, offering a warm smile.

"No, I want this."

Even though he was trying to hide it, Rainwater could see the uncertainty in Mackay's eyes. Morrison however looked supremely confident as he removed his glasses and handed them to Clara.

"Hold on to these for me would you?" he said, his eyes never leaving Mackay. "I'm not sure if you're brave or stupid, Mac, so I'm going to go easy on you." He said, pulling his sweater off and exposing his slim torso.

Although Mackay was physically superior of the two, there was a danger about Morrison that everybody could sense.

"Don't," Mackay said, pulling off his sweater and handing it to Rainwater. "I won't be going easy on you, that you can count on."

"Don't worry," Russo said, leaning close to Mackay's ear. "I told him he isn't allowed to kill you. I still need you to drive this boat."

"What if I kill him?"

"If I thought that was even a remote possibility, this wouldn't be happening." Russo replied, flashing a cruel smile as he stood and addressed the group.

"Here's how this will go down. The two of you will go into the storeroom. You have five minutes to beat the shit out of each other, after which, this is over and we get back to work. Understood?"

Mackay nodded, Morrison bounced from one foot to the other, his eyes never leaving his opponent.

"In that case, let's do this before our creature gets too far ahead of us."

Russo nodded to one of the armed guards by the door, who pushed it open, exposing the bare steel walled room.

"Let's get this over with," Morrison said, striding into the room and waiting for Mackay.

"Hey, you don't need to do this. It won't bring Ox back. Let it go." Rainwater said quietly.

"I can't, lad. I need to do this."

Without another word, he strode into the room.

"Okay, the five minutes begins when the door is closed. Try not to make a mess." Russo said, and nodded to Mito, who closed and locked the door.

With the workforce clear of the aquarium, Trautman and Royston stood by the controls for the water pumps. Connected by a series of underwater pipes, the pumps were located in six separate locations around the edge of the holding tank. When activated, they would open, sucking in thousands of gallons of seawater per second. A complex filtration system would ensure nothing other than pure seawater would be pulled into the bowl. A secondary system, much like those found in water parks, would manipulate the water once in the bowl, creating currents and waves, in essence turning the aquarium into a miniature indoor ocean.

"I hope you and your guys put this together right, Trautman."

"Don't worry about that, just activate the pumps and we can all go home and get some shuteye."

Royston Nodded and both men started flicking on the master switches. A dull hum filled the air as the console illuminated in sequence.

"Okay," Trautman said, glancing at Royston, "let's fill her up."

Almost immediately, gallons of seawater began to spew into the massive holding tank, the sound echoing around the cavernous walls with a mighty roar.

"Pressures look good," Trautman bellowed over the noise. "All pumps are functioning. I told you my boys wouldn't let me down."

Royston nodded as he watched the water level slowly begin to rise.

"Anyhow, I better go tell our insistent owners we've started to fill this son of a bitch," Trautman said, clapping Royston on the shoulder. "Keep an eye on those gauges, I'll be back in five."

"Okay that's it. Time's up." Russo said, motioning to Mito to open the door.

Mito did as he was instructed. Morrison walked out, sweat beading on his brow. His knuckles were bloody, and apart from a cut lip, his narrow face was unmarked. He grinned at Clara, and held out his hand for his glasses.

"Thanks," he said as he slipped them on, making his way down the corridor towards his quarters. Rainwater and Clara pushed past into the room, ignoring the stench of blood and sweat.

Mackay was on the floor, curled against the wall. Despite the size and weight advantage, it was obvious he had been no match for Morrison. His breathing was wet and ragged, and as he looked at Rainwater and Clara through puffy, half-closed eyes, he even managed a bloody smile.

"Well, that didn't go how I expected," he wheezed, spitting blood onto the floor.

"Jesus, Mac," Rainwater blurted, helping his friend to his feet. "Someone get him a doctor," he yelled to those gathered outside, who were watching with indifference.

"He's a slippery little bastard," Mackay gasped as Clara got under his other arm and supported him as he tried to walk. "He really knows where to hit too."

"You were lucky," Russo said from the doorway. "He could have easily killed you."

"He needs help, we need to get him to a doctor." Rainwater said as MacKay's legs buckled.

"No doctors. No more distractions. We had a deal. I held up my end, now it's his turn to do the same."

"He could have broken ribs, internal bleeding," Clara said. "Please, help him."

"I'll have our physician on board look him over as soon as we're on the way. Here." He handed Clara a half bottle of scotch and a first aid kit. "Give him some of that. It should stop his shakes and bring him round a little –"

"You son of a bitch," She hissed as Russo grinned in response, not missing a beat.

"– then clean him up. I don't want him bleeding all over the wheelhouse. I want him ready to get underway in fifteen minutes."

"He's in no fit state to do anything, look at him!" Rainwater screamed.

"I see," Russo shot back, and strode across the room, smoothly pulling his pistol from inside his jacket and pressing it to Mackay's head.

"In that case, maybe we should put him out of his misery?"

"Itsokayitsokay…" Mackay mumbled. "I'll be ready, I'll do it…"

Russo smiled, and rather than remove his weapon, pushed it harder into Mackay's forehead.

"I could crush you right now, all of you," Russo hissed. "Despite that, I'm still trying to do the right thing. You should all remember that if you want to get out of here alive."

He stepped back and slipped the gun back into its holster, and took a deep breath.

"Fifteen minutes. Don't make me come and find you."

Russo made his leave, prompting the watching crowd to disperse and go back to their duties.

"We need to get off this boat," Rainwater whispered as he helped to sit Mackay on the floor.

Clara didn't reply, but the look in her eye told him she felt exactly the same way.

CHAPTER 49

Dexter lay in his bunk, staring at the roof of his cabin. Even though he had tried to pull himself together, he couldn't rid the image of Russo pointing the gun at his face, from his mind, or the deep, numbing fear it instilled. He had never known fear before, not real fear anyway. The closest thing to it was when he got lost in the Amazon during an expedition to study chimpanzee populations, and spent three days without food or water trying to find the rest of his team. As frightening as that was, it didn't remotely compare to the outright horror as he looked at the sightless eye of the gun that had been trained on him. All he could think about was how close he had come to the end of his life. Game over. No second chances.

He hadn't been to church since he was a boy, but as he looked down the void of the gun barrel, he prayed anyway, mumbling to a god who he had long ago stopped believing in for the pursuit of science. As he stood waiting to die, he thought about all of the things he never did, or would never get to do. He would never finish his book on Darwinian evolutionary theories. He would never reconcile with his drunk of a father who had, on more than one occasion held out the olive branch. He would never ride a rollercoaster or have children of his own.

He looked around the windowless room and tried to ignore the unease that crept through his guts. These were bad people, that much was obvious, and whatever was going on was way above his and Clara's heads. They were biologists, not soldiers or pawns in some elaborate game. Part of him – the repressed Dexter who was full of confidence and swagger – wanted to fight and find out what the hell was going on. The other Dexter, the one who was shy and timid and afraid he might find himself looking down the business end of another gun, was refusing to cooperate. That side of him was saying he was best to keep out of it, to let these people do whatever it is they wanted to do as long as he got to go on living. It was a selfish outlook, and one that the confident inner Dexter didn't yet have the fight to overcome, and so he remained in place on his bunk, thinking of a million reasons to do something proactive and just as many to stay where he was. As he lay fighting with his conscience, the engines rumbled to life, and they were underway again, the room swaying and rocking as the boat rolled through the water. Confident inner Dexter told him to get out of bed and see what the hell was going on, but he was quickly silenced by his cowardly counterpart, who told him whilst he was out of sight he was out of mind, and as a result, out of trouble. As before, there was no real fight. He stayed where he was, unaware that the *Victorious* was heading straight down the throat of a storm.

CHAPTER 50

The *Victorious* sliced through the giant swells of the storm that tried to capsize the boat. As they neared the centre, the rain had transformed into snow, which flurried against the wheelhouse windows making visibility next to impossible. Inside, the tension was palpable as they sat in the darkness. Mackay peered out of the window, making minor adjustments to the controls as he tried to second guess the direction of the waves. He had barely spoken during the six hours he had been in control of the vessel, apart from demanding that the lights be extinguished so he could better see the landscape. Rainwater had no idea how anyone could possibly navigate in such conditions. The visibility was so poor that he could barely see the bow of the boat as it crested each wave. Each roll of the boat took his stomach with it, and with every one, he was sure they would go over. Somehow, the vessel stayed upright.

Even in the gloom, Mackay's wounds were clearly visible, and the entire right side of his face now had an ugly blue-purple bruise. He seemed smaller somehow, as if whatever happened in the room with Morrison, had broken him on the inside as well as the outside. The tension even seemed to be getting to Russo, who was watching Mackay between intermittent glances at the radar screen.

Clara was listening to the radio, noting the weather updates as they came in. As unlikely as it seemed, an uneasy alliance had been built centred around survival.

"We're coming up on the ice pack," Clara said, her voice sharp and loud in the otherwise silent wheelhouse.

"Did anyone hear what I said, I said we-"

"We heard you," Russo said, giving her a quick glance. "It's under control."

"You need to abort, you can't go through the ice field. It will tear this boat apart. Mackay, tell him."

"His boat. His problem." Mackay grunted, his eyes never leaving the window.

"Just make sure you keep on that signal. No matter what it takes."

A huge wave broadsided the boat, rocking it violently as it forged ahead. For a sick, horrifying moment, Rainwater was sure they were about to capsize. The vessel creaked and vibrated, sending Clara's charts sliding across the floor, even Russo looked afraid, gritting his teeth as he watched the cold, black Antarctic ocean threaten to swallow the boat. Somehow, the *Victorious* managed to stabilise itself, and the rollercoaster ride continued.

"Got a portside list," Mackay said, still not taking his eyes from the window.

"What does that mean?" Russo shot back. Mackay didn't reply.

"It means the boat is leaning to one side rather than going straight," Rainwater said, bracing as the vessel rode another sickening wave and smashed back into the ocean.

"Why would it do that?"

"Ice most likely clinging to the superstructure. You need to get some men outside to break it up. If we get hit broadside again, we could go over, and then this mission of yours is finished."

"We can't send anyone out there. We need to carry on and take our chances. We've already lost too much time."

Rainwater was about to respond, when the sound of something clattering against the hull stopped him.

"What the hell was that?" Russo said to nobody in particular.

"Ice," Mackay replied as another small iceberg clipped off the hull.

"Already?" He said, snatching the binoculars and trying to see through the blizzard.

"This is what we've been trying to tell you. This storm is going to be throwing these things at us at speed, it won't take much to put a hole in the boat, and then we're all screwed." Rainwater said as he snatched the binoculars from Russo and peered out into the storm.

The ocean was still an undulating mass, like a rippling, living creature as its froth tipped waves continued to barrage the vessel. As if that wasn't reason enough to worry, the water was now littered with icebergs, which, much like the *Victorious*, were at the mercy of the elements.

"The main ice pack is just ahead, you see it, Mackay?"

Rainwater looked to his friend, who didn't answer, nor did he acknowledge the intermittent thuds and scrapes as the boat was hit by the chunks of floating ice.

"Mackay?" Rainwater repeated.

"It's all ice here. Antarctic waters." He mumbled in return, still staring straight ahead.

"You think it's going back to the shelf don't you?" Clara asked Russo.

"The shelf?" Rainwater said, looking at Clara.

"The Ross Ice Shelf. It would be a perfect habitat for a creature like this. Maybe in some underwater cave or hollow or something."

"See, Dr Thompson? When you strip away the moralistic pettiness, it really is exciting isn't it?" Russo said, grinning at her.

"It won't matter anyway," Rainwater said, glancing out of the window. "Because if we don't fix that list, we won't make it long enough to find out."

"And I say again, who would you have me send out there in these conditions?"

"What about him?" Rainwater said, nodding towards Mito. "Or do you need to keep your little pet close at hand?"

Mito sneered as Russo considered the situation. "No," he said eventually, "I'll take the chance our captain can pilot us safely through the storm."

"You really don't know what you're up against here do you?" Rainwater said as another chunk of ice slammed into the hull of the boat. "This isn't a game. We're all at risk, every single one of us. You have a responsibility to—"

"My responsibility is to capture this creature."

"No, your responsibility is to making sure the crew of this vessel is safe. You either need to fix this problem, or get out of this storm."

"And I say again, who will you have go out to do it? My crew are soldiers, not fishermen."

"I'll do it."

Russo and Rainwater turned towards Andrews, who was already shrugging into his jacket.

"Why on earth would you do that?" Russo asked.

"Because he's right. You've lost sight of your responsibilities. This mission was never supposed to be about capture or using this fish as the basis for the next great military weapon. This was meant to be about discovery."

"Come on, surely you aren't still bitter about me treading on your toes? You'll get ample opportunity to study our fish once it's safely captured. That is, as long as you remember which side you're on."

"This isn't about sides. It's about survival. Frankly, I couldn't give a shit about the mission or this fish. Not anymore. You're a cancer, and all I want to do is survive long enough to get off this fucking boat."

"Don't put this on me," Russo said, pointing a finger at Andrews. "You knew what we were getting into. Don't pretend you're some innocent victim caught up in this."

"I knew what you were planning, I just didn't know how far you'd go. You outrank me, and I've been around long enough to know I have a job to do. Don't begin to think you can butter me up and play nice. I see through you, Russo. I know how you operate."

"Then you know what the consequences are for getting in my way."

"Drop the threats. They won't wash, not anymore, and you don't need them." Andrews said as he zipped his jacket.

"And why's that?"

"Because I know you won't rest until you complete this mission, so the best thing I can do is make it as smooth as possible, starting with de-icing this boat. I can't do it alone though. I need help."

"I'll do it." Rainwater said, stepping forward.

Andrews nodded. "We need more hands. Two at least. What about him?" Andrews said, nodding towards the towering Mito. "We could use his muscle."

"Done." Russo said. "You can also take Miss Thompson's assistant if you can get him out of his room. The earlier incident has shaken him badly I'm afraid."

"Okay, that's four. How long until we hit the worst of the storm?"

"Three hours or so." Clara said. "You need to be done by then no matter what. It's going to be bad."

"We better get a move on." Rainwater cut in as the boat was rocked by another wave crashing broadside into the hull.

CHAPTER 51

The four men stood by the hatch door, each carrying a sledgehammer and wearing protective rain gear as they prepared to head out onto deck. Rainwater looked at them in turn. Andrews looked ready and determined, Mito was defiant and cocky, a cigarette hanging out of the corner of his mouth, and finally there was Dexter. He had taken some convincing to come along and looked to be the most afraid. Rainwater wondered how long any of them would last before they broke.

"Okay," Rainwater said as he pulled on his beanie hat, realising that though he was a rookie, he was going to be by far the most experienced man on deck. "Be careful. Watch each other and let's break as much of this ice off as possible. Dump it over the side. That stuff can really hurt you if you get hit by it."

"Don't be so dramatic," Mito said. "You talk like it will be bullets flying around out there."

"You might be surprised."

"And why would that be?" The giant soldier shot back as he blew smoke in Rainwater's face.

"Because, I guarantee you the conditions out there are unlike anything you have ever experienced."

It was a good line to end on, and without waiting for a response, he pushed open the hatch door. Although the conditions were frightening enough from the wheelhouse, out on deck, it was altogether more terrifying. Rainwater led them from the safety of the ships innards, the wind biting his flesh and whistling around his ears. The thundering sound of the ocean as it threw great walls of freezing water in the air was the only thing able to blot out the incessant howling of the wind.

The deck rose and fell, rolling under their feet as they shuffle stepped towards the portside rail, which was only a thigh height away from tossing them into the freezing Antarctic sea. Mito's cigarette was plucked from his mouth and spiralled away from the vessel as he too now pulled a black beanie hat over his ears. He seemed a lot less confident.

"Okay," Rainwater shouted, barely audible over the wind. "Start on the external structure and whatever you do, keep your concentration. If you dislodge some of this ice and it comes down on top of your head, it could kill you."

"This is too dangerous," Dexter said, his stubble already flecked with snow.

"We have to do this. We don't have a choice." Rainwater shot back.

A jolting scrape shook the boat as it ploughed into another iceberg.

"Let's get to it. Two on the outer rail, two on the inner structure. Let's get this done as quickly as we can. Big guy," Rainwater said to Mito, "you come with me. You two start clearing that rail ice. Keep an eye on the water, if a rogue wave hits us, it will sweep you off the deck and into the ocean before you know it."

"Shouldn't we have life jackets?" Andrews asked, looking out at the undulating seascape.

"No need," Rainwater replied with a sick smile. "By the time we could turn around and come back for you, you would already be dead. Besides, I doubt Russo would turn this boat around anyway. Just keep that in mind, and lets clear as much of this ice off as we can."

"Got it," Andrews said, testing the weight of his hammer and staggering towards the portside rail, Dexter in tow.

"Come on," Rainwater said, "let's use that muscle of yours." Rainwater said as he swung the sledgehammer into a built up growth of ice on the outer roof of the door.

"You do this for a job?" Mito said as he too swung the hammer at the roof, bringing a great slab of ice crashing to the deck. "You must be crazy."

"No more than working for an egotistical prick like Russo," Rainwater countered as he swung again, putting more effort in than normal to try and match Mito's power, but falling short and only managing to crack the ice rather than shear it away. With the wind howling in his ears, and his fingers already numbing from the cold, he thought it would be a miracle if they all survived the night.

They worked in silence for more than two hours, too cold and exhausted to bother speaking or bickering. Rainwater's back and shoulders were on fire, his nose and ears numb as he continued to break away the build-up of ice. Even the muscular Mito seemed withdrawn, his earlier bravado replaced by a frown as he continued dislodging the ice build-up. Rainwater paused to look out to sea, breathing in sharp ragged gasps as he saw night finally start to become day. He checked his watch, and tapped Mito on the shoulder.

"Twenty more minutes then we have to go in."

Mito nodded, his eyes half lidded with exhaustion.

Across the deck, Andrews was also close to exhaustion, his body punished, his mind fried by the constant fear from flirting on the edge of death. From his position on the rail, the violence of nature was all too evident, the salty smell of the ocean all to close as it pounded the hull with incessant regularity. He glanced over to Dexter, who hadn't spoken a word for more than an hour. Like Rainwater, Andrews was sure he would be first to crack, and was surprised to see he was in fact, still reasonably fresh, and was still swinging his hammer with the same vigour they had all started with and had one by one faded as conditions took their toll. His hair was frozen to his head, his glasses frosted over, and yet, he still brought the hammer down on the ice, over and over again with metronome like regularity. Andrews had to admit, it was impressive. It seemed the frightened scientist was made of sterner stuff than all of them.

Although Andrews didn't know it, on the inside, Dexter was screaming. He could no longer feel his hands, and his body had long since gone beyond agony. He had heard about how some people could push themselves to new levels of tolerance when faced with extreme circumstances, in fact, he had been planning on writing an article on that very subject before he had agreed to come with Clara's on this god-forsaken voyage. He had intended to write about how such things were impossible, and a person's limits were just that – limitations that could not be surpassed – he knew now he was going to have to change his thesis, as he had long ago passed that point where he couldn't go on and was operating on some unknown plane. He was aware of the pain in his body, and the merciless bite of the cold. He knew the fear was there, a thick thing he could taste at the back of his throat with every single crested wave or thud of iceberg on the hull.

He was also aware he couldn't take anymore.

It seemed only he had any sense left, and nobody else could see, although chasing this creature under any circumstances was bad, chasing it into a category three storm was paramount to suicide. As his body had shifted to autopilot and taken care of the physical aspect, he had been quietly plotting how best to take control of the boat and steer them to safety.

Between swings, he glanced to Mito. He was Russo's main source of intimidation. He would have to go if there was to be any chance of taking over the boat. He was sure once they realised what was happening, Rainwater and Andrews would help. From the little snippets of information he had picked up, it seemed the only person who wanted to be out here was Russo. Everyone else was acting under protest.

He looked at the heavy hammerhead as he swung it against the rail, splintering a huge chunk of ice, which tumbled into the ocean. It would make a great equalizer. Casually, he turned and started to walk towards Rainwater and Mito, heart pounding in his chest, throat dry as the aches and pains in his body finally started to make themselves known. Mito's back was like a target, his slick yellow rain jacket a homing beacon. Despite his fear, his inner voice was calm, reassuring.

Hit him in the spine first, once more in the head. Do it quickly. Do it humanely.

He felt nauseous at the thought he was about to commit murder, but that reassuring inner voice was right there to sooth and correct him.

No, it's not murder. You are doing what needs to be done for the greater good. You are doing what you need to do for Clara.

That last thought seemed to settled his nerves a little, and he readjusted his grip on the hammer, and prepared to strike.

Rainwater saw Dexter's blue jacket out of the corner of his eye, and half turned towards him, intending to tell him they had to go back inside soon. Everything that happened next only took an instant, but seemed to play out in slow motion. He knew what Dexter was planning to do. He could see it in his eyes. They were wild and glaring, his teeth gritted as he reared back to swing the hammer at Mito.

"Look out!" Rainwater shouted.

Mito half turned and saw Dexter swinging the hammer. Even as big as he was, there was no way he could defend himself. It was at that point, as he was certain Mito was about to be killed that the sixty foot wave slammed into the boat, washing over the deck, hitting Mito, Rainwater, Andrews and Dexter like an express train. The boat rolled to the point of capsize, then righted itself. In the wheelhouse, Clara and Russo stared out of the window and the carnage below.

CHAPTER 52

Rainwater blinked saltwater out of his eyes, and drew in a great breath of air. He was on his back wedged against the portside rail. The deck was strewn with chunks of ice, which had been dislodged by the giant wave. His relief at surviving morphed into panic as he scoured the deck for the others. Andrews was further up the rail and on all fours, coughing water and looking dazed. He saw Mito next, his face twisted into a grimace as he staggered to his feet and stalked towards Dexter, who was doing his best to scramble away from the giant soldier. Dexter somehow squirmed past his pursuer, and headed towards the interior hatch. As Mito followed, he smoothly drew his pistol and aimed for Dexter's leg.

"No, wait!" Rainwater said, before he was silenced by the snap of gunfire. Even though the boat was still bucking and rolling, Mito was accurate, the bullet hitting Dexter in the thigh and bringing him down.

"Little motherfucker!" Mito raged as he stalked towards the wounded scientist.

Dexter was crawling on his belly, whimpering as he tried to escape. Whatever bravery he had found before the wave hit had deserted him, and he was back to being a frightened man who was in the wrong place at the wrong time. Rainwater got to his feet and ran across the deck to intercept.

"You stay back!" Mito screamed, briefly pointing the gun at Rainwater who threw his hands up and stopped in his tracks.

"This son of a bitch was going to kill me. If that wave hadn't hit, he'd have caved my skull in."

"But he didn't," Rainwater said, trying to reason with Mito. "Put it down to the stress of the situation getting on top of us."

Mito put a boot on Dexter's spine, stopping his progress. "I don't think so," he said, pointing the gun at the back of his head.

"Please," Dexter whimpered, "I really don't know what came over me…"

"You can't kill him! He didn't mean it!" Rainwater said, taking a step forward. A powerful hand restrained him, and he looked at Andrews, who shook his head slowly.

"Don't get involved," he said, nodding towards the wheelhouse window.

Rainwater looked to see both Clara and Russo watching proceedings. Clara's mouth was moving, and although he couldn't hear her, Rainwater knew she was screaming for Mito to stop. Russo was simply watching, a half smile on his lips.

Mito levelled the weapon at Dexter's head, and looked to the wheelhouse window to Russo.

Time seemed to freeze as Rainwater watched, sure this was all designed to teach Dexter a lesson. After all, he was no threat, he was just a frightened man who had been pushed to the edge and snapped.

Mito, don't.

Rainwater opened his mouth to say it, when Russo nodded. The single rapport of gunfire was almost lost in the storm. Dexter immediately stopped struggling as blood began to spread from underneath his head in a rapidly growing pool. Rainwater couldn't quite believe he had gone through with it, and could only watch as Mito flicked the safety back onto the weapon and slipped it into its holster, then turned towards Andrews and Rainwater, his face twisted into a rictus of rage. Rainwater wasn't looking at Mito though. He was looking at Russo in the wheelhouse, who was watching proceedings with a slick smile etched on his lips. Of Clara, there was no sign, and that was a good thing, for it meant she was spared the sight of her assistant's body sliding across the deck with every rise and fall of the boat, leaving a bloody trail as it went.

"Everybody inside," Mito said, glaring at Andrews and Rainwater. Too numb to argue, the pair did as they were told, and started walking towards the door. Rainwater couldn't help but glance at Dexter's corpse as he passed it. He knew now there were no lengths Russo wouldn't go to, and nothing he wouldn't do to get what he wanted.

Everything had changed.

CHAPTER 53

Clara took a sip of the whisky and set it back on the table in the galley kitchen with shaking hands. Rainwater sat opposite of Clara, wondering what to say to try to console her. No words came, and so he looked at her pale face, and her bloodshot eyes, as she stared into space. How could he possibly try to tell her everything would be all right when they were on board with a man who knew no limits? He wasn't in any way equipped to do that, and so he let her grieve and drink, as he listened to the thrum of the engine and the increasingly regular sound of icebergs smashing off the hull. The storm had been brutal, but against all odds, the boat had come through unscathed, and was now heading south, the temperature plummeting as they followed the creature.

Mito had gone to the wheelhouse when they had arrived back in the boat, followed by a furious Andrews who was baying for blood.

"Why are you here?" she asked as she took another sip of her drink and wiped her makeup streaked eyes with the palm of her hand.

"I uh… Thought you might not want to be alone."

"No," she said, shaking her head, "I mean, why are you *here*, why are you looking for this thing? The rest of us are here by accident, you seem to be the only one out here by choice."

"To be honest, I've been asking myself that same question. This creature sank my boat, and killed my dad and uncle and a close family friend. For a while, all I could think about was revenge and killing this thing. Now…" he cleared his throat and stared at the half empty whisky bottle. "I really don't know why I'm out here."

Clara poured him a drink and then topped up her own glass.

"I thought this was a scientific mission, a chance to study something new, a missing link in the evolutionary chain. Dexter…" Her lip trembled and she took a deep breath. "Dexter didn't want to come. He thought it was a bad idea. I didn't listen to him."

"There was no way you could have known what was going to happen out here. He must have thought a lot of you, to follow you out here."

"I loved him like a brother," She said, taking another drink. "I always knew he wanted more, but we never spoke of it. I was never interested in him like that, but I still loved him. Does that make sense?"

"Yeah, it does actually." He mumbled. "It's about the only thing that does make sense right now."

"He'll kill us. You know that don't you?"

The way she said it chilled him more than the freezing conditions outside, and he looked her in the eye. There was intensity, a glint of determination and anger. He took a drink of the fiery whisky, grimacing as he swallowed it.

"I'm going to kill him."

Rainwater hoped it was the grief and alcohol talking for her, but she was incredibly lucid, and he saw she meant it.

"That's not a road you want to be heading down. This seems bad now, and it will for a while. Remember that away from all this, you have a career, a life. Don't let getting revenge on Russo ruin that for you. People like him always get what they deserve in the end."

"No they don't," she said with a disgusted sneer. "People like him always get away with it and come out smelling of roses. He'll make sure all of us loose ends are tied long before we get back to civilisation, if we ever do that is."

"We got through the storm. At least that's something to be grateful for."

"True, but we're heading towards Antarctic waters. The temperature's going to plummet and the icebergs are going to increase in size and density. This boat isn't equipped to deal with those conditions. Russo either doesn't care, or won't acknowledge it. Either way, it's going to get bad."

"I fished on the Bering Sea, and that can get pretty bad."

"Not like this," she said, shaking her head.

"The further south we go, the denser the ice pack will become. A boat like this isn't built to cut through it. The smaller, thinner part of the ice field will be manoeuvrable easily enough. That's what will draw us in. The second we're through, it will close behind us."

"You mean we could be trapped?"

"If the ice has nowhere else to go and it gets dense enough, yes."

"Great," Rainwater muttered as he drained his glass. He looked at Clara, but she was staring past him at the door.

Russo stood, arms folded as he looked at them both. He wore an expression, which Rainwater was sure he had been practicing in the mirror – just the right mix of grief and sorrow.

"I wanted to talk to you about what happened," he said, stepping into the room.

"You better get out of here," Rainwater said, wondering if his bravery was due to the booze going straight to his head.

"I'm not here to cause trouble," Russo replied, speaking to Rainwater but watching Clara. "I really feel we need to talk about what happened."

"What's to discuss? You killed an innocent man." Clara hissed as she drained her glass and immediately poured another drink.

"I didn't kill anyone."

"You gave the order. That makes you responsible in my book, even if you didn't pull the trigger yourself."

"Come on, be fair. He was hardly innocent in this. He had attempted to attack one of my men who could have been severely injured or killed. Can you blame him for retaliating?"

"Don't you think shooting him is a little too much?" Rainwater cut in.

"You don't understand, I have to be seen to keep discipline with the crew. If I lose control I—"

Rainwater lurched out of his seat and swung a looping punch at Russo. His knuckles connected with jaw, sending Russo staggering into the fridge freezer, which opened and spilled its contents onto the floor.

Russo didn't go down, instead, he touched his fingers to his bloody lip, and spat on the floor. Rainwater stood defiant, trying to ignore the throbbing pain in his hand. Russo didn't fight back. Instead, he pulled off a length of kitchen roll and held it to his lip.

"Any other time, you would have been dead for doing that." He said as he examined the bloody tissue and touched it back to his lip. "I understand you're upset, so on this occasion, I'll let it slide."

"Get out of here," Rainwater said, balling his fists.

"I did what I could, if you chose not to accept the olive branch so be it. It's on you. If you try anything like that again, I won't be responsible for what happens."

CHAPTER 54

Russo went directly to his room, still holding the tissue to his lip. Slamming the door shut behind him, he tossed the tissue on the dresser and looked at himself in the mirror, surveying the damage. He was surprised at how haggard his reflection had become. His eyes were sunken and dark from the lack of sleep, and a fluffy salt and pepper stubble was well on the way to becoming a beard. He tried to see past the things he had done, and that he had been forced to do to complete the mission. He hadn't realised it before, but he was starting to look...

Old.

People saw him as a monster. They didn't understand what he had to put up with, or the difficult decisions he had to make. He had seen the way people were looking at him, the disgusted, fearful look in their eye, and he was starting to wonder if he was close to losing the crew.

Mutiny on the Victorious.

He smiled, and his swelling lips screamed in anger, transforming it to a wince.

No.

He wouldn't let that happen, not when he was so close to the end. He tried to figure out when he had last been able to sleep without his conscience nagging at him about how far he had to go to get the job done. That was the side other people didn't see, the personal toll that taking on a mission took on him. His superiors wanted results, and had already spent millions of dollars in both building the Florida facility and researching the state of the art capture and cloning facilities they intended to use. The message was clear. They had done their part, and everything now depended on him. A pretty tall order for someone earning just over seventy grand a year before taxes. He kicked off his shoes and lay on the bed, ignoring the uncomfortable mattress as best he could as he stared at the roof. As tired as he was, he knew what would happen. It was as if lying down was some kind of trigger to make him become wide-awake and unable to sleep. For three nights, he had tried to get a couple of hours rest, only to find himself unable to drop off, distracted by the billion things racing around in his head and the nauseating motion of the boat as it ploughed towards the southernmost tip of the world.

He pulled the roll of mints out of his pocket and looked at them. They weren't mints of course, not really. They were a special mix of narcotic, made up for him by a guy in LA and packaged to look like harmless breath fresheners. Apparently, most of the A list stars did their drugs this way now. In the age of social media and everyone and their dog carrying a camera, it was the safe way to feed a habit. For a price, you could have your own personal cocktail made up and packaged in such a way that nobody would know any different. His brand was a mixture of anti-depressants, cocaine and aspirin – all with minty fresh breath thrown in for good measure. He didn't like to call himself an addict, especially as he prided himself on his supreme level of self-control. Even so, he hadn't accounted for how long they would be at sea, and now that he had run out, he was becoming increasingly agitated. He took the last anonymous white tablet from the package and turned it over and over in his hands, trying to ignore the screaming panic in his belly at the thought of not having any more to take after this last one.

I don't need them. I take them for recreation. I control them. They don't control me.

Which was all well and good, he thought as he stared at the miracle pill, except that it was bullshit. Even now, he could feel how much his body craved that numbing cocktail. He half wondered if they were what made him so able to make the tough decisions he was forced to make. What would he do when the aches started, the stomach cramps and spasms, as his body tried to adjust to functioning without its precious medication?

Save it. Save this last one until you really, really need it.

It was a good idea, and yet as he lay there, his stomach fluttered and his brain fired with ideas, thoughts, hopes, dreams, guilt, need, pleasure, and pain. This was way too much to expect any one man to handle without a little chemical rebalancing.

It's not like I'm some crack addict holed up in a squat somewhere.

Although that was true, he still didn't like the idea of coping without his precious pills. Not when there were already so many things he had been forced to do to get this job done.

You're stronger than the pills. You don't need them. You can kick them anytime.

The voice in his head was convincing, even if he had heard it all before. He had threatened to put himself in rehab on more than one occasion, only to find himself breaking out in sweats and speed dialling his supplier to FedEx him a fresh supply.

This time.

He promised himself as soon as this mission was over, and he had delivered the creature to his employers that he would check himself into rehab, and take himself a long vacation. Somewhere that was warm and away from civilisation, somewhere with sandy beaches and no roads or nightclubs, – perhaps the Maldives. For now though, he had a job to finish.

He popped the last pill into his mouth and closed his eyes, trying to get some sleep and not think about what he would do when those pains started, and how he might cope next time a tough decision had to be made. He prayed for sleep, knowing that his body desperately needed the rest. However deep down, he knew it wouldn't come. His body would make him stay awake.

Don't give it a choice. You're in control. You are the master of your own body. You can sleep if you want to.

He looked at the alarm clock by his bed. It was only a little after five in the afternoon, (not that time mattered when you had chronic insomnia and addiction to manage) and he was determined to force himself to get some much needed shut-eye.

You are in control, you can do this if you want to.

He swallowed the pill, and closed his eyes, slowing his breathing, trying to empty his head, determined to prove to his body who was in charge.

Five hours later, and sick of staring at the same spot on the roof, a frustrated Russo got off the bed, showered, changed, and headed back towards the wheelhouse. He was trying not to acknowledge the need in his gut for more of his precious drugs, which was already starting to present itself, and to think less about what tomorrow would be like, never mind the day after. Pushing the worrying train of thought to one side, he walked out to stand beside Mackay and drew a breath.

The open ocean was gone. In its place, the water was littered with giant icebergs that drifted gently in the waters as far as the eye could see. The entire deck of the boat was thick with ice, and ahead, looming on the horizon, lay the impressive and intimidating Ross Ice Shelf.

CHAPTER 55

The creature moved with grace around the mountainous icebergs that hung below the waterline. Back in familiar territory, it changed course, heading towards the dark fissure in the wall of the ice that dwarfed even the creature's mammoth frame. Angling into the pitch-dark underwater chamber, the animal weaved around the twisting ice formation and deeper into its lair. Two miles away, the *Victorious* pushed on through the dense ice field as driving snow fell from white skies overhead. In the wheelhouse, Russo was staring at the Radar screen.

"It's gone into the shelf." He said to the room. "Mito, get Andrews, tell him I need him here, now."

Mito headed below deck as Russo turned to Mackay, who was still staring out of the window and hadn't slept for three solid days.

"Stop the boat, now."

Mackay didn't acknowledge, instead increasing speed towards the tightly packed ice field.

"I said stop the boat." Russo repeated, wincing as the *Victorious* collided with a large iceberg, which scraped down the side of the hull.

"Are you out of your damn mind?" Russo yelled, reaching for the controls. It was the exact moment Mackay had been waiting for since he had been forced to take over. In a single fluid motion, he pushed the boat to max speed, and then lunged at Russo, clamping his massive hands around his throat and shoving him to the ground as the boat raced towards the shelf.

"You deserve this you prick," the Scot raged through gritted teeth.

Russo clawed at his massive forearms, unable to free himself from Mackay's vice like grip.

"I'll see you die before you get to that fish you son of a bitch," Mackay hissed as Russo's eyes bulged out of his head.

Mito heard the commotion and raced back into the wheelhouse, dragging Mackay off his employer, and laying into him with vicious punches.

Spluttering and staggering to his feet, Russo joined him, both of them beating the prone Mackay to a pulp.

"Hey," Rainwater said, racing from the galley, tackling Mito without thinking. The four were now engaged in a brawl on the confined space of the wheelhouse, as confused soldiers and Clara looked on.

"Look out!" She screamed.

The *Victorious* lurched out of the water as it clipped the immense iceberg on the starboard side, the entire hull groaning as the thunderous impact made the boat shudder. All through the vessel, people were thrown like ragdolls. Glass shattered, alarm bells rang as the boat half slewed on top of the iceberg. The lights flickered as the rear of the vessel slammed back into the water. Propped on a natural shelf just below the waterline, three quarters of the mangled *Victorious* was out of the water, only its stern still fully in the ocean. Silence befell the wheelhouse as the forward motion of the boat stopped, wedging the vessel in a landscape of compacted ice.

Confused crew members got to their feet. Mito had a nasty looking gash on his head, and Rainwater had a bruised cheek where he had been hit during the brawl. He pushed himself to his knees, as he looked around the destroyed wheelhouse. Everyone bore the same expression, all except for Mackay. He was sitting on the floor, staring at Russo, smiling a bloody toothed grin.

"You idiot!" Russo screamed, wiping blood from his nose. "Have you any idea what you've done?

Get them out of here!" Russo raged, pointing at Mackay. "All of them, lock them up."

"Good luck catching your fish with no boat." Mackay said as he was hauled to his feet by Mito.

"All of you are going to go down for this. I swear to God. I'm going to make sure you spend the rest of your fucking lives in the worst hell hole prison I can find." he screamed, the veins bulging out of his neck. "Lock them away, I don't want to see them again until we get a rescue boat out here."

"Yes sir," Mito said, nodding to two soldiers who led the trio away.

"The rest of you…get out. Leave me alone."

The crew looked at each other, and then at Russo.

"Didn't you hear me? I said out! Everybody!" he screamed.

This time the crew made a swift exit, leaving Russo alone. When they were gone, he paced the wheelhouse, which now angled uphill towards the bow. His guts gnawed for his medication and his nerve endings tingled with need, both of which were becoming harder to ignore. He leaned on the control console and closed his eyes, letting out a deep sigh as he looked at the landscape beyond. The ice shelf was tauntingly close, the ocean between the boat and it, was completely frozen over – packed with more ice than he had ever seen in his life. The snow continued to drive down, and the wind howled through the broken window beside him.

"What's going on up there?" Andrews said to Morrison as he passed him in the corridor.

"It looks like our mission is over," Morrison replied. "Seems our temporary captain deliberately ran us aground."

"Are we going down?"

"No, as luck would have it, we've got ourselves perched up on an iceberg, otherwise we would all be taking a cold bath right now. We're going nowhere."

"Where's Russo?"

Morrison jabbed a thumb over his shoulder. "Wheelhouse, says he doesn't want to be disturbed."

"I don't care what he wants anymore. It's time we put a stop to this."

"Good luck," Morrison said, and then walked away. Andrews jogged up the steps and entered the wheelhouse, choosing his words carefully as Russo stared out of the window.

"We need to call for help," he said, unable to believe how old and broken Russo looked.

"We're so close," Russo whispered. Andrews struggled against the gradient as he stood beside him.

"It's over, you must know that right?"

"How bad is the damage?" Russo asked, chewing on his lip.

"Hull is damaged. We're also wedged up here on this iceberg. Luckily for us, it's not going anywhere because of the ice field."

"Is the boat seaworthy?" Russo asked, half turning towards Andrews.

"No. It isn't. In fact, if it wasn't for the sheer luck of us riding up this iceberg, chances are it would be underwater right now."

Russo nodded, and turned his face back to the window, looking out at the arctic storm. Andrews was astounded by how he seemed to be withering by the second.

"Its right there Andrews. *Right there*." He said, nodding to the towering ice shelf.

"This isn't all bad. You know where this creature's lair is. Another crew can come out and finish the job. You did everything you could."

"And what, they take all the credit? Would you say that's fair?"

Andrews opened his mouth to answer, and then stopped. Russo was trembling, and a light sweat lined his brow.

"Well, do you?"

"No," Andrews said, deciding it was better not to ask if Russo was okay. "Even so, this isn't about fair. It's about survival. You have this thing tracked and you know where it is. I would say that's a pretty successful mission under the current circumstances."

"We both know that tracker only has a day or so before the battery dies."

"That doesn't matter now. You know where it is."

"What? Somewhere in the ice? Do you know how big the Ross Ice Shelf is? Even something as big as our fish will be like a needle in a haystack." Russo's eyes were on stalks and he thrust his trembling hands into his pockets, leaning forwards to counter the angle of the boat.

"Why don't you go get some rest? Let me call it in." Andrews said.

"I'm fine."

"You don't look fine."

"I said I'm fine." He snapped.

They were silent for a moment, both watching the snow flurry outside.

"Let me call it in," Andrews said again, hoping Russo was too out of it to argue. "We need some help out here."

Russo didn't answer, so Andrews shuffle stepped across broken glass towards the radio, his heart plunging into his stomach when he saw it. The console was destroyed, circuit board and wires hanging out of the shattered casing.

"What the hell happened here?" Andrews said, testing the radio anyway before throwing the useless receiver against the wall, where it bobbed on its bungee style chord.

"Smashed it." Russo said, still staring out at the snow.

"What the hell did you do that for? We need to contact the Coast Guard, we have injured people on board!"

"I had to," he whispered, still staring out of the window.

"What are you talking about, are you out of your mind?" Andrews bellowed, grabbing Russo by the shoulder and spinning him around, unable to help but recoil when he saw Russo's twisted grin.

"The mission goes ahead. No Coast Guard. Not until we have what we came for."

"There are crew on board who need medical attention."

"I called in the transport ship before I smashed the radio. It's on its way here. They'll take our injured on board as well as our fish."

"This is crazy, listen to yourself!"

"Don't mistake my determination for insanity." Russo shot back, his eyes darting as he grinned at Andrews.

"Look at you, you look like hell. You're obviously sick, and it's affecting your judgement. How the hell do you expect us to complete the mission when we're stranded?"

Russo turned back to the window and nodded towards the mass of ice between the boat and the shelf.

"I think we can walk to the wall from here across the ice, then use our climbing gear to get on top of it."

"You can't be serious," Andrews said, shaking his head and ignoring the tight ball of fear in his gut. "This isn't a stroll we're talking about here, it's the Antarctic Ocean."

"Which is frozen enough for us to cross on foot."

"You can't know that. If you do this, people will die."

"People die every day. It's something neither you nor I can change."

"No," Andrews said, walking towards the door. "This has gone too far. Job or no job, I'm done. I'm not going to go down in flames with you on this one, Russo. Not a chance."

"Fine."

Andrews was expecting to have to argue with the sweating, twitching Russo, and was stunned into silence by his unexpected agreement.

"I don't think you would be much assistance past this point anyway. Besides, I need someone with seniority to stay here with the *Victorious* for when the transport ship arrives."

"*You* are going out there?"

"Of course I am. I've come too far to sit back and watch from the boat. All I need from you is to complete your end of the mission and send the drone over the shelf."

"You really do intend to do this, don't you?"

Andrews said, waiting for a reply that didn't come.

"Yeah, I'll send the drone," he said with a sigh. "After that, I'm done. The sooner I'm off this boat and away from you, the better."

"That works for me. How soon can you have it in the air?"

"You'll die out there, Russo. You know that don't you? What you're planning...its suicide."

"Your concerns have been noted. How long for the drone?"

"I can have it in the air in twenty minutes." Andrews said with a sigh, knowing any attempt to talk Russo out of his crazy plan was futile.

"Good. Let me know when it's done."

Andrews didn't reply and left Russo staring out at the window at the ice that had almost completely encased the boat.

CHAPTER 56

The M180 drone was a brand new prototype developed especially for operating under extreme weather conditions. The size of a large bird, the 180 was initially developed for the civilian sector to plot and monitor underground lava flows at Yellowstone national park. It was equipped with an array of sensors – the most impressive of which was a state of the art multimillion dollar thermographic imager, which was able to detect extreme fluctuations in temperature below the earths surface. In Yellowstone, the underground lava flows had shown as bright white heat against the surrounding rock formations, here in Antarctica, shades of blue and purple were more likely to be on display. The 180 was also fitted with high definition video and audio recording software, as well as sensors to detect air pressure, wind speed, and the minutest fluctuations in the surrounding atmosphere. Powered by multidirectional rotors, the unit had a range of around three miles and was remotely operated by a pilot who could navigate the unit with pinpoint precision.

Andrews was lead developer of the system prior to his involvement with Russo, and had been tasked with modifying the unit for short range military reconnaissance missions. Now, he was beginning to think his expertise with the prototype was the only reason Russo had decided to hijack his meeting and ensure he was a part of the programme. How Russo knew about the 180 was something which had troubled Andrews for some time. It was meant to be off the books, one of many above top secret research projects designed to further bolster the security of the country and its allies. He made final checks to the unit, and ensured that the video feed was online, the super high definition cameras picking up Andrews and the room with perfect clarity. Taking a last look over the prototype unit to ensure that it was fully operational, he called Russo and told him that they were ready to go.

Fifteen minutes later, Andrews was in the control room, the twin monitors showing the frozen deck of the *Victorious* and the

Ross Ice Shelf beyond. Russo paced back and forth, chewing on his fingernails that were already raw and shredded.

"Are you sure it will function in the cold?" he asked as he watched the monitors.

"I'm sure. I have this under control." Although he didn't quite smile as he said it, Andrews enjoyed the fact that he was now in charge, and Russo was waiting on his every move.

"Well, let's get it in the air. There's no time to waste."

Andrews nodded, and despite his growing disdain for Russo, he couldn't help but be excited that his new project was about to go into action. He powered up the drone, the image on screen shuddering as the rotors whirled to life.

"Okay, everything looks good to go." He said, taking a firm grip of the twin control sticks and gently pulling them towards him. Out on deck, the unit gently lifted into the air, cutting through the falling snow.

"I need to check to make sure that everything is in order here. I'm going to do a quick recon around the boat."

Russo didn't answer, instead, he stared at the computer screen as the drone made a slow orbit around the stricken vessel. From outside, the damage was more evident.

"You see that?" Andrews said, pointing to the screen. "That's all that was stopping us from sinking."

Russo could see it now on screen, the way the iceberg formed a natural ledge for the *Victorious* to perch on, keeping it from sinking into the black depths of the Antarctic.

"Okay, everything looks to be in order. Let's go take a look at this ice shelf."

Andrews teased the controls, expertly making the drone climb away from the vessel and across the icepack. The drone moved into the shadow of the ice shelf, and came to a stop in front of it, its face smooth and solid.

"Okay, let's take her up." Andrews said, making the drone ascend. For what seemed like an eternity, the screen was filled with the mountainous white face of the shelf.

"How high is this thing?" Russo asked, a note of concern in his voice. Andrews checked the instruments.

"A hundred and thirty seven feet so far."

Russo whistled through his teeth as the drone continued to climb. A little after two hundred and four feet, the screen exploded with light as the shelf ended and glorious sunshine cut through the falling snow.

"Man, now that's a sight for sore eyes." Andrews mumbled as the Drone moved over the tip, now hovering above the shelf. "Two hundred and seven feet from bottom to top. You have one hell of a climb ahead of you," Andrews said, enjoying the increasing uncertainty in Russo's face.

"What's that?" He said, pointing to a dark smudge on the screen.

"Looks like a crevasse. Let's go take a closer look."

Andrews flew the drone closer to the smudge, and saw that it indeed was a crevasse, a narrow gouge cut into the shelf.

"Thought so, "Andrews said more to himself than actually in conversation with Russo. "This whole place is filled with these. Some of them are smooth as glass and cut right through to sea level. Others start narrow and grow into huge caves or chambers. You fall into one of those deep ones and you won't be getting out again."

Andrews had hoped to further unsettle Russo, but saw if anything that he was growing in confidence.

"This is it. A perfect place for a creature of this size to remain hidden. Begin the imaging process."

"You know there's no guarantee you'll find a way to get to this thing even if it shows up, right?"

"I disagree. You said so yourself, those fissures can grow into chambers, which in turn will feed back into the water. That's where we will find our way in. All we need to do is to find the right one."

"If you say so. I still think it's a suicide mission."

"Noted."

"Alright," Andrews sighed, "let's take a look and see if we can locate this cave of yours."

He flicked a switch, and the display changed from the vibrant high definition display to bright blues and blacks, as the thermal imaging device was activated.

"I don't see any heat source," Russo said as he stared at the screen.

"You won't, not yet anyway. This is brand new technology. We can't just read it in real time. The beam is located underneath the drone on its belly. We need to fly directly over any points of interest, and then fire the beam straight down. We should see the results instantly over on the second screen here. Let me show you."

Andrews piloted the drone over the fissure and pressed a button on the console. A few seconds passed before the second of the two computer screens was filled with an image that was mostly blue apart from the black cut across it, and was edged with lighter purple shades.

"See how the black gets lighter on the edges? That's melt water. Over time, these cracks fill with snow that freezes and melts, each time making the hole wider. This one only looks to be around twenty feet deep. In another thousand years, it could be a chamber hundreds of feet wide."

"So it's not what we're looking for?" Russo asked.

"No, you aren't that lucky. We're looking for something a lot bigger. There are a few more anomalies ahead, let's go check those out."

"How will we know when we find it?"

"Believe me, you'll know when you see it."

Russo nodded as the drone moved towards its next waypoint.

CHAPTER 57

The room where Rainwater, Clara and Mackay had been held previously, was now being used as a makeshift medical centre, and so Mito had locked them into one of the unused crew quarters. Although cramped, this one at least had two bunk beds and a small window. The bruised and beaten Mackay sat on one of the bunks and gingerly lay down, folding his hands behind his head.

"You okay?" Rainwater asked as he sat on the opposite bunk.

"I am now that prick has been stopped, although these beatings are starting to take it out of me."

"How long had you been planning to ground the ship?"

"Since they forced me to take over. There was no way I was about to let that wanker cause any more pain."

"Speaking of pain, how are you holding up?" Clara asked.

"I've been worse, I'm just sore, that's all."

"So, what do we do now?" She said.

"Not much we can do." Rainwater replied. "Coast Guard will have been called. They'll come and evacuate the boat and we can all go home. As far as plans go, it was pretty genius, Mac."

"Not really," Mackay replied as he folded the pillow under his head and kicked off his boots. "I just used the conditions against him. That dickhead has no idea what he got himself into. Believe me, the second I get back to the world, I'm going to the press. I'm bringing this prick down."

"Do you really want to go there? I mean the backlash could be—"

"I'm prepared to risk it," Mackay said, cutting Clara off. "I convinced Ox to come out on this trip, and because of that, he's dead."

"That wasn't your fault. You couldn't know what would happen." She said, sitting beside him at the foot of the bed.

"That don't change the way I feel about it. Surely you know all about that." He said, looking over at Rainwater.

"I do," he replied, "but the longer I'm here, the more I want to get back to normality. I'm sick of all the death and bloodshed. I want to go home."

"I'm sure we will, as soon as the Coast Guard arrives." Mackay said, closing his eyes.

"What do we do until then?"

"Nothing. We sit here and wait."

"I'm sorry for dragging you into this, Mackay. You were right. I should have left this well alone."

"Forget it, lad. You didn't twist my arm. I knew well enough what was on the cards the second I came out here. Nobody's to blame."

Rainwater wanted to thank Mackay, or at least say something. Try as he might, not a single word came to mind. He walked to the window and looked out at the snowscape.

"Hey, something's going on out here."

Clara and Mackay joined him as he looked out of the window.

Mito watched as the crew busied itself preparing equipment out on deck. The snow for the time being had stopped, and now rucksacks of provisions and supplies sat alongside rolls of rope and assorted climbing gear. Morrison walked towards the towering soldier and stood beside him.

"Having a clear out?" he asked as he started to roll a cigarette.

"You haven't heard?" Mito replied, his breath fogging in the frigid air.

"Heard what?"

"The crazy bastard has found it. We're heading out on foot."

"Out?"

Mito nodded to the compacted ice landscape that encased the boat. Morrison followed his gaze and craned his neck up the ice shelf to the summit.

"He can't be serious. It's suicide."

"I tried to reason with him, but he won't listen." Mito replied, shrugging his shoulders for emphasis.

"How can he be sure it's there? The shelf is huge. It covers a ton of area."

"He says they have a hit on the thermal imager. Looks like some kind of crevasse that opens into a cave system at the water line. Russo seems to think that's where our creature is."

"And he's heading in on foot? What happened to the reinforcements? What happened to waiting for the containment team?"

Mito shook his head. "He won't wait. They've been delayed by the storm and won't get here until tomorrow. He wants to move on it now before it heads out to feed again."

"It's crazy. It'll never work. Not with so many untrained people out there."

"You don't have to convince me. I'm with you all the way. I'm just following orders. He told me to put a team together ready to head out on foot, and that's exactly what I'm doing."

"Where is he?" Morrison asked, unable to help taking a second glance at the intimidating ice shelf.

"Control room. I don't expect you'll change his mind. You know how he is."

"I'm going to go talk to him."

"Well, I hope for all our sakes you can convince him not to do this. I don't get paid enough to die for some damn fish."

Morrison nodded, tucked his unsmoked cigarette behind his ear, and headed towards the interior of the boat.

Russo zipped up his bright red winter jacket and adjusted his hat, the dizzying mixture of adrenaline, fear, and withdrawals from his medication proving to be enough to keep him going. The cramps and sweats had been awful to the point where he thought he would rather die than continue to cope with the crippling agony, yet, he somehow got through. True enough, he felt weak and on edge, and his headache had grown into a thunderous migraine, but he was still going. There was a knock on the door, which only served to scratch at his already hypersensitive nerves. Morrison entered without waiting for a response, sitting in the vacant captain's chair and lighting his cigarette as Russo finished his preparations.

"You know this is a suicide mission." He said as he exhaled a plume of blue grey smoke.

"You sound like Andrews."

"That doesn't mean I'm wrong."

"That ice is plenty thick enough to take our weight."

"And you know that how exactly?"

Russo didn't answer, and instead busied himself with double checking his backpack.

"The men are scared. None of them want to do this." Morrison said, watching Russo carefully.

"Then they should have done something else for a career. This is a job that has risks. Every man on this crew knew that going in. The ice will hold."

"Maybe so, but that's just the start isn't it? Even if you make it across, you still have to find a way to scale that ice shelf."

"We have ropes. Axes. Climbing equipment. We'll make it."

Morrison grinned. "Maybe you have all the equipment, but I have to wonder if you have the men with the skill to get you up there?"

"Isn't that why I'm paying you?" Russo snapped, glaring at Morrison.

"I suppose so," he replied, ignoring the thousand yard stare and enjoying his cigarette. "You need to understand this isn't going to be a walk in the park. I know many a professional climber that wouldn't risk climbing an ice shelf. It's gonna cost you extra."

"How much?"

"Another fifty grand will do it. I'm not a greedy man."

"That seems like a lot of money."

"I'm worth every penny." Morrison replied with a grin. "Even as good as I am, it might not matter anyway."

"Why?"

"Climbing rocks is easy. You just need to plan and take each hold as it comes. This shelf... well that's a different story. For starters, they're unstable. At any point, an entire section could fall into the sea. If that happens, we all die. Then there is the ice itself. It can look solid enough, but can break away at any time. Make no mistake. There are no guarantees here, no matter how good a climber you think you are. I don't think fifty grand is too high a price under the circumstances."

"Please," Russo snorted, "don't tell me you have morals now. Maybe you should stay here with Andrews and wait for the containment team to arrive."

Morrison grinned. "You don't scare easy do you?"

"I don't scare at all."

"I do." Morrison shot back, blowing smoke out of his nostrils. Russo looked at him with his eyebrows raised. "You seem surprised." He said, watching Russo shuffle from foot to foot.

"I thought you were our fearless survival expert. It doesn't bode well if you are afraid too."

"That's where you have it all wrong," he replied with a faint smile. "See, a healthy dose of fear keeps the senses sharp. It keeps a person alert. In my experience, without fear, a person is more likely to do something stupid and put themselves at risk."

"Well, you can trust me that I won't do that. I pride myself on my planning."

"I know," Morrison nodded, "which is why I ask myself why you're doing this? More importantly, what do you hope to do if you find this beast in its lair? As far as I can see, you're powerless."

Russo opened his mouth, and then snapped it shut. Morrison had a point.

"Look," he said, "I don't pay you to think. I pay you to make sure we survive. I'll give you the extra fifty thousand if that's what it takes. I want the team ready to go within the hour."

Morrison stood and flicked his cigarette out of the broken wheelhouse window.

"Whatever you say, boss. Just don't say I didn't warn you. As long as you know, money or no money, I can't guarantee you that you will live long enough to see this fish of yours."

"Maybe I'll surprise you."

"Maybe," Morrison said with a shrug, "or maybe we'll all die out there in the ice. I suppose once we set out from here, all bets are off the table."

"I don't know about you, but I certainly want to live."

"Yeah," he said, walking past Russo, "don't we all."

CHAPTER 58

"They're leaving." Clara said as she stared out of the window.

Mackay and Rainwater joined her, watching the group of twelve men in matching red winter clothing shrug into backpacks, and hook coils of ropes over their shoulders.

"Maybe they're just getting ready for the Coast Guard to arrive?" Rainwater said, not believing it himself.

"I doubt the Coast Guard will be coming at all." Mackay said, tapping on the glass. "I see that prick Russo with that big son of a bitch Mito. He wouldn't be out there if we were just waiting to be picked up."

"Surely they aren't about to try to cross the ice?" He said, glancing at Mackay.

"I wouldn't put it past em'. Especially considering the lengths he's gone to so far to get what he wants."

"You think he would really risk trying to cross that ice on foot and climb the shelf?"

"I think at this point he's willing to try anything."

"We need to do something," Rainwater said.

"May not have to," Mackay muttered as he returned to his bunk and lay down. "If they are planning to walk out over the ice, chances are the arseholes will kill themselves anyways."

"So what do we do?"

"Nothing. Let them get on with it if that's what they want to do."

"We can't just sit by and watch," Clara cut in, sitting on the edge of the second bunk.

"I don't see what choice we have. Might be an idea to get comfortable. We could be here for a while."

"If they all go out there and something happens, we'll die in here."

"They won't leave the boat completely empty. My guess is there will be a skeleton crew on board in case they need to radio back for help. Relax, nobody will forget us." Rainwater said, watching as preparations continued outside.

"Hey, they really are leaving," Clara said, as she watched Russo and his men climb over the edge of the boat and begin to cross the ice.

"Crazy bastards," Mackay said as he and Rainwater joined Clara at the window.

Russo immediately realised he had made a mistake. The idea had seemed entirely plausible from the boat, however, now they were walking across frozen ocean, and it took a tremendous effort of will to keep going. He could feel the frightened and hateful eyes of his crew on him as he followed Morrison, trying as best he could to ignore the cracking under his feet with each step. It was like a giant game of Russian roulette. Morrison had taken great pleasure in telling Russo how the landscape – although seemingly solid – was actually a series of icebergs that had been frozen together. He made a point of explaining that as long as they didn't step on the joints between the bergs directly, they should be fine, but also pointed out that because of the snowfall, actually spotting them would be nigh on impossible. Russo glanced at Morrison ahead. His shoulders hunched, hands thrust into his pockets. His breath pluming as he traversed the ice. Of them all, he was the only one who still seemed unafraid, and looked to be taking some form of sick delight in the worries of the rest of the team. In single file, they inched towards the giant ice shelf, which up close was even more intimidating as it towered above them.

We will never be able to climb that thing.

He had been repeating it over and over to himself as they neared, and only pride stopped him from abandoning the mission.

Just keep moving. One foot in front of the other.

The advice was sound enough. The reality of the situation was that he was beyond afraid. He glanced over his shoulder. The *Victorious* was already no more than a ghostly shadow in the swirling snowstorm.

Forwards then.

Time passed and lost all sense of meaning. Shadows lengthened and the sky started to grow dark, and still the ice held. Russo started to wonder if they might yet make it.

The *Victorious* was eerily quiet since the crew had ventured onto the ice. The night had been long, and what little sleep Andrews had managed to get was broken with nightmares of dying out here alone because of Russo's incompetence. He walked the deserted corridors of the stricken vessel, grateful for the time to think about what to do for the best. There was no way to contact the outside world. No way to raise the alarm and get help if the boat slipped from its perch and started to take on water. The wind rocked the stricken vessel, and Andrews couldn't see any way Russo and his team could have possibly survived the climb in such awful conditions.

He walked out on the deck, grateful for the warming sun on his face despite the intense bite of the wind. He lifted his binoculars and scanned the ice shelf, expecting to see bodies littering the base of the shelf, of tell tale dark pools where the team had fallen through the ice to their death. To his surprise, he saw none of those things. He could see the blue climbing rope swaying against the face of the shelf.

The crazy bastard made it.

He lowered the binoculars, and looked out at the dense field of ice that had locked the stricken *Victorious* in its grasp as far as the eye could see. He suspected recovering the boat wouldn't be an option, and it was destined to a future at the bottom of the Antarctic ocean, a relic to showcase Russo's blind incompetence and blinkered need to succeed at all costs.

"Screw this," he muttered under his breath, grateful actually to hear a human voice amid the silence. He knew exactly what he had to do.

"How did you sleep?" Rainwater asked Clara, rubbing the back of his neck.

"I didn't really," she replied. "I really could use the bathroom though."

"Tell me about it."

Both of them looked at Mackay, who was asleep on his side, snoring loudly.

"Looks like somebody had a decent night anyway," Rainwater muttered.

Clara chuckled and walked to the window.

"Any sign of activity?" Rainwater said as he pulled his boots on.

"Not that I can see."

"At least the sun's up," he replied as he joined her at the window, squinting at the glare.

"That might not be such a good thing."

"Oh, why not?"

"If the ice starts to melt and break up, the boat could slip free and sink. We would drown in here."

He didn't reply. The thought of a horrifying, claustrophobic death in the tiny, locked room was the worst thing he could imagine. His thought process was broken by the sound of the door being unlocked. Clara and Rainwater shared a quick glance, and then were joined by Mackay, who was roused from his sleep and stared bleary eyed at the door.

"What the hell do you want?" Rainwater said to Andrews.

"Relax, I'm not here to cause trouble. Russo's already done enough of that. I'm letting you out."

"I thought Russo ordered you to keep us locked in here?" Mackay said.

"Russo isn't in charge anymore."

"And now you expect us to trust *you*?" Clara said.

"Do what you want," Andrews shrugged. "I'm going to make coffee. It will be in the galley if you want some."

The trio watched him go, and then looked to each other.

"What do we do now?" Clara asked.

"Well, I don't know about the two of you," Mackay said, rubbing his eyes, "but coffee sounds good to me."

CHAPTER 59

They listened as Andrews filled them in about the discovery of the fissure and Russo's plan to go to it on foot.

"He's crazy," Clara said, shaking her head. "That thing is too big to function out of the water. It's not possible that it has dragged itself into a cave."

"I agree," Andrews replied. "He seems to think there's some kind of underwater entrance which opens into a pool or lagoon of some kind inside the ice shelf."

"That's plausible. Even so, I don't know what he hopes to achieve by going to it on foot."

"No, me either. All I know is this entire situation has gotten out of hand, and even if he can't admit it to himself, Russo is out of control."

"I doubt they made it up the face of the ice shelf. Not in those conditions last night." Mackay said as he drained his coffee cup.

"They did."

Everyone looked at Andrews, who squirmed in his seat. "Russo radioed in early this morning to say they had reached the top of the shelf and were proceeding to the crevasse. He wanted to know how far out the containment vessel was."

"The crazy son of a bitch." Rainwater muttered. "I can't believe he actually made it."

"Can't you stop him?" Clara asked Andrews. "He's a liability to himself and everyone in his command."

"He doesn't answer to me."

"He must answer to somebody."

"I don't know anything about that."

"Couldn't you call the Coast Guard? Maybe have somebody come and pick us up?"

"Can't," Andrews said with a shake of the head. "Russo destroyed the radio. He wanted to make sure nobody stopped him from completing his mission. All we have now are shortwave walkie-talkies. There's nothing else we can do."

"We could go after him."

Everyone looked at Rainwater, who in turn lowered his gaze to his empty coffee cup.

"What I mean is, we can follow him and put an end to this."

"You are startin' to sound as crazy as he is, kid," Mackay said.

"You don't think I thought of that?" Spat Andrews. "I tried to talk him out of it, the guy won't listen."

"Maybe words aren't enough anymore. Maybe action is what we need."

"Didn't you listen to anything I told you? Who knows how far up the chain Russo is. I can't do anything."

"Bullshit," Rainwater snapped back. "You have a duty to protect us don't you?"

"Well, I…"

"Isn't that what you government types do? Protect us from things like this? Surely you must see now that we have to end this?"

"And how do you suggest we do that?"

"Russo's hell bent on capturing this thing, correct?" Rainwater said.

"Yes," Andrews snapped.

"Then we have to destroy it."

"This isn't some kind of bug you can crush under your shoe. This is a giant. Even if we wanted to, we can't."

"I know a way." Clara said.

All eyes turned to her. "I know a way we can stop him. It won't be easy. In fact, it's not even guaranteed to work."

"What did you have in mind?" Rainwater asked.

She finished her coffee, took a deep breath, and told them her plan.

CHAPTER 60

The mid-morning sun continued to shine from pale blue skies. Rainwater, Clara and Mackay looked out over the field of ice and the shelf beyond.

"We can't do this," Mackay said, pulling his hat over his ears. "Ice is melting all over the place. It's too dangerous."

"We have no choice." Rainwater said, glancing at his bruised and beaten friend. "You sure you don't want to stay here? You don't have to come."

"Screw that, I'm not staying here. I'd rather take my chances on the ice. Besides, Morrison is out there, and I still have unfinished business with him."

Rainwater nodded as he shrugged into his backpack.

Andrews joined them on deck, his face a mixture of admiration and concern.

"You sure there isn't anything I can do to talk you out of this?"

"Just make sure you let this containment team of yours know what the situation is when they arrive." Rainwater said as he peered over the bow of the boat.

"I will."

"And be ready for us."

"How will I know when it's done?"

"Trust me, you'll know."

The foursome stood awkwardly for a moment, unsure of how to proceed.

"Well," Andrews said, squinting at the sun. "You better make a move. This ice is melting fast."

"Agreed," Rainwater replied, trying to ignore the tightness in his stomach and the thundering tempo of his heart. "Okay, let's get to it."

He hooked his leg over the bow and carefully started to lower himself over the edge by the same ropes Russo and his men had used. Carefully, he distributed his weight onto the ice, ready to scramble back up the rope if it broke beneath him.

"Okay, come on." He said to Clara, who with much more grace than he managed, slid down the rope and stood beside him.

Mackay followed, and the three of them looked out over the white landscape in between them and the ice shelf.

"Watch out for those," Clara said, pointing at the cracks in the ice. "It will be weak in those areas. If we fall through, there's a chance we won't make it back out again."

"Great," Mackay said, his cheeks already flushed from the cold.

"Well, let's get to it. Sooner we reach the shelf the better."

Andrews watched them walk for a while, then retreated into the deserted vessel and poured himself a large whisky. Not for the first time, he couldn't wait for this hellish mission to be over.

They didn't speak as they traversed the frozen ice field. Words hardly seemed appropriate anyway. The only sound was the crunch of snow underfoot and the occasional frightening crack or groan of the ice as it struggled to take their weight. As they left the *Victorious* behind, it was plain to see the ground on which they walked would soon be reclaimed by the black depths of the Antarctic Ocean, which waited for them to falter. Now, in a place far beyond fear, Rainwater led them on, knowing there was no going back. He focussed on putting one foot in front of the other, and aiming for the climbing ropes Russo and his team had left behind on the face of the ice shelf.

"This is insane," Mackay muttered as they moved into the shadow of the ice shelf. "We've no business out here."

"Let's just keep moving." Rainwater replied, unable to fault Mackay's assessment of the situation.

"You really think we can climb that?" he asked between ragged breaths.

Rainwater glanced at the imposing shelf, then over his shoulder at the ice that they had just crossed.

"We have to."

"At least in the shadow of the ice shelf, the ground should be more stable underfoot." Clara cut in.

"I'll take that. We need all the help we can get." Rainwater muttered as they reached the sheer face of ice.

Mackay whistled through his teeth. "Damn, that's... pretty high."

"At least they left the ropes behind." Rainwater said, tugging on them to test their strength.

Clara stepped forward, checking the ropes and craning her neck to the summit.

"You see where they went up before us?" She said, pointing at the face of the ice shelf, which was pocked with gouges from the pick axes used by Russo's team. "If we follow their route, we should be fine."

"I uh... I'm not too good with heights." Mackay muttered.

"You'll be harnessed in to these support ropes. Believe me, this would have been a hell of a lot more frightening if we had to free climb."

"You're sure you know what you're doing?" Rainwater asked as she clipped herself to the rope.

"I know enough, although I'm only really a hobbyist climber. It's how I relax. This is unlike anything I've ever done before."

Rainwater looked back towards the stricken *Victorious* and the ever thawing ice field on which they stood.

"It looks like going back isn't an option now anyway. What's the best way to approach this?"

"First, you need to take off those rucksacks. You won't be able to climb whilst wearing them. We can tie them with rope and feed it out as we climb. Once we hit the top, we can haul them up after us."

"Got it," Rainwater said, shrugging the heavy rucksack off his back. "Anything else?"

"Don't be tempted to rush. Take it slowly. Make sure each handhold is strong. If you get tired, let the rope take your weight. We need to communicate with each other at all times."

Rainwater nodded. He was impressed at the way in which she had taken control of the situation, and even though he was way beyond the conventional level of fear, he was confident in her ability to see them safely to the top.

"Okay, let's go," she said, pulling out her pickaxe and slamming it into the face of the ice shelf. With agility, Rainwater could only ever dream to have, she started to ascend; making the initial few feet look easy as she waited for them to follow. Mackay glanced at Rainwater, who shrugged his shoulders.

"Next time you try to talk me out of something, remind me to listen to you." Rainwater muttered.

Mackay chuckled and swung his own pickaxe at the face of the ice shelf. "Aye, I'll do that," he said with a wink.

Rainwater managed a smile, and he too started to climb, knowing certain death now surrounded them on all sides, and the worse was potentially to come.

Like a huge, deep scar cutting through the top of the ice shelf, the crevasse had smooth, glass like walls interjected with razor sharp jutting shards of ice. Curving at a forty five degree angle, the crevasse narrowed into a near vertical shaft beyond which Russo's thermal readings suggested it opened again and should be traversable on foot. As he had looked into the inky depths, he had almost given in to his urge to quit, and only carried on because success would mean he would be able to return to the real world and get a fresh supply of his beloved medication.

Morrison stood beside him, checking his harness as he prepared to abseil into the abyss. Even he was now showing the strain of their predicament, his face taught and frightened as he licked his cracked lips.

"I don't like this," he said to Russo as he peered over his shoulder into the darkness.

"It will be fine. Once we get to the fifty foot mark, it should be walkable."

"Should be?" Morrison snapped back with a strained grin. "You don't sound too confident. Maybe I should have asked for an extra hundred grand instead."

"The readings suggested it was walkable."

"Did the readings also tell you exactly what risks are involved with doing this?"

"I'm sure you can't wait to tell us."

"Believe me, I don't enjoy it, but you need to know the facts."

"Then tell us all quickly so we can move on. The transport vessel will be close now."

"Well in that case, I'll be brief. This isn't like abseiling off a roof or down a mountain side. These walls are smooth as glass. There's no way to keep a foothold. In places, water will have gouged holes, narrow, inescapable shafts that lead nowhere. The slightest slip, the tiniest mistake could see any one of us fall down one of these voids."

"All the more reason to be careful. I'm sure none of us want to die."

"If you fell in one, you would. Or at least, I know I would. Better to go quickly than suffer a slow and agonising death. The irony is even if we survive and make our way to this chamber, none of us really win. Not when this creature is down there."

"And as I told you that aspect is completely under control. Do you think I would drag us out here if I didn't have a plan?"

Morrison sneered. "A few days ago I would have said no. Now I'm not so sure."

"Oh, and why might that be?"

"You've become a victim of your own success. There are no limits for you, not anymore."

"It sounds like you're ready to desert me in our time of need."

"Don't worry," Morrison replied, leaning back and taking the strain on the rope. "You don't need to start thinking about pushing me into one of those death holes. As long as I get paid, I'll do whatever you say."

"Let's get moving then. We don't have much time."

He nodded and started to inch into the crevasse, his feet struggling for purchase against the slippery surface.

"Careful as you come," he muttered, letting out a little more line. "It's a bastard to stay upright on."

Russo followed suit, and along with Mito and the rest of his team, began to lower themselves down the slope. As they edged below ground level, claustrophobia enveloped him, and the need for his medication became a living entity – a thrashing, enraged thing in his stomach that demanded his constant attention. Counting back from ten, he dismissed it, concentrating his efforts on keeping his footing.

"There was a guy once," Morrison said, his voice reverberating off the walls that surrounded them on all sides. "A guide on Mount Everest. He knew it well and made his living from taking people up and down the mountain. Anyway, he falls into this crevasse. Maybe he didn't see it, maybe it was covered with a snow bridge. He—"

"Snow bridge?" Russo asked, the story already repulsing and fascinating him as they inched away from the comforting glare of the sun.

"Yeah. Dangerous things. Looks like solid ground, but in reality, it's just a few inches worth of barely frozen snow. You step on that, it ain't holding you up. Anyway, this guy, he falls into this crevasse. Falls maybe a hundred and fifty feet."

"Holy shit," Russo muttered as Morrison went on.

"He probably died instantly. At that depth, bones would shatter on impact. Ice here is as hard as rock. Even if he survived the initial fall, he wouldn't have lasted long. Hypothermia would set in soon enough. Can you imagine how it would be? Lying broken and in agony and just waiting to die?"

Russo kept his eyes on his feet as he inched down the incline. He could feel Morrison looking at him and the smile etched on his lips.

"You could have picked a better time for this story. Why now?"

"Because I need you all to respect this place for how dangerous it is. Make no mistake. Death could snatch any and all of us in an instant and there wouldn't be anything we could do about it. Just... Keep it in mind."

Morrison had reached the edge of the slope, and looked into the vertical drop below.

"I don't see a ledge. You sure it's here?"

"I already told you. The imaging says it was."

"Wait here for a minute," Morrison said, adjusting his position. "Let me go first and make sure we aren't all wasting our time."

Without waiting for a reply, Morrison abseiled over the edge and into the darkness. Russo waited, unsure if it was paranoia of the lack of drugs that were making him feel as if everyone was staring at him.

"Hey, boss," Mito said, snapping Russo from his train of thought.

"What?" he snapped.

"Are you sure about this?"

Russo looked the soldier in the eye, and the fear was plain to see. He felt a pang of remorse, and remembered the mission.

"You can go back to the surface if you want to," Russo hissed. "Be aware though that when we get back, you can expect a future confined to the inside of a prison cell."

"Be reasonable. None of us signed up for this."

"You signed up to protect your country, and that is exactly what this is. To refuse is to spit on our flag."

Mito clenched his jaw, and although Russo knew he wanted to say something, the big man declined.

"The next person who mentions this will find himself court marshalled. Make sure the rest of the men know that." Russo whispered.

"Hey, Russo!" came Morrison's voice, echoing off the crevasse walls.

"Yeah?"

"Looks like that machine of yours was right. Come on down. You'll need to power up those UV lights though. Its pitch dark down here."

Russo looked at the men, who were in turn staring at him. "Well you heard him. Power up your lights."

Russo twisted the activator on the underside of the vertical tube light attached to the breast of his outer jacket. The crevasse walls were immediately illuminated in a green hue, which cast their shadows into long, disfigured shapes.

"Okay, let's go." He said, making sure to sound as confident as he could manage. As the crew watched, and with more outward confidence than he felt inside, he dropped over the ledge and plunged into the darkness.

Around two thirds of the way up the face of the ice shelf, a terrifying revelation overcame Rainwater.

He could go no further.

He clung to the ice, his arms and shoulders screaming in protest, his heart thundering at a tempo which reverberated around in his head. He couldn't move. Even though the sun had been shining, the wind was still strong, tugging at him and making his coat flap, snapping angrily against his body. Just ahead, Mackay was making steady progress, and although slow, he at least still had control of his limbs. Above them both, and almost at the top was Clara, who was showing her range of skills by climbing the ice shelf with relative ease.

Rainwater knew he should call out and tell them he was unable to move, but his tongue wouldn't operate, and was stubbornly forcing him to remain silent. He looked down, and immediately regretted it, as a rush of vertigo surged through him.

"You okay, lad?" Mackay shouted from above, his eyes glinting in the sun.

Tell him yes.

Do anything.

Hell, a nod would do.

He still couldn't move, and was increasingly certain he had found the place where he was going to die. Not at sea like he feared, but on the side of the Ross Ice Shelf, clinging like a frightened child to it until the wind snatched him away.

He could hear distant voices – Mackay and Clara in discussion and calling to him. The wind rocked him, cutting through his layers of clothing and biting into his skin. It was somehow comforting. In fact, he thought if he closed his eyes for a few minutes, he might be able to ignore the situation. After all, his eyes *were* heavy. Surely, nobody could begrudge him a little rest from the demands of the climb.

"Hey."

Rainwater's eyes snapped open, and he blinked away the soup in his brain. He looked at Clara, who had descended back down the ice, and now hung beside him.

"You can do this," she whispered.

He wanted to reply, to explain calmly to her that although he appreciated the effort she had gone to come back, his body was simply refusing to cooperate. Of course, he couldn't, and so returned his gaze to his gloved hands, which were still stubbornly clinging to the ice. Clara put her hand on top of his, and he looked at her.

"Remember what I said. Take it steady."

He did as he was told, his body shifting into some kind of autopilot as he finally started to ascend. It was easier with Clara beside him, and he was grateful for her presence.

"Thanks," he said as they moved closer towards the summit.

"What happened?"

"I don't know…panicked I guess. I've never been too good with heights."

"So you decided to climb an ice shelf?"

He couldn't help but smile. "Yeah, well. I've never been one for taking the sensible option either."

"So I see. Are you going to be alright now?"

"With the climb?"

"Yeah."

"I have to be. Going back doesn't look like an option anymore."

Clara looked over her shoulder, and was surprised to see how much the ice field had broken up.

"It's a good thing we set off when we did. Crossing the ice would be impossible now."

"Whatever happens, we have to see this through to the end. There's no going back."

Clara turned her attention back towards the climb, and with Rainwater's words bouncing around in her head, she started to understand not only was the future uncertain, it was going to take a minor miracle for them to make it back to civilization in one piece.

The fissure had widened into a walkable passage as Russo had predicted. However, although the width had been easily determined, the height had not, and now Morrison led them single file down the narrow passage, which was too small to stand upright in as it wound deeper into the ice. Half crouched and with their shoulders brushing the walls, they walked in single file. Mito was suffering more than most, and was grunting and muttering as he tried to force his broad shoulders through the incredibly tight confines.

"This is crazy," Morrison whispered, his voice amplified by the walls. "This thing is getting narrower, not wider."

"Just keep going," Russo replied, turning side on to push past a particularly narrow section. "It shouldn't be far now."

" I love how we are risking our lives on should be and shouldn't be," Morrison shot back, flashing an oozing smile over his shoulder at Russo, which was cast into long probing shadows by the UV light on his jacket.

"I thought you were happy as long as you got paid?"

"I'm still here aren't I?"

They moved on, squeezing their way deeper into the glacial ice.

"It's getting pretty tight up here," Morrison said, squeezing with some effort between two jutting pieces of ice. "How far do you think it is before this thing opens?"

"Soon," Russo grunted as he too squeezed between the narrow ice, unwilling to tell Morrison they probably should have already arrived at the opening.

"Don't you find it crazy that we're probably the only people ever to set foot in this passage?"

"I didn't realise you were the type to get all sentimental."

"That wasn't my point."

"Oh, and what is?"

"My point is nobody else would be stupid enough to do something as insane as this."

Russo snorted in response, as Morrison shifted position.

"Hang on, the tunnel is getting wider here."

Russo joined Morrison in a small, smooth chamber that tapered off as it descended deeper into the ice. Below, another narrow fissure awaited them. Morrison grimaced as he began to remove his backpack and uncoil another length of rope. Russo however, smiled.

"That's it. Through there is where it opens to the chamber where the creature lives."

"That looks pretty narrow," Morrison said as he prepared the climbing rope.

"I have to see," Russo shot back, and began to inch down the incline, his boots barely giving him purchase.

"Whoa, wait a second," Morrison said, grabbing Russo's jacket sleeve. "We need to get the safety ropes set up and…"

"Forget the ropes, I have to see it now!"

"I can't let you do that," Morrison said, conscious of the watchful gaze of Mito and the others as they joined them in the chamber.

"You can't stop me, I'm going down." Russo said, further inching his way down the dangerously slick incline.

In a single motion, Morrison dropped the ropes, grabbed Russo by the collars of his jacket, and slammed him into the wall.

"Now you listen to me," he hissed, his nose inches from Russo's. "Up there, you were in charge. Down here, you do as I say."

"Let me go. I'm paying you. I control you!" Russo said, squirming under Morrison's grip.

"You're paying me to keep us alive, which is exactly what I intend to do."

"This is my mission!" Russo said through gritted teeth. Morrison only smiled as he leaned in close and whispered in Russo's ear.

"There are a lot of people here in this hole who would like nothing better than to see you fall and break your snivelling little neck. Believe me, I've wished it on you more than once. However, like you, my reputation means a lot to me, and so does my money. Let me make one thing absolutely crystal clear. My financial gain is the most important thing in the world to you right now."

"To me? Why?"

Morrison smiled his lion's smile. "Because that's the only thing stopping me from throwing you to the wolves. Make no mistake. You could have a tragic accident here and nobody would ever question it. Places like this, in the dark with danger all around…These are my places. This is where I thrive. You want to stay alive, then you do *exactly* as I tell you. Now I don't know what kind of drug you're in withdrawals from right now, but…"

"I'm not on anything I…"

"I really don't care. All I know is, you're putting us all at risk. The next time you step out of line will be the last. Got it?"

Russo nodded as Morrison released his grip.

"Now just give me a minute to get these ropes ready, and then we can go take a look."

Russo nodded, watching as Morrison returned to uncoiling the ropes. Despite the cold, another intense warm sweat was surging through Russo, and he could feel the glaring eyes of the team – *his* team– 9 of the best who he had personally assembled for this mission on him. Now however, cast in flickering green hues, their shadowy faces were full of hate, and betrayal.

My God, they want to kill me.

Just as he was trying to deal with that idea, another popped into his head which over ruled all others.

They want to take over the mission. They want to take the credit for my hard work.

He looked at them again, focusing on their devious, shadowy faces.

Yes.

That was it. He was sure of it.

How can they be stopped? How can you re-establish superiority?

Even as he said it in his head, his hand went to the pickaxe on his belt, its weight reassuring against his leg. He wondered how they might react if he were to plunge it into Morrison's head. Would that act alone, the sight of blood which would look black in the glow of the UV lights be enough to make them toe the line long enough for him to complete his mission?

Stop it.

That was the rational side of him. The side before the drugs, before the lack of sleep, and before the pressure. It had certainly been a while since it had made itself known, and Russo allowed it a chance to say its piece.

You're being paranoid. It's the withdrawals talking. You need Morrison to get you out of here.

Maybe his rational side was right, or maybe it wasn't. Either way, the desire to slam the business end of that pickaxe into Morrison's skull was becoming overwhelming. In fact, he was starting to *want* to do it.

And what? Mr Rational screamed at him. *You go to prison and someone else takes the credit for all the hard work you've put in?*

"Okay, we're ready," Morrison said, interrupting the conversation playing out in Russo's head. "We go together, understood?"

Russo didn't answer, watching his team carefully as he approached the rope and clipped his harness to it.

"Just like the last time, lean back and take it steady."

Morrison led the way, Russo following on the second rope, unable to tear his eyes away from his team, who were standing at the top of the slope. He couldn't really see their faces – the shadows were too heavy in the green hue of the lights, but he could feel them staring at him with hungry eyes.

Bastards.

Turning his attention back to the climb, and trying to ignore the pains that slammed through his body, he inched his way to the jagged horizontal opening at the bottom of the slope.

"Looks tight," Morrison said as they came to a halt. "We'll have to go in here on our bellies."

"Is that safe?" Russo said as claustrophobia threatened to overcome him.

"None of this is safe. If you want to turn back, now's the time."

Russo looked at the jagged black mouth, and tried to imagine how it would feel to be crawling through it on his stomach, his face only inches from the ground, and his back pressed against the thousands of tons of ice above him.

Was it really worth it? He asked himself as he contemplated what he was about to do.

Was it worth the stress, was it worth the risk?

These were questions that would always be answered with one of his imitation mint antidepressants. Without them, those questions wouldn't go away so easily. The truth was that he was ready to give up. He was tired, both mentally and physically, but he was also stubborn, and wasn't about to let his team see any sign of weakness that they could exploit. He looked at the hole, then to Morrison, making sure to look him dead in the eye.

"Let's do this." He said simply, managing a smile that felt as repulsive on his lips as it must have looked.

"For the record, I'm advising against this," Morrison said as he fed more rope into the black depths. "You have no idea what's down there."

"I know exactly what's down there." He whispered. "And it's waiting for us."

Morrison dropped to his knees and peered into the fissure, unclipping his light from the front of his jacket to see better inside.

"Looks like it gets pretty narrow. No more than two men at a time. Looks like it levels off a little way down, but it's hard to say."

Russo was terrified to the point of thinking he was going to throw up. Confined spaces were one of the few things he hadn't been able to train his mind and body to ignore, and the hole in front of him looked like his own personal hell.

"You don't look so good," Morrison said.

"I'll be fine, I'm just… Excited."

"There's no shame in being afraid. I've been in some of the worst hellholes on this planet, but this place is giving me all kinds of bad vibes."

"It's exciting isn't it? The thought of climbing into hell itself?" Russo whispered.

Morrison frowned at the haggard, bearded spectre in the dark.

"I guess it is." He muttered.

"Shall we proceed?"

"I guess so."

The pair ducked their heads into the opening and dropped to their bellies, army crawling through the narrow passage, Morrison, as always led the way with Russo slightly behind. As they delved deeper, Russo could feel the weight of the ice pressing against his back as he pulled himself along. Whenever the thought of collapse entered his mind, he forced it aside, counting back from ten until the idea went away. At the point when he was sure it was too tight to progress further, the chamber began to widen. Just a little at first, then big enough to crawl on all fours, and then large enough to stand in.

He heard Morrison draw breath a second before he saw for himself, joining him in a surprised gasp.

The pair stood and looked at the scene below. In that one instant, all of Russo's plans changed. Nothing had prepared them for this.

"I don't believe it…" Morrison muttered, his eyes wide and staring. He looked to Russo for some kind of a response, and was chilled by what he saw.

Russo was smiling.

CHAPTER 61

Andrews had shaved his five day beard growth and put on his best suit. He adjusted his tie and assessed his reflection, trying to see it as an outsider would. He looked exactly how he should – a high ranking government official who still had his sanity. That was key. Making a minute adjustment to his tie, Andrews walked through the deserted ship and out on the deck. In the distance, he could see the decommissioned battleship making its way through the ice, smashing through the field with little effort. They would be here soon enough, and if they followed procedure, would send a boarding party to the stricken the *Victorious*.

Andrews hoped so. He had his evidence prepared, and was ready finally to discredit Russo and try to regain a little of his self-respect. The addiction had been easy to prove, as were the murders for which he was responsible. The only thing that remained was convincing those higher up the chain that their chosen project leader had become a liability. If that meant he was pulled from the entire operation, so be it. It had after all, been a complete clusterfuck from the start anyway. Taking a deep breath, Andrews watched the battleship draw closer. It was time.

Russo couldn't believe what he was looking at. Even in his wildest imagination, he couldn't have pictured such a perfect scene. The narrow crevasse had opened into a gargantuan bowl – a stadium like natural formation of ice. High above, golden shafts of Antarctic sun streamed through holes in the arched roof of the giant ice cave. Down below, the platform on which Russo and Morrison now stood fell away at a natural incline, before meeting the ocean that had formed a huge underground lake. As impressive as it was, Russo had barely paid it any attention. Instead, his focus was on the creature. It lay motionless, its enormity perfectly visible in the crystal clear waters. Around it swam three of its young. Each roughly the size of a fully grown elephant, the offspring of the creature stayed close to its parent.

"Did you know about this?" Morrison whispered as he looked at the scene below.

"Of course I didn't," Russo snapped, staring open mouthed. "But this is a game changer, make no mistake."

"If this thing has offspring, there must be another one somewhere."

"I doubt it."

"Are you serious? These things had to come from somewhere."

"Believe me, if there were more than one of these things, we would have detected them." Russo whispered as the rest of his team started to enter the chamber and stare at the spectacle below.

"So how do you explain this?"

"Some creatures, for example, certain species of frogs and seahorses are asexual. They don't need a mate to produce offspring."

"You think that's what we have here? That's a pretty big leap, Russo."

"Not really. Look." Russo pointed to the water's edge, which was littered with whale bones.

"This isn't a new home for these creatures. My suspicion is they have always existed here, generation after generation of them living and dying in this space."

"How would they feed?" Morrison asked as he gawped at the creature.

"This location ties in with a recent collapse of the shelf before we first detected the Bloop signal again. My guess is the mother had been trapped here, and the collapse opened the chamber wide enough to allow her finally to get out into the open ocean.

"That still doesn't answer how it was able to feed, to sustain itself for all these years if it was trapped."

"Actually it does. Let's assume there was some kind of access tunnel or canal leading to the ocean, but it was too small for our creature to escape through. That doesn't mean nothing was able to come in. Look at those whale bones. There are a hell of a lot of them. My suspicion is that the whales were drawn here, who knows, maybe some rudimentary form of sonar enticed them straight into the creature's lair."

"All I hear is more if's and buts. You really don't know anything about these creatures, do you, Russo?"

"No I don't," he snapped. "I intend to find out. That is the beauty of this. We have discovered a missing link in the evolution of this planet. A subspecies self-contained for thousands of years, living and dying in its own miniature eco system. It actually makes sense now."

"What does?"

"Why this creature went on a rampage when it was set free. Can you imagine the sensory overload it must have felt when access to the ocean was finally granted? For years it must have been able to sense its surroundings teeming with life, but was unable to act on them."

"So why come back? If it had been stuck in here for so long, why not stay out in the world?" Morrison asked.

"Isn't it obvious? After we tagged it and it was hurt, its natural instincts told it to return to the one place where it felt safe."

"This is all well and good. You still haven't told me what you intend to do or even why we're here."

Russo checked his watch, and then turned to Mito, who along with the others had joined Russo and Morrison in the cave. "Give me the radio." He said simply, holding out his hand.

Mito handed it over, unable to tear his eyes away from the creature. Russo grinned at Morrison, for the first time able to forget about his agonising withdrawal pains.

"It's time we did a spot of fishing."

Andrews looked Commander Tomlinson in the eye, watching for a reaction. The pair was sitting at the table in the galley of the battleship. He had told the commander all about Russo and how he had gone off the rails. As Andrews had relayed the information, the sandy haired Tomlinson had simply stared impassively, his blue eyes watching Andrews's reactions for any hint of a lie.

"And you say Agent Russo has some kind of addiction?" Tomlinson said in his southern twang.

"That's right." Andrews replied, tossing one of Russo's empty mint tubes on the table. "I found that in his room. I'm sure you can get some residue from the inside if you wanted to prove exactly what he's been taking. When he left the ship, he was exhibiting classic withdrawal symptoms."

"And you say there have been, uh, casualties?"

"Deaths, Commander. Murders. Let's call them what they are."

"These are wild accusations. Do you have any proof?"

"Aside from my own testimony, actually I do. There are three other people who were on board who can verify my report. They've gone after Russo to try to stop him, but have written and signed statements as to what happened before they headed out over the ice. Those are right here," he said, handing the folder of papers to Tomlinson.

"This is a very serious situation."

"Yes sir, it is," Andrews shot back. "What I need to hear from you is what you intend to do about it. It's obvious to me this has all gone too far."

"Absolutely. I agree completely. What we need to do is ensure we resolve this with the minimum of...uh, shall we say embarrassment."

"I get that, Commander. Believe me. I know how things work here. Resolution with the minimum exposure or risk. I get it."

"I'm glad you understand. Do you know anything about what is happening here?"

"Not really. I don't have the security clearance."

"You do now." Tomlinson said.

"Our task was to capture this creature with..."

"I know this part. I picked up pieces along the way," Andrews cut in. "I don't get exactly how you intended to get the thing from the ice to the boat and contain it."

"The idea was simple really. We suspected this creature always had a lair, a place where it felt safe. Russo's job once he'd found it was to frighten the creature out into the open and in to the waiting transport bay of this research vessel."

"How do you frighten something so big?"

"The idea was to use a series of underwater concussion grenades. Russo was under instruction to toss them in the water and drive the creature out of the cave system."

"That still doesn't explain how you intended to get it on board the boat. Besides, wouldn't that compromise the integrity of the cave?"

"The structure of the cave system was a concern, however, we felt by using underwater charges, the damage to the outer structure would be minimal. Of course, as with anything there are certain risks. As to getting it on the boat, we intended to rely on using what we know about these creatures."

"Let me guess. You have bait in the holding tank, right?"

Tomlinson nodded. "As you know, this creature has an almost insatiable hunger. Our research showed much of the marine life in this area has vacated what they deem to be the creature's territory. In the end, it was fairly straightforward thought process. The holding tank contains a recently killed whale. We were to send a series of underwater vibrations that we hoped the creature would hone in on, sensing either a creature in distress, or a rival to its territory. The hope was that in its curiosity, it would swim right into the holding tank and we could close it up behind."

"You're talking in past tense. I hope that means you fully intend to call this off."

"Yes," Tomlinson nodded. "This has already gone too far, and if Russo is half as unstable as you say he is, then we need to remove him from this situation."

Tomlinson's radio crackled to life, as the unmistakeable sound of Russo's voice filled the room.

"Speak of the devil," Andrews said. "Mind if I sit in whilst you give him the bad news? Forgive me if I seem mistrusting, but a hell of a lot has happened since this mission began."

"By all means, stay and listen. I fully intend to make our stance on this situation completely clear."

"What do you mean stand down?" Russo hissed into the radio. "Everything's ready and in place."

"That's a direct order agent," Tomlinson's voice crackled over the radio. "This mission is over. Return to the surface. A chopper will pick you up and bring you and the rest of your team in. You have a lot of questions to answer."

"You don't understand, we're so close. Have you any idea what we've risked to get here?"

"The only thing you have risked are the lives of good men and the integrity of our government."

"That's easy for you to say in your big fucking boat with your fat salary," Russo croaked, his eyes wide. "I put myself through hell to complete my mission and these are the thanks I get?"

"You went way beyond the call of duty here. We all know that."

"That's what I do!" he screamed, his voice reverberating around the cavernous space. "That's why you hired me. I do whatever it takes."

"Even as far as murder?"

gladly do without it as long as he could guarantee his survival. He turned to Mito.

"We need ropes. As many as we have. We also need to fashion a harness, maybe some kind of netting."

"Those things are too big to pull out of the water." The burly soldier replied.

"In open water maybe. If we can get them to the edge where it's shallow, we might stand a chance."

He glanced at the icy water, and felt his stomach roll.

"Let's get to work," he said quietly, before kneeling and unrolling the spare rope from his rucksack.

CHAPTER 62

They had managed to lure one of the young to the shallows, and against all odds, more in blind luck than any kind of skill, Mito managed to snare the head of the ten foot creature, and was wrestling along with the rest of Russo's team to drag it from the water. Its agitated parent swam in furious circles, charging towards the shallows and breaching, and then retreating back to the deep. Unable to get to its distressed calf, the creature had taken to racing at speed around the perimeter of the bowl, slamming into the walls and causing the ice to crack and splinter.

"Pull!" Morrison grunted as he and the six other men dragged the juvenile creature further into the shallows, its slick body now exposed to the chilly air. In direct response, its mother breached the surface, and charged into the ice wall, the sound echoing around the bowl at incredible volume.

"That thing's going crazy, we should let it go," Mito said as he kept a close eye on the wake that raced around the lagoon.

"It can't get to us here, it's too shallow," Morrison replied as he pulled harder. "Let's get this thing out of the water and we can get out of here."

The makeshift harness was hooked over the creatures head, pinning its flippers and underdeveloped tentacles to its side. The men pulled again, sliding the creature further towards land.

"That'll do it," Russo said, watching from the edge of the water.

He had deactivated the explosive and clipped it back onto his belt, and now grinned as he waded into the water to his knees, ignoring the cold bite against his flesh.

"It's beautiful," he said as he laid a hand on its thrashing body.

"If you're gonna kill this thing, then hurry up, we can't hold it much longer. By the way, the big one is reacting, she might bring the entire place down on us." Morrison said through gritted teeth as he and the rest of the men struggled to hold the creature in place.

Russo grinned and unhooked the pickaxe from his belt.

"Just wait until Tomlinson sees you," he said, rearing back with the axe.

"Stop!"

Russo turned to see Clara, Mackay and Rainwater as they made their way towards the edge of the water. Mackay was armed with the handgun he had borrowed from Andrews. Rainwater held the bulky backup T7500.

"I think you recognise this, don't you?" He said, pointing the business end at Russo.

"I believe that's mine."

"Then I don't need to tell you what this is capable of."

"You realise that isn't an explosive device don't you?"

"I know. If I fire it into the roof, the concussion blast will still bring this cave down and put any chance of you completing this mission at an end."

"You intend to bury us alive?" Russo said with a smile, as the furious creature slammed into the wall causing a large chunk of ice to fall from the roof and crash into the water.

"We aren't all as barbaric as you pricks," Mackay said, glaring at Morrison who was still struggling to restrain the creature. "Anyone who wants to leave, now's the time."

"We don't want to hurt anyone, but we're sealing this cave. This creature is too dangerous to live in today's world. We have to put an end to it." Clara cut in, gawping at the restrained newborn still thrashing around in the shallows.

"I understand," Russo said, unhooking the explosive from his belt and activating it. "Nobody's leaving. I need these men to help me with this creature. As soon as I have my trophy, you can do what you will."

"You aren't in control here. Not anymore." Rainwater said, looking Russo in the eye.

"I'm always in control. Always. You know why? Because when it comes to it, I'm prepared to do what you won't."

"The way that thing is smashing into the walls, bomb or no bomb, the roof is going to come down and we'll all die here." Rainwater said.

"You don't have the guts. You can do whatever you feel you have to, but I'm going to kill this creature and take my prize."

"Don't! I'm warning you." Rainwater said, turning the T7 on Andrews.

"You don't have the guts to use that. You don't even have the guts to use the family name," Russo sneered as the enraged beast breached, leaping from the water and smashing down on its back, sending an arcing wall of freezing cold spray washing over them.

"I'll do it, I swear I will," Rainwater said, pointing the weapon at the roof.

"You drop those ropes now," Mackay said to the men holding the creature in place, pointing the gun at them to emphasize the point.

"Ignore him, keep a hold of it," Morrison said, flashing a cocky smile at Mackay.

"Last chance. Drop those ropes and get out of here. I won't tell you again."

"You don't have the guts," Morrison said with a sneer, readjusting his grip. "You don't have what it takes to kill a man."

"He's right," Russo cut in, his deranged smile growing wider. "You're fishermen, not soldiers. Do you think you'd ever get away with the murder of a government official, or any part of his consultation team, you would-"

A gunshot echoed around the vast chamber, stopping Russo in his tracks.

Morrison fell to his knees in the water, the entry wound perfectly visible above his right eye. He fell against the creature, sliding into a sitting position, blood and brains dripping onto his chest and into the water. Mackay lowered the weapon, turning his cool gaze towards Russo.

"That makes me and him even. Now you just give me an excuse to put one in you too."

Even Rainwater and Clara were staring at Mackay in shock, unable to comprehend what they had seen. Russo was about to respond with a smart comment, something about how Mackay should have come to work for him, when the furious creature breached the water, slamming itself against the outer wall of the chamber. Already weakened, a huge section of the roof collapsed onto Russo, narrowly missing Mackay. Russo lost his grip on the grenade, which rolled towards the edge of the water. Rainwater drew breath, and was about to tell Clara to run when the explosive detonated, and the world exploded into white light and pain.

Screams reverberated around the chamber.
Ice splintered.
Debris fell.

Searing agony in his chest and leg brought Rainwater's world back into focus as he tried to shake off the intense ringing in his ears. He surveyed the scene. There were bodies scattered in and around the water. Some were incomplete. From his vantage point, he could see a severed leg bobbing across the surface of the water. Clara was on all fours, coughing and wiping away the blood, which now matted her hair against her cheek. She had been lucky. Mito was face down on the ice, his dead eyes staring into the floor from the pulpy remains of his face. One bloody arm hung out of the mound of ice that had landed on Russo.

Rainwater got to his feet. The air was filled with pained moans of the wounded and dying. Some of the more fortunate of Russo's men had been out of the blast zone and were now helping their colleagues to safety.

Through the ringing in his ears, he could just about hear Clara screaming. He followed her line of sight, past the ice that had buried Russo towards Mackay. He was sitting in the water, leaning against the stranded juvenile creature, which had escaped mostly unscathed from the blast.

Mackay's entire left side was a burnt, charred mass of flesh. He was holding his stomach, and Rainwater could see soggy entrails protruding from between his fingers. Rainwater knelt beside him, blinking away tears as he held his friends' free hand.

"Hang on, Mac, we'll get you some help, we…"

"Don't." he said, his voice calm and accepting. "It's done. I'm finished."

"We can get you out of here, and get you to a hospital…"

"Come on, lad, look at me. We both know I'd never make it. Besides, I killed a man. At least this way I won't have to spend the rest of my years in a prison cell."

Ice began to fall from the roof with more regularity as the agitated creature continued to race from one end of the lagoon to the other, slamming into the outer walls and causing the water to lurch in ever increasing waves across the surface.

"She smells the blood. We need to get out of here." Clara said, finally able to hear again after the volume of the explosion.

She tried to help Rainwater to his feet, but he was still holding onto Mackay's hand.

"Mackay, I'm sorry…"

"Don't apologise." He mumbled, looking at Morrison's body, which was slumped next to him against the creature. "Maybe it's what I deserve."

"I won't leave you here," Rainwater said, his voice wavering.

Clara put a hand on his shoulder.

"We have to go. It's not safe here."

"Not unless we all go together."

"She's right, this place won't hold much longer." Mackay grunted.

Reluctantly, Rainwater released his grip on Mackay's hand as Clara helped him to his feet.

"You aren't going anywhere!" Russo screamed as he staggered towards them. His face was a mess, his eyes wild and white as they peered out of his blood mask. His right arm hung limply at his side, in his shaking left, he held a pistol that he was pointing at them as he splashed through the shallow edge of the water.

"You ruined everything!" he raged. "I had this under control. I'd won!"

"Look around you, Russo. It's over. You're just making it worse." Rainwater said as he backed away, pushing Clara behind him.

"Fuck you!" Russo screamed, lurching towards them and firing the gun until it was empty.

Searing agony exploded through Rainwater as one of Russo's wayward bullets found their target and threw him to the ground. Clara screamed and stumbled, trying to back away from Russo who turned his attention towards the stricken creature in the shallows, grinning at Mackay as he passed.

"I came here to kill this thing, and that's what I intend to do," he mumbled, and then turned back towards Clara. "Lucky for you I'm out of bullets, but I still have this."

He grabbed the pickaxe out of the bloody water at Mackay's feet and approached the creature. Mackay grabbed his legs as he passed, and was kicked away by Russo, who glared at the wounded fisherman.

"Just die quietly. You don't have long left." Russo said as he staggered against the creature, wincing as his injured arm banged against it.

"Neither do you." Mackay said with a bloody grin as he tied one of the ropes harnessed to the creature around Russo s ankle, knotting it securely. Rainwater saw him do it, and despite the agony that raced through his body from both explosion and gunshot wound, he got to his feet and charged towards the stranded creature, attempting to shove it back towards the deeper water. Mackay was too weak to stand, so he pushed his back against the girth of the creature. Russo realised what was happening and let out a high pitched scream, and then dropped to a sitting position in the icy water to try to untie the knot around his ankle.

"Clara, come on," Rainwater said through gritted teeth, trying to ignore the sight of his own blood pooling against the grey blue body of the creature. Clara joined them, yet still, the creature didn't move. Just as Rainwater was about to give up, some of the surviving soldiers came to help. Slowly but surely the creature began to move.

"What are you doing? You work for me. Traitors! You will all pay for this," Russo shrieked as more ice fell from the roof as a result of the adult creature's incessant assault.

The soldiers ignored him, and knowing it was fruitless, Russo gave up trying to untie the knot and was furiously hacking away at it with the pickaxe as best he could with his one remaining useable arm.

The creature shifted slightly, and then all at once, slid into deeper water. Rainwater and the soldiers fell to their knees, Clara held onto Mackay and watched the creature swim towards its parent. Russo unleashed a guttural raw scream as he was dragged leg first into the water, eyes wide with defiance as he was pulled under. The furious beast continued to circle and slam into the sides of the walls, bringing more ice crashing around them.

"Is everybody out?" Clara said to one of the soldiers.

"Apart from us," he replied.

"Then let's get the hell out of here."

"I heard that," the soldier said as he and his colleague staggered for the exit.

Rainwater looked to the T7500, which was discarded on the floor.

"How bad were you hit?" she asked, looking at the blood seeping through his fingertips as he clutched his shoulder.

"It's not too bad."

"Can you move?"

"Yeah, we have a bigger problem though," he said as he nodded towards the T7 on the ground.

"Remote was damaged by the blast."

"Then forget it. We need to get out of here."

"I'll do it manually."

"You can't stay here," Clara said, staring through the blood that covered her face. "Let it go, we need to get out of here."

"We made a commitment to end this. That's exactly what we need to do."

"The plan was to remote detonate, which we can't do now. Let's forget it. You don't need to become a martyr."

"People are dead because of me. This is what I deserve."

"Don't give me that hero crap," she said, glaring at him. "I lost someone too. We won't do their memory any good if we stay here. There'll be another chance."

"There won't, they'll come in and take it if we leave now. We have to finish it. You know I'm right." He said, looking Clara in the eye.

"I'll do it," Mackay gurgled. "We all know I'm gonna die here anyway. Let me go out my own way."

Clara looked at Rainwater. They both knew Mackay was right.

"You know what to do?" Rainwater whispered, feeling nauseous at the idea of leaving Mackay.

"Aye, I know what to do. You two get out of here. Just get me out of this bloody water first. I can't feel my legs," he said, trying to smile but only managing a grimace.

Rainwater and Clara dragged him out onto the ice, propping him against a jutting natural ledge. The ground beneath him immediately turned red with blood, which ran towards the water's edge. Rainwater positioned the weapon, helping Mackay get comfortable with it.

"Aim for the roof," he said, choking back tears "This whole thing should…"

"I get it," Mackay said, finding a smile. "Now get out of here, both of you."

Clara started to help Rainwater to his feet, when Mackay grabbed him and pulled him close, whispering in his ear. Clara looked on as Rainwater listened, nodded, and finally stood, wiping tears from his eyes.

"I will. I promise," Rainwater said, backing away to stand beside Clara as another huge chunk of ice fell from the roof and slammed into the water.

"Go, get out of here. I'll give ya as long as I can. Got any smokes?"

Blinking through tears, Rainwater grabbed his half pack of cigarettes from his pocket and handed it along with the matches to Mackay.

"Mackay…"

"Don't say anything. Just go. Remember what I told you." He wheezed

"Come on, we have to leave," Clara said, watching as the creature slammed into the wall, its impact sending a huge splintering crack towards the roof. She kissed Mackay on the head, and hugged him with her one free arm.

"I'll never forget what you did for us today," she whispered.

"You look after that lad. Make sure he stays on the right track," he replied, now also crying. "Go on the pair of you. Get out of here." Mackay said as he lit a cigarette with his shaking hands.

"Come on," Clara said, hooking an arm under Rainwater's and helping him climb towards the fissure where the soldiers were waiting to help them. As they neared the exit, they looked back one last time to see Mackay sitting amid a landscape of bodies and severed limbs, propped against an outcrop of ice and smoking his cigarette whilst the furious and agitated creature circled its young, protecting them from the carnage on the surface.

Mackay held up one bloody hand, waving them off then closed his eyes and continued to smoke.

Blinking through tears, both Clara and Rainwater started to crawl through the fissure, the soldiers helping when Rainwater couldn't manoeuvre by himself. All the time they waited for the explosion, for that sound which signalled that Mackay's ultimate sacrifice was complete. They reached the rope leading out to the surface of the ice, and were relieved to see more troops. Teams of men ferrying the wounded onto the surface.

"Come on," one of them said to Rainwater, strapping him into a harness as Clara was put into a second carrier.

"Anyone else back there?" The soldier asked one of the other soldiers.

He glanced at Rainwater and Clara, and then shook his head. "No, we're the last."

"Okay," he replied, before speaking into the radio strapped to his shoulder. "This is alpha two-zero seven. Last of the survivors coming topside now. We're coming out."

The winch began to hoist them to the surface, the soldier following on a second hoist. The blinding sunlight that greeted them felt like a different world. They were helped out of the harnesses and ushered towards the waiting helicopters. Inside the cave, Mackay smoked the last cigarette in the pack. His throat burned from smoking so many consecutively, but he knew he wouldn't need to worry about anything as trivial as Cancer killing him.

"He sighed and looked at the wake which still moved over the surface of the water.

"Okay you bastard," he grunted as he lifted the concussion bomb into position. "Time to put an end to this."

He steadied his aim, pointed the weapon at the roof and closed his eyes, and then muttered a quick prayer before pulling the trigger.

The chopper was already in the air and angling towards the battleship when the deafening roar of the collapse reached them. They watched as hundreds of tons of ice imploded and plunged into the sea. Rainwater felt Clara's hand grasp his as they watched the spectacle.

"You were damn lucky to get out of there," the soldier said, shouting above the noise of the rotor blades.

"I don't feel lucky," he muttered.

"You got a name, for the log?" the soldier asked, holding up the clipboard.

"Yeah, actually I do." He said simply, then closed his eyes and turned away from the window.

Twenty hours later, Commander Tomlinson entered the medical bay and strode towards Rainwater. His shoulder wound had been dressed and the minor burns from the grenade explosion tended to. Clara sat beside him, watching as the commander approached.

"Doc says you're a lucky man, Mr Rainwater."

"I don't feel lucky."

"Not often a man gets blown up, shot, escapes an ice collapse like that and lives to tell the tale. How do you feel?"

"Like shit. So what happens now?"

"That's what I'm here to talk to you about actually." Tomlinson said, sitting in the chair beside the bed.

"What happened here is a series of unfortunate events. We don't want to cause you any undue stress or issues down the line."

"Let me guess, you want us to sign non-disclosure agreements right?"

"It seems you're a man who doesn't like to beat around the bush. Very well, I can respect that. Frankly, this incident is an embarrassment. By law, we should open this to an investigation, and the truth is that I suspect we won't like what we will find. Besides which, it's almost re-election time, which means the folks in the White House are mindful of the stories that come out in the press."

"Let me save you the trouble," Rainwater said with a sigh. "I've had way more than enough of this. All I want is to get home and start living a normal life. If it means we get to do that, I'll sign anything you like."

The relief on Tomlinson's face was plain to see as he stood and beamed at the two of them.

"I'm glad to hear it. Let's put this mess behind us and move on, shall we?"

"That's all I want."

Tomlinson crossed the room and hesitated by the door.

"We will be back in US waters shortly. I'll have someone bring you those NDA's to sign then you are both free to go. We will of course cover all medical expenses and funeral costs for those lost. It's the least we can do. All the same, I would be tempted to forget everything that happened out here."

He waited, expecting a response or some kind of thanks. Rainwater and Clara looked at him, enjoying watching him squirm.

"Well, I have lots to do. Rest well, Mr Rainwater. This ordeal is finally at an end."

EPILOGUE

Tomlinson stood in the dark, inhaling deeply on his cigarette, feeling neither pleasure nor satisfaction from the act of smoking. His migraine had grown into a thunderous thing, and he hoped by spending some time in the darkness that it may help the feeling to pass. The survivors had all signed their NDA's and were in the process of being booked out and released, and also reminded that any breaking of the confidentiality agreement would result in swift and full punishment by law. He didn't think it would be a problem though. Like him, they had all had enough of the entire situation.

"You shouldn't be smoking in here."

Rather than stop, Tomlinson took another deep drag. "On the list of things that shouldn't have happened these last few weeks, my smoking is probably dead bottom of the pile."

Andrews walked out of the shadows and stood beside the commander. "Beautiful, isn't it?" he said, looking over the enormous holding tank.

"Would have been if things hadn't gone to shit. It's probably better this way anyway," Tomlinson said as he exhaled. "That thing would have been too damn big to transport. Safely anyway. It's better off dead if you ask me."

"I agree," Andrews said taking the offered cigarette and lighting it. "No matter which way we look at it, we had a lucky escape."

The two were silent for a while, and stared into the darkness.

"Want to take a look at it?" Andrews said, glancing at Tomlinson.

"Why not, suppose it's not every day you get to see something so unique."

Andrews flicked a switch, illuminating the array of underwater lights in the holding tank. Inside, the juvenile creature swam in lazy circles, still dragging Russo's body behind it by the leg.

"Talk about lucky," Tomlinson said. "We opened the tank doors to cut the whale carcass loose and this little bastard swam right in and started to feed on it. Couldn't believe it. Happened before the explosion. Thing must have bolted straight out of the cave when they pushed it back into the water."

Andrews nodded, watching Russo's bloated corpse make another lazy rotation. "Ironic really. Russo spent the last few weeks of his life chasing this thing, and even in death, can't get close enough to it."

"I don't know about that, but I'll tell you this. I'm happier transporting this one to Florida rather than that big son of a bitch."

"In time, this one will grow to the same size. Hell, maybe bigger, who knows."

"So, it doesn't matter that it's not the adult?"

Andrews shook his head. "No. Same DNA. It really makes no difference."

"The only thing I wonder about, is what might happen if things go wrong."

"Like what?"

Like if this thing grows to maturity then decides it doesn't want to be contained in Florida anymore."

"It's a secured facility. It's perfectly safe."

"Maybe it is. Nobody has ever really dealt with anything like this before, have they?"

"True," Andrews said, dropping the butt of his cigarette and crushing it under his boot. "It's all about discovery. That's what Project Blue is all about. Russo didn't see that. For him it was all about the black and white of the capture. He saw the objective, but didn't see why it had to be done."

"Maybe," Tomlinson muttered. "Anyway, shut down those lights, I don't want to look at his damn corpse anymore. I just hope it was all worth the effort and we can learn something from this animal."

"I'm sure we will," Andrews said as he reached over to the light switch. Pausing to take a last lingering look at the magnificent creature, he flicked the switch and plunged the holding tank into darkness.

FIN

CHECK OUT OTHER GREAT DEEP SEA THRILLERS

MEGA
by Jake Bible

There is something in the deep. Something large. Something hungry. Something prehistoric.
And Team Grendel must find it, fight it, and kill it.
Kinsey Thorne, the first female US Navy SEAL candidate has hit rock bottom. Having washed out of the Navy, she turned to every drink and drug she could get her hands on. Until her father and cousins, all ex-Navy SEALS themselves, offer her a way back into the life: as part of a private, elite combat Team being put together to find and hunt down an impossible monster in the Indian Ocean. Kinsey has a second chance, but can she live through it?

THE BLACK
by Paul E Cooley

Under 30,000 feet of water, the exploration rig Leaguer has discovered an oil field larger than Saudi Arabia, with oil so sweet and pure, nations would go to war for the rights to it. But as the team starts drilling exploration well after exploration well in their race to claim the sweet crude, a deep rumbling beneath the ocean floor shakes them all to their core. Something has been living in the oil and it's about to give birth to the greatest threat humanity has ever seen.

"The Black" is a techno/horror-thriller that puts the horror and action of movies such as Leviathan and The Thing right into readers' hands. Ocean exploration will never be the same."

CHECK OUT OTHER GREAT DEEP SEA THRILLERS

PREDATOR X
by C.J Waller

When deep level oil fracking uncovers a vast subterranean sea, a crack team of cavers and scientists are sent down to investigate. Upon their arrival, they disappear without a trace. A second team, including sedimentologist Dr Megan Stoker, are ordered to seek out Alpha Team and report back their findings. But Alpha team are nowhere to be found – instead, they are faced with something unexpected in the depths. Something ancient. Something huge. Something dangerous. Predator X

DEAD BAIT
by Tim Curran

A husband hell-bent on revenge hunts a Wereshark...A Russian mail order bride with a fishy secret...Crabs with a collective consciousness...A vampire who transforms into a Candiru...Zombie piranha...Bait that will have you crawling out of your skin and more. Drawing on horror, humor with a helping of dark fantasy and a touch of deviance, these 19 contemporary stories pay homage to the monsters that lurk in the murky waters of our imaginations. If you thought it was safe to go back in the water...Think Again!

CHECK OUT OTHER GREAT DEEP SEA THRILLERS

LAMPREYS
by Alan Spencer

A secret government tactical team is sent to perform a clean sweep of a private research installation. Horrible atrocities lurk within the abandoned corridors. Mutated sea creatures with insane killing abilities are waiting to suck the blood and meat from their prey.

Unemployed college professor Conrad Garfield is forced to assist and is soon separated from the team. Alone and afraid, Conrad must use his wits to battle mutated lampreys, infected scientists and go head-to-head with the biggest monstrosity of all.

Can Conrad survive, or will the deadly monsters suck the very life from his body?

DEEP DEVOTION
by M.C. Norris

Rising from the depths, a mind-bending monster unleashes a wave of terror across the American heartland. Kate Browning, a Kansas City EMT confronts her paralyzing fear of water when she traces the source of a deadly parasitic affliction to the Gulf of Mexico. Cooperating with a marine biologist, she travels to Florida in an effort to save the life of one very special patient, but the source of the epidemic happens to be the nest of a terrifying monster, one that last rose from the depths to annihilate the lost continent of Atlantis.

Leviathan, destroyer, devoted lifemate and parent, the abomination is not going to take the extermination of its brood well.